I am a moon. My mother is definitely a moon. My father—he's a hard one to classify. I'd say he's a star, but a distant-burning kind, burning away in another galaxy. You'd need something more than the Hubble telescope to see him properly. No, all my hopes are on Jeremy, my little brother. He has the makings of a star, I swear. He'll make enough light for us all. . . .

I've divided the human race into stars and moons ever since I began reading the sky. It's a tidy and satisfying system, one you can rely on. Before that, I classified people in another way—herbivores and carnivores. (I was a herbivore, of course. Moons usually are.)

Anyway, the thing that I'd like you to consider is, if you're a moon like me, you won't make your own light. You'll borrow it. You'll go in for a lot of appeasement gestures, like smiling too much and wagging your tail.

And it was being a borrower that got me into all this trouble in the first place.

ALSO AVAILABLE IN DELL LAUREL-LEAF BOOKS:

BORROWED LIGHT

ANNA FIENBERG

ACKNOWLEDGMENTS

I found these sources extremely helpful in the research for this book:

Timothy Ferris, *The Whole Shebang*, 1997
Rose Wyler and Gerald Ames, *The Golden Book of Astronomy*, 1955
Michael Hoskin (ed.), *The Cambridge Illustrated History of Astronomy*, 1997
ISIS, Women's International Cross-Cultural Exchange,
Women's World, June, 1986
Margaret Atwood, *Alias Grace*, 1997,
for her thoughts on mesmerism and spiritualism
Many thanks also to the Sydney Observatory for their kind assistance

Published by
Dell Laurel-Leaf
an imprint of
Random House Children's Books
a division of Random House, Inc.
1540 Broadway
New York, New York 10036

Visit us on the Web! www.randomhouse.com/teens
Educators and librarians, for a variety of teaching tools, visit us at
www.randomhouse.com/teachers

ISBN: 0-440-22876-X

RL: 5.1

Reprinted by arrangement with Delacorte Press

Printed in the United States of America
February 2002

10 9 8 7 6 5 4 3 2 1

OPM

BORROWED LIGHT

PART
1

*I*t was the discovery that the moon has no wind, no water and no air that changed things for me.

That, and the feeling of being inhabited.

When I was sixteen, these two discoveries lay side by side in my mind, as separate and solid as stones. In time they connected, until, looking back, I could never see one without the other.

I first saw the surface of the moon through a telescope in my garden when I was twelve. That same year I learned that stars were all in the process of dying.

I was shocked. My grandmother and I were standing

near the azalea bush, our bare feet moist with dew. We were "reading the sky," as she put it. We did that often. In summer it was lovely, the cool grass tickling our toes. Stars sizzled above us. It's amazing how just one crumb of information can change a person's view of the world. I thought stars were incredibly glamorous after that. And tragic.

Stars, said Grandma, live only as long as they have fuel. Then they degenerate into white dwarves, or are defeated by gravity and slither into black holes. It's a ghastly end, but, as I told Grandma, at least stars have a life. Their fiery hearts storm with atoms, creating unimaginable heat, turning hydrogen into helium. They make their own light!

Now, take the life of a moon. It just follows a planet around, like a dog on a leash. Same old orbit, same old neighborhood. Padding along, it catches light rays like bones thrown by stars.

I am a moon. My mother is definitely a moon. My father—he's a hard one to classify. I'd say he's a star, but a distant kind, burning away in another galaxy. You'd need something more than the Hubble telescope to see him properly. No, all my hopes are on Jeremy, my little brother. He has the makings of a star, I swear. He'll make enough light for us all.

You might think, to look at me, that I am a star. If you just gave me a passing glance, that is, out of the corner of your eye. Did you know that children can't see well out of the corners of their eyes? They don't develop good peripheral vision until about eight years old. It's something to watch out for, particularly when your little brother is crossing the road. Little kids don't see a thing, believe me.

Anyway, if you're over eight, and therefore glancing at me quickly from the corner of your eye, you'll see my long wavy dark hair. You may notice I am very slim (from worry, not weight watching). I have a straight nose with elegant nostrils shaped like bass clefs. My music teacher told me that, when she couldn't think of anything else encouraging to say. People have complimented me on my smile. Tim, my ex-boyfriend, said it was sexy. I work hard at my smile.

People often search for kind things to say when they meet me. I think they sense my eagerness to please. Maybe they can even see my tail wag. My mother says that if you can't say anything nice, don't say anything at all. My father is often lost for words and spends a lot of time on the other side of the planet.

Here in the shadows, lying on my side in bed, I am sixteen again. I watch the line of my body curving out and in like a violin. But if you look properly, you'll see it's only my hip bones that stick out like mad. I *really* look like a starving cow in a drought. When Jeremy falls asleep with me he slings his leg into that hollow of my waist and snuggles up. I love that. I pretend he's my baby, my little calf. At least I used to. Now I can't bear to think about it.

It's late, and I'm tired. My eyes ache. I can't sleep. My skin is tingling with nerves. Outside, it looks so peaceful. The house lies in fields of silence, the neat lawns and careful gardens threaded together with moonlight.

It won't last, though. Moonlight changes the world for a while, but it's like a magician who does only illusions, not transformations. When it moves on, the moon leaves nothing behind. The sun would give you a warm spot.

If you really want to know, I've divided the human race into stars and moons ever since I began reading the sky. It's a tidy and satisfying system, one you can rely on. Before that, I classified people in another way—herbivores and carnivores. (I was a herbivore, of course. Moons usually are.)

Anyway, the thing that I'd like you to consider is, if you're a moon like me, you won't make your own light. You'll borrow it. You'll go in for a lot of appeasement gestures, like smiling too much and wagging your tail.

And it was being a borrower that got me into all this trouble in the first place.

Some people have photographic memories. They can tell you the color of their baby blanket, the prize they won in kindergarten. Those people could tell you the date, too, of any personal event, as if it were etched there in the top corner of each memory frame. I can't. I remember only feelings. And smells.

Once, when I was little, we went on a holiday to a farm. I sat down in the chicken yard, to talk to the hens. I got chicken manure all over my skirt. The stink was enough to make you pass out. When I ran into the kitchen crying, everyone laughed. "Ugh, you smell *fowl*!" they crowed, radiant with their own wit.

I remember nothing about the pony rides or the cow called Daze I was supposed to have milked so happily. Since then, whenever I smell garden fertilizer, I blush like a madwoman.

It's a defect in my character, this "feeling" memory. You can't really *tell* feelings—imagine someone recounting a long anecdote, without place, setting or time! Just, "I felt this, I felt that, but I don't know when. . . ." It's like being lost in a landscape with no signposts.

I have a mountain of other defects as well, which you will discover if you continue with this. For instance, I read constantly, even at the dinner table. My mother says it's rude. Not a good example for Jeremy. (It's also unhygienic, as pages get stuck together with sauce spots.) But I like to expand my general knowledge. I pick up a lot of interesting facts through reading—it's a side effect, like the rampant fungal growth that occurs with antibiotics. Did you know, for instance, that a bulldozer is as heavy as seven hundred seven-year-old children? Such facts provide a kind of social glue; you can bring them out whenever there's a gap in conversation.

But astronomical facts are the best. They are in a class of their own. They enlarge the perimeter of your life, sweeping you away, past the dinner table, above the arguments and the silences and the washing up. They signpost the way to other worlds you might want to live in.

In another twenty years, if I'm still alive, I'll want to remember this sixteenth year properly, the way other people remember. Not just the feelings and smells. So I'm writing this while it's still clear. I'll put in my own signposts, and the feelings can just drape over them like swamp weed.

Do you remember the bad things in your life more than the good? I tend to remember disasters. I must have a special section in my brain that says Line Up Here, Disasters

Only. This annoys my mother, who says I had a perfectly decent childhood. And maybe she's right, because compared to the catastrophe that happened when I was sixteen, the sum of all the painful events of my childhood would be as microscopic as those first single-celled bacteria climbing up the lips of volcanoes.

*T*hat year, when I was sixteen, I had to make a decision. You ought to know I'm terrible at decisions. I'm the biggest procrastinator I've ever met. I lie around for ages imagining both sides (I actually lie on my bed a lot, it's another defect of mine) and keep feeling sorry for the side that loses. It's like a ghost standing at the end of my bed.

My ex-boyfriend, Tim, is always saying, "I decided to do it on the spur of the moment!" When he says that, you can see he feels heroic—he throws his head back and laughs, and his teeth (carnivorous) glint in the sunlight. You can see he is a daring, impulsive guy—a real risk taker. Well, he is a star, after all. A real one. That's why I was attracted to him.

But do you know, I don't really believe in spur-of-the-moment decisions. Not now. I think so many things lead you to make that decision. The swish of your mother's dress as she walked past your cot, the tang of your father's soap, the dreams you had when you were three. There are things you can't remember, jostling like wrestlers in a crowd, trying to push to the front of your mind. I can feel them sometimes, it makes me hold my head, I feel a pressure that tingles in my scalp, like tears pricking my eyelids. The wrestlers sometimes make me cry, but I can't see their shape or expression, they just press on me when I'm doing nothing—pulling the sheets up on my bed, watching television.

Life is one big question mark, if you ask me.

*T*his disaster, at sixteen, is without comparison. It is the worst thing that ever happened to me.

Worse than the time I drank too much green ginger wine and passed out on the kitchen floor at Simon Throng's party. I woke up to find that my hair was full of potato crisps and everyone else had gone home. I hate green ginger wine, anyway. I'd only had one glass, then two, because everyone else was doing it. The girls had looked so cool, summer legs crossed, fingers laced around those elegant, long-stemmed glasses.

This disaster was worse, too, than the time I came home from a party with my dress inside out. I'd gone parking with Tim at the botanical gardens. By day the gardens are soft and inviting. At night there are sharp things in the grass that poke into your back and stinging things that make you think of deadly funnelweb spiders. You're supposed to be carried away with your lover's caresses, but it's not easy when you think every breath might be your last, due to the funnelweb. Somehow Tim removed my dress, and I helped, of course, because I am always obliging and consider others first. (You do that to excess if you're a borrower.) Being naked in a public place, surrounded by spiky objects, doesn't excite me, if you really want to know. As soon as it was polite, I slid my dress back on. I rode home, safe now, wrapped from neck to knee in natural cotton. I wasn't aware that my labels were flapping—and everyone could see I was size ten, made in Thailand, and needed a warm machine wash only.

*T*hese painful events were temporary. After a while they lay buried, like sharp metal objects you step on in the sand. I wince sometimes, just as I'm falling asleep, and remember them.

But the disaster I'm about to confess to you is definitely the worst. It had the shock value of a giant meteor crashing to earth. Have you heard about the meteor that fell in Winslow, Arizona? It made a crater two kilometers wide. Well, when I heard the result of my test, my mouth fell open just like that.

"You're pregnant," the doctor said. "I'm afraid the test was positive."

He was afraid? What about me?

Everything became very quiet after he said that, like when you dive underwater. Without sound, I saw things so clearly. The doctor's hand rested on the desk. It was pale, with fine black hairs sprouting below each knuckle. There was something pubic about the hairs, so I looked away. Next to the hand was a small fish tank. I peered closer. Inside was a long pinkish thing that looked like it was still evolving.

"A lungfish," said the doctor kindly, giving us both a bit of time. "Of the order Dipnoi. It has lungs as well as gills."

"I know, and in certain species it builds a mucus-lined mud covering to withstand extended droughts."

The doctor looked annoyed. He was used to bringing out his information like a present. I was supposed to go, *"Oh!"* Normally I would have. I'd have smiled a lot, too, and fallen about with amazement. (Because I'm a borrower, remember. We try to fulfill people's expectations at any given moment.)

Only that day I didn't feel like it. I just didn't feel like it.

I think his hand was extended to comfort me. I was too numb. The silence thing had come back. In the moments after an explosion there is no other sound. The doctor's mouth was opening and closing, and without the words he looked quite funny, like the telly when the mute button is pushed. Funny and vulnerable. I didn't want to worry about *him* on top of everything else, so I switched back to looking at the lungfish, of the order Dipnoi.

But I couldn't help thinking of all our fishy ancestors crawling up from the sea millions of years ago. Slithery slidey blotches, wriggling with pride—"Look, I've got lungs and you've only got gills, ner ner!" I remembered that a human fetus makes gills in the early weeks, only to destroy them later on.

I wondered if I had a little fish inside me.

I could feel tears welling up, warm as those primordial swamps. Suddenly the lungfish pressed against the glass. My tears spilled their banks. I wanted to let the poor thing out. The water would gush over the table, drowning the files and the neat penholder with the doctor's name inscribed in gold, and the pink plastic pelvis of a female perched in the corner. But I couldn't rescue it. Nobody could. The creature seemed frozen in time, eternally procrastinating—

animal, mineral or vegetable?——while all its brothers and sisters had made up their minds a millennium ago, embracing a muddy bank, or sliding down under a wave.

"Whatever decision you make," the doctor said, picking up his gold pen, "I'd be glad to help."

I wanted to blurt it out then, and howl. His face was all crumpled with concern. Soft, like rumpled sheets. I could have laid my head in his lap.

"Thank you," I said, and stood up. I waved to the lungfish. I couldn't manage anything more.

*W*hen I came home from the doctor's, nobody seemed to notice anything different. I didn't really expect them to. Everyone in our family has eye trouble. The world goes blurry at a distance of two centimeters outside their own skins. I forgive Jeremy, of course. He is only five. And anyway, the day I got home, he was worrying about much larger things.

He was wearing his bike helmet again, inside the house. "Oh, Jem," I said, "it won't do you any good, even if a meteor does land on our house. That one in Siberia turned into a fireball and killed fifteen hundred reindeer when it fell. Where's Mum?"

I've thought for a long time now that maybe I should stop teaching Jeremy to read the sky. For me it's exciting, it's a way out of here. There are definite possibilities. But Jeremy just seems to worry about things falling on him.

Jeremy shrugged and the helmet shifted sideways. It was

10

too big for him, anyway. "Mum?" He wrinkled his forehead. "She's in the living room, talking to those dead people."

We both sighed. I sat down heavily on a kitchen chair and pulled Jeremy onto my lap. The helmet hit my chin. From the living room we heard a voice. "O beloved spirits, come in peace, we are ready for you." We held our breath in the kitchen. Jeremy snorted. I could feel his shoulders shaking. The silence was thick in that room. We'd seen it. It hung suspended, like layers of cigarette smoke.

We heard a low murmuring. There was a moaning and wailing, the sounds reeling together through the silence, and then, like a solid shape spinning up from a potter's wheel, a clear cry came. It made goose bumps stand out on my skin. Jeremy pulled his helmet down.

Someone was crying. It was a hopeless kind of crying, as if it came from the bottom of a well. I could hear Mum doing her comforting routine. It was Wednesday, I realized, and I couldn't have picked a more depressing day to make my discovery.

Wednesday was séance day. Every Wednesday, for as long as I can remember, I've come home to a darkened living room, moist with sad ladies. Curtains are drawn, the air is trapped and still, the dining table is pushed into the middle of the room. Sitting around it are eight or nine women, usually my mother's age or older. They all have one finger on a glass that is moving jerkily around a Ouija board, telling stories of misfortune. My mother says they are trying to contact the spirit of a loved one who was too rapidly snatched from this world. When I come in from school, she glances up at me with irritation and purses her mouth into *shhh* position. It makes her mouth look like a dried plum. "There's fruit in the bowl," she whispers. "Can't talk now."

She may as well swat me. Jeremy often sings in the bath, "Shoo fly, don't bother me, I do not want your company." Sometimes I worry that he feels like I do.

Once I tried to talk to Mum about the ladies. "You're too young to understand," she said. But she let me join a meditation class she runs on Thursdays. That was a disaster (of the temporary kind). We all lay on the floor with our shoes off, me and ten women, while my mother took us down some stairs and into a cellar—imaginatively speaking, that is. It was quite pleasant on the second stair, where she said some wild lavender was growing. Could we smell it? So restful it was, wriggling our toes in the carpet, hearing gentle sighs all around.

But when we got to the fourth and fifth stairs, we were going below ground, and Mum's voice became softer. It was musty in this place, where no lavender grew, and I could hardly hear her. I was dying to open my eyes. The silence was suffocating. You could even hear people swallow. "Be aware," my mother whispered to us, "don't fall asleep. Look around. Remember."

Suddenly there was a loud fart, like a car backfiring. I jumped. It was the lady with the floral dress. She was fast asleep.

Everyone pretended they hadn't heard. I started to laugh. I couldn't help it. I might as well have tried to stop breathing. I kept my mouth locked for a while, but I kept hearing that fart in all the silence and soon the laughs were ripping my throat open, huge tugging lions of laughs, and in the end I just gave in and lay there on the carpet, shrieking. It was the best laugh I've ever had.

Afterward my mother wouldn't speak to me.

I tried to tell her that it was only because I was so relaxed by her meditation, and I'd loved the lavender bit. And that later, in my room, the laughs had turned to sobs, because I'd felt so lonely laughing on my own. But she wouldn't listen. She's only interested in her ladies' sorrows. I realize now you can only join her secret circle of sorrow if you are forty and over. If you're exactly like her. Otherwise she doesn't want to know.

My mother has some secret mission to mop up the sorrows of all the women in the world. She hasn't bothered with training from health courses or naturopathy or Gestalt therapy or religion—nothing with a certificate and a bit of respectability. Not my mother. She trusts nothing. Only her own "instincts"! And the muttering of the dead. She writes pages and pages in her diary about her discoveries— perhaps she's inventing her own therapy. She spends a lot of time staring into space, looking for signs from the natural world. Putting it down like this, she sounds quite creepy. But I suppose I'm used to it. Jeremy's the one I worry about.

It's not that she doesn't do things that mothers are supposed to do. She makes our lunches and cooks our dinner, and asks us about our day. She doesn't look like the mother in the Addams family. Although, come to think of it, she is rather willowy and dark and intense-looking. And sometimes, I have to admit, she forgets to comb her hair. She wears it long, like mine, but she has quite dazzling streaks of gray in it now. When she remembers to brush it, her hair flows down her back like wine. I tell her to heighten the color in it, that a deep burgundy would look great, but she says she couldn't be bothered, that I shouldn't care so much about appearances—then I get a lecture on spirituality, et cetera, and the inner world, so I drop it. Dad just raises his eyebrows and shakes his head in that oh-she's-hopeless way. He tries to share a conspiratorial grin, but that irritates me, too. I'm not going to be on *his* side, old fussyboots.

No, the thing is, she might ask questions but she doesn't listen to the answers. When Jeremy or I start on a story—what someone said at school, what happened at swimming lessons—her eyes glaze over, settling into a vacant stare.

I call it her dead-bird gaze.

I'd never tell her about me. About *my* misfortune. I don't know her well enough.

*I*t was hard to finish dinner that Wednesday night. Now I had a proper diagnosis, I surrendered to the nausea that had been bubbling away. I excused myself and ran to the bathroom. I flushed the toilet to disguise the noise and was sick into the tumbling blue water. After that, I could face the avocado salad. Mum says avocado possesses every vitamin known to man, so we eat it a lot. I was voraciously hungry and on the verge of throwing up at the same time. It's a dreadful combination of sensations, if you really want to know.

We had dinner early, because Dad was going away at the crack of dawn the next day. He likes to have plenty of time to pack and fuss and check he has all his socks. Be Prepared is his motto. He must say it at least fifty times a day. He doesn't object to avocado salad because it's an efficient fruit. You can economize with avocado, he says. I bet he'd eat space rations if he could. He prides himself on his big O—organization, that is. Mostly he makes jokes about Mum's cooking. Not the funny ha-ha jokes, more the sneery, condescending snipes that leave an uncomfortable silence while you decide whose side you should be on. I feel sorry for Mum then. She looks down at her plate, but when she looks up again she's wearing her dead-bird gaze.

It didn't matter to me that my father was going away the next day because I wasn't going to tell him my terrible news, anyway. I couldn't imagine such a thing. He'd be outraged at my lack of organization. Where was my preparation? My preplanning? My feasibility study? Distant stars like him have absolutely no empathy for moon behavior. They don't understand that we are helpless against the stark gravitational pull of other bodies and are doomed to follow.

That evening I went into my room and lay on my bed. I was panicking. Often I do my worrying here, but that's pale pink compared with the scarlet of panic. It makes you feel like you are dying and need an ambulance. That your heart's going to explode out of your chest. Red everywhere. It's like listening to a siren that won't stop. I just wanted it to stop.

"You're pregnant," the doctor had said. His voice rang in my head. The lungfish gasped at me from the glass. Two words that were going to change the rest of my life. Two words, but they made a sentence.

I would have to make a decision. I would have to decide. But there was nobody to ask.

I met Tim at a party. I'd been nervous for two weeks, ever since I got the invitation. The girl who invited me was two years older, and she drank green ginger wine like milk. She had five earrings in one ear and seven in the other. She looked like a warrior, and she said "Well, fuck *me*!" whenever she was surprised. She was surprised quite often, and her exclamation always sounded more like a threat than an invitation.

Anyway, I still don't know why she thought of me. Perhaps she did that quick-glance thing (being way over the age of eight) and thought I looked passable—a decorative asset for her party, like streamers to hang over the windows, and balloons at the gate. Or maybe she just needed more girls.

A week before the party I decided to buy a new dress. After all, it's not every day you go to the house of Miranda Blair, urban warrior extraordinaire. I thought of getting an orange streak in my hair, too, and maybe some black lipstick (like Miranda), but I knew, deep inside, that a moon like me couldn't carry it off.

Still, I must have been feeling daring, just a little bit nuclear, because I bought a bright red dress. It was really short, too, and its silky skirt shone and rippled round my hips like petrol on fire.

"You'd have to be mighty sure of yourself to wear a dress like that," a customer said as I left the shop. I cringed, right down to my bones. You could accuse me of anything, but not *that*, I swear.

I wore it, just the same. But it was hell, if you really want to know. As I walked into Miranda's hallway, I could hear the music blaring from the rooms up ahead. I was alone. There was a full-length mirror on the wall, and I glanced to see if I had any parsley between my teeth. God, I looked like a lonely flamingo, picking its way through a forest of bottles. Those absurd long legs were as skinny as stilts. I hung on to the wall for a moment, wishing like mad I'd worn the old black dress that covered my ankles.

The house opened up into a huge room crammed with people. I quickly searched the faces for someone I knew. No one looked back at me, or smiled, or even lifted an eyebrow. Maybe there was a policy not to talk to flamingos. I wandered over to the sliding glass doors and peered out at the night. There was a chance I could look cool and a bit mysterious, standing on my own, contemplating the sky.

Actually, there was a luscious full moon that night. It shone steadily down on the lawn, picking flowers out of the dark. I haven't always been so derogatory about the moon, you know. I admire its generous nature, offering a torch to the night, sharing its light around—even if it is borrowed.

It was a relief, the night sky. Such a comfort, like an exotic but well-known family you can confidently return to. There was Venus and, to the left, Jupiter, both glowing with the steady shine of planets. Long ago Grandma told me that the song "Twinkle Twinkle Little Star" was surprisingly accurate. "Planets shine and stars twinkle," she'd said, "depending on how turbulent the atmosphere is, of course." I saw stars quivering with life and turbulence.

Someone turned up the music. I could feel the drumbeat thumping through the floor, into my feet. It pushed into my body, thrusting its heartbeat over mine. It was like a drug, that music, it could take you over, and I wished to God it would. It pulled me down from Venus and Jupiter and the quivering stars, but it did nothing to cover me. Over the music I heard someone laugh, and then someone else, and suddenly I was convinced they were laughing at me. Maybe I was ridiculous standing there in that neon dress, blaring like a Coca-Cola sign.

I tried to stretch down the hem of my skirt. My cheeks were on fire. I wished I'd stayed home with Jeremy. I wondered if he'd worn his bike helmet to bed. Surely Mum would have noticed.

The lights were dimmed, and I watched couples slow-dance into the shadows. They looked like figures in an oil painting, the colors of their limbs fading into each other, so you couldn't see where one body began and the other finished. I would have given anything to dissolve into someone like that, but I bet all my bones would get in the way.

That was when Tim emerged out of the shadows. I'd seen him at school—Timothy Cleary, surfing idol, skin like honey, eyes like magnets. Unattainable as planet Jupiter. But he was walking toward *me*! Maybe he'd mistaken me for someone else. I couldn't bear to see his face sag with disappointment. I nearly fell over his feet.

"Hi, I'm Callisto May," I said, all in a rush. I edged him

over to the light where he could see me better. "Are you looking for someone?"

"Someone like you," he sang. It was an old sweet song, and he had a lovely voice. I wasn't a good judge, though, because I would have given him a music award even if he'd sung like a gorilla.

There is a God after all, I thought fleetingly, and made up my mind to tell Grandma. But I knew she'd say it was just the power of pheromones.

We chatted for a while, our voices straining over the beat of the music.

"Are you a good friend of Miranda's?" I asked.

He shrugged. You could see the muscles in his shoulders gliding under his skin. *He must be very strong from all that paddling in the surf,* I thought. *I bet he could pick me up with one hand.* I felt a delicious ripple of excitement, like notes rising up the piano.

"Yeah, I guess so, we've known each other for years. She was my girlfriend for a while." He grinned. "She's a gutsy lady!" His voice was admiring.

I nodded in a nonchalant manner. But I was alarmed. That piece of information changed things for a moment. I wondered if Tim approved of blowing up garbage bins and bullying Year 7 girls. I hoped he wasn't as dangerous as Miranda. But he smiled at me again and lifted a curl from behind my ear.

"You have great hair, Callisto."

I put garbage bins and bullying firmly away.

"Do you go to Whale Beach much?" he continued.

I had a sudden vision of Tim and his friends sitting on

19

their towels, looking at girls in bikinis as they strolled past. I'd heard that they rated the girls one to ten. Big breasts scored high. I shuddered and stepped back for a minute. The hair in his fingers pulled tight.

"Ow!" I gasped. I said it under my breath, so I don't think he heard, because he went on holding the hair.

"I don't think I've seen you there," Tim went on. "We go most weekends—you know, the guys, José, Phil, Bob and me. There's the best waves at Whale Beach, and José brings his dog sometimes. He can have a good run around in the park there, off the leash."

"What kind of dog is it?"

"An Alsatian. He looks fierce but he's as gentle as a possum. I used to have a dog but he died last year."

Tim's eyes were suddenly shinier, and he looked down at our feet. I took his hand and pressed it. It was very warm and I could feel the pulse in his wrist. I wondered if I should ask him what kind of dog his had been, or maybe he didn't want to talk about it. But if I didn't ask, he might think I didn't care. I couldn't decide. Also, that little beat under my finger was distracting. It made me see that Tim was vulnerable, he was a human being like me, dependent on food and drink and air to keep that beat going. We had something in common, as long as I kept holding his hand.

We let the music into our conversation then. It filled the sea of dark between us with just the right words. I stopped agonizing about the dog.

Later Tim went to get a drink and I wondered if he'd ever come back. I needed to go to the toilet, but what if I missed him when he returned? I stood there squeezing my thighs together.

And there he was, blue eyes from a postcard sky, threading his way carefully through the room, bringing two glasses of green ginger wine.

I wish I could say we talked all night, but what with the music and the phenomenon of irresistible attraction between two bodies, we began kissing quite soon.

That was something to remember, that first kiss. Tim put his arms around me—honey-colored, with little golden fireflies of hair—and drew me toward him. He looked at me, carefully, for thirty whole seconds. That's a long time—you try it. While he was looking, I counted silently. It was less excruciating that way. No one had ever looked at me for that long. Except Jeremy, perhaps. But that's because he was dying for me to tell him what happened when a planet collided with a meteor swarm.

Once a reporter came to our school and interviewed lots of students. "Pretty Callisto May," wrote the reporter a week later in the newspaper. Can you believe it? Everyone else just had their name in the paper, without the adjective. I read that phrase over and over again. There it was, in black and white, a judgment made by the world. Well, I couldn't agree. What about my spiky hips, my disappointing breasts? I wanted to run after the reporter, ask him if he'd noticed the hairiness of my arms, my scrawny legs, with the knobble bone on the ankle that could cut paper. Where were the womanly curves? Couldn't he see the shadow of a mustache? Did he usually wear glasses? No, if he'd taken more than a glance out of the corner of his eye, he never would have written "pretty Callisto May." That was for sure.

But at Miranda Blair's party, on the third of March, Tim Cleary looked at me for thirty seconds. When he was finished, he still wanted to kiss me. I smiled so much my face ached. I was caught in his gaze, trapped in sunlight. Every cell of me was in focus, every movement seemed larger than life. I was exquisitely aware of my breathing, my bass clef nostrils, the itch under my tongue, the twitch beginning in my mouth. I felt beautiful for the first time. Tim Cleary picked me out with his eyes, he selected me, *me!* and suddenly I was alive.

His mouth was hard and soft at the same time. I was amazed that a boy's lips could be so silky, like the most secret parts of a girl. And behind the lips were the teeth and jaw, pushing and determined, carnivorous. I was excited, scared, breathless, thrilled. He didn't close his eyes while he kissed me. Neither did I. I wasn't going to miss anything. His eyes stared into mine. I didn't know what would happen next. But I would do whatever he wanted. He'd given me the best gift in the world. I leapt for it eagerly, borrowing his warmth and making it my own, the way the moon borrows light.

School was very different after the third of March. Miranda Blair, urban warrior, let me join her tribe. I ate my avocado sandwiches with her on the wooden seats under the oak tree. I stood on guard at the toilet door while she had a smoke. I bought some black nail polish. And I got my ears pierced.

Grandma said that if I was so determined to do my ears, she'd take me to the hospital herself—she has a friend who is a matron there. I bled profusely, as if I were in a major car accident. As I said to my mother when I got home, "I don't know why I can't just do things normally and go to a chemist like everyone else. It's over in two minutes, isn't it, with that little gun the chemist uses? And you haven't got white-coated doctors rushing around talking about transfusions." My mother just shrugged and muttered something about Grandma's absurd faith in doctors, and then she did her dead-bird gaze. Still, it gave me another bloodthirsty tale to tell the warriors. I was becoming an expert in tall tales.

Miranda had wanted to know all the details about my night with Tim. I'm sure she still fancied him herself. "What did he say? Did he lick your earlobes? Did he put his tongue down your throat?" Miranda and her friends orbited about me like satellites around a new sun. Every time I told a new Tim story, the awe grew like a sudden rise in temperature. I couldn't quite believe it. It made me glow, even if it didn't feel real. I gave them little bits, like seeds spat out. I tried to keep all the juice to myself. I couldn't exactly remember what Tim had said that night, but I was becoming a whiz at making it up. I remembered only looking into his eyes and seeing myself, like the goddess Venus emerging from the sea.

I was continually nervous. It made my mouth dry, all this inventing, and I licked my lips a lot. They became chafed and an ulcer bloomed on the tip of my tongue. It's hard kissing with an ulcer. It hurts and you feel like a leper. But I didn't like to say no.

On Sundays I went to the beach with Tim and "the guys." I usually wore a T-shirt over my bikini. I explained that I had a family failing. Skin cancers popped out on our backs after five minutes' exposure to the sun.

I sat on the beach for hours, sweltering, while the guys surfed the waves. I didn't like to read, because I might miss one of Tim's best "tubes." He always asked me afterward if I'd been watching. When they were finished, the boys would race back over the sand, surfboards cradled under their arms like awkward pets. Tim would leap upon me, all dripping and slippery, with his cold wet lips on mine. His hips pressed into me, digging us into the sand.

The cold of his skin was welcome, but I could hear the sniggering of his friends behind us, and I died quietly of embarrassment. Gently I'd nudge Tim off my bones, and he'd sit up and hunt around for a beer.

José often brought his dog, Tito, to the beach. But he had to be careful about taking it onto the sand. There was a big sign near the toilet block with a picture of a dog and a great red slash through it. One Sunday José brought his spray can and splashed the sign with purple. When he'd finished, I told him the dog on the sign looked like an alien from Mars. No Aliens on the Beach, he wrote happily along the top. So José brought his Earth dog down to the shore.

Tim laughed with the rest of us, but I could see that he was worried. When a lifesaver jogged up an hour later, Tim stepped in. "Sorry, mate," he said, "but my friend José here doesn't read English. His dog came out with him from Chile."

"Well, it's a two-hundred-dollar fine for a dog on the

beach," warned the lifesaver. "So you better tell your friend. Okay, guys, *hasta la vista!*" He waved in a friendly way to José and jogged back up the beach.

"*Hasta la* what?" said José. He was angry with Tim. He'd been dying to tell the lifesaver all about alien dogs. But Tim just caught him in a headlock and they wrestled to the sand.

Tim was different like that. He drank till he was legless, he surfed in electrical storms and acted wild at parties. But he liked things legal and tidy. His parents were quite strict. I had never met them, but he told me many stories of his mother and her Hygiene Household. It sounded as if she scrubbed and vacuumed and dusted and washed for eight hours a day. She sat down to dinner with a paper towel in her hand. She was washing up before the family had finished dessert. Visitors had to sit on special covers laid carefully over the sofa, so as not to soil the brocade.

"Does she ask guests if they're toilet trained before they come in?" I only wanted to make him laugh. But he didn't. He frowned at me, and his lips clamped together.

"She's not that bad. She's just house-proud. My father says the best thing about the day is coming home to a tidy house. So I suppose she makes him pretty happy."

After that I didn't say another word of criticism about Tim's family, even if he was railing against them. I suppose I wouldn't like it if Tim started going on about my mother. And he had enough material, all right. When he came to pick me up for our first date, Mum answered the door with beetroot juice all over her nose. He didn't say anything, but she must have seen him looking. "It's a cure for skin cancers," she explained. "It works wonders."

Later, when we were driving away—we were going to José's house to watch a video—Tim didn't mention my mother. I thought that was very decent of him. He never made beetroot jokes or anything. She must have looked so weird, standing there like the victim of a dog bite. It's strange how you can go about detesting your own family, but if anyone else criticizes them, it's like a knife in your heart. I learnt a lot of things from Tim.

But I was always nervous. I don't know why. The trouble with my breathing started then. I was constantly breathless. I developed bronchitis, which wasn't very attractive because it made me bark like a dog. Often I'd come down with it the night before a big party. With my hollow chest and barking cough, I could have been someone in an opera dying of consumption.

Since real disaster has hit, these anxieties look tiny, like ants at a distance. You'd think I'd have enjoyed being popular for once. But I felt like someone in a bad disguise. Any minute I would be discovered.

I suppose I am superstitious, like my mother. Deep down I think something terrible will happen if you go against the divine order of things. Moons shouldn't dress up as stars, even if they are only pretending.

*I*f you really want to know, there were some parts of going out with Tim that I didn't like. But when I came home, I'd fall on my bed and lie there for hours. I'd watch the room floating with moonlight and scenes from my life would be silvered. Here on the bed I could change things. I was like a film director, freezing some scenes while I had a good look at a particular expression, a certain gesture. I played the first kiss scene over and over again. I felt Tim's hands stroking my face, his tongue tickling my ear, the music beating its way into my body. It made waves rise up in my belly like the tide coming in. I'd wanted that song to last forever—"Fire," it was, and I'd never forget that, no matter what disasters happened later. I wanted that moment to last, to freeze that frame. Tim with his arms around me, shining down on me while I quivered in his light. I could feel his heart hammering hard against mine, the music vibrating through the floor, running like sap through my toes.

On my bed, I'd replay that scene until I was exhausted. I was a star actor in a million-dollar movie. Then other moments would creep in. I'd chop the film there, letting the bad scenes fall into the dark. I'd grind my heel into those. I'd crush them down into the bottom of my mind, until no crack of light was emitted.

Sometimes when I was lying on my bed at night Jeremy would wake up. He had a piercing cry, like a car alarm. "Aargh, aargh, aargh!" he'd scream, and I'd run panting across the hall into his room to save him from mortal combat. Usually he'd be dreaming about Batman caught in a meteor shower, or Robin falling off the moon.

That Wednesday night, following my discovery at the doctor's and Jeremy's fight about the helmet (he'd wanted to wear it to bed, just in case), he had fallen asleep in about five seconds flat. He stopped fighting exhaustion and helmet removal, and turned over. "Batman out," he said, and closed his eyes. He became as limp as seaweed, letting the tide suck him in.

I'm amazed at the way small children fall asleep like that. They just give in, like little animals without backbones. I wish I could.

Anyway, there I was on my bed, panicking in my own world, when I heard his cry. I ran into his room and saw him sitting up straight in bed. His fists were clenched on the sheets, and he was mumbling something. I crept over to him. "You're not the boss of me, scumbuggit!" he hissed. "This is an extortion rain!" I smiled at him, even though he was asleep. Jeremy's had "glue ear" for ages, and he doesn't always hear the exact Batman dialogue, but he certainly gets the tone right.

I tucked my hand under his shoulders and laid his rigid little body back under the bedclothes. It was like trying to fold a plank.

I went back to my bed. There were books strewn all over it. I was supposed to be studying for a history exam. But I kept thinking about Jeremy's glue ear. There were little hollow plastic things you could put into the Eustachian tubes, I'd found out, which widen the area and let it drain. Grommets, they were called. I'd told Mum all about it—it was only a minor operation, it took about fifteen minutes and it would stop Jeremy looking so intense all the time. When you talk, he watches your lips like mad, so he doesn't miss anything. How is he going to act cool in high school and look as if he doesn't care when he's there hanging on your lips?

But Mum won't take him to the doctor. She doesn't believe in them. I keep telling her, doctors aren't like witches or giants, they do exist, and her ignoring them isn't going to make them go away. She just shrugs and points to catastrophes like thalidomide that left thousands of babies crippled, and "rests her case." Grommets are hardly thalidomide, I say, for God's sake. But she just continues to experiment with five drops of juice from an onion whenever Jeremy gets an earache. So now he smells of onion as well as looking intense, which is a very nerdy mixture, if you ask me. Poor Jeremy, I think he is destined to be a star, but he'll have to fight the clotting dark matter of his family if he's ever going to get there.

Jeremy's like me—he worries about a lot of things. Things that will probably never happen. I'd hate to tell him that reality is often even more dreadful than anything he could imagine.

That afternoon, when we were sitting in the kitchen, whispering very quietly, Mum tiptoed out of her séance and told us to go away. "Where?" said Jeremy. "Wherever," she said, waving us off. So I took him down to the swimming center.

We strolled down there in the afternoon sunlight, and we both cheered up a little. I bought Jeremy an ice cream and he sat on the edge, dangling his feet in the pool.

I watched his legs moving like scissors through the water. When he'd made enough foam he drew his legs up under him and rested his chin on his knees. I counted three grazes and one bruise.

"Why won't your mind do what you want it to?" he asked.

We both looked down at his toes while we considered. Bubbles clung to invisible blond hairs like beads.

Jeremy often asks questions that philosophers have been pondering for centuries. He has a very high IQ, I think. He says it only gives him more room to worry.

"What don't you want to think about?" I asked.

"Oh, nothing. Let's not talk about it. Batman out." He finished his ice cream and sat hanging on to the stick. His mouth was slightly open as he gazed at the other children zipping in and out of the pool. He had a cold and I supposed he was breathing through his mouth. His ears would play up again soon, for sure. When Jeremy laughs, his black eyes disappear into two crescent moons, and his whole body wobbles like jelly. But he wasn't laughing then.

"Calling Robin to Batman, come in, over," I said.

Jeremy swung round, lit up and wired. "Batman here, what's happening on planet Jupiter, Robin?" His whole face changed. Batman and Co. were the only beings on earth that could deflect his attention from meteors and gravity. He began to giggle, tapping his leg in a private rhythm of excitement. This was the game, and it was never long enough for Jeremy.

"Well, Batman," I said in my rocket radio voice, "I've heard there's a problem on planet Earth, but I can't see what it is from up here. Could you zoom in and have a look around?"

Jeremy sprang up and searched the horizon. He narrowed his eyes and sighed. "The sun is shining and the children are playing, over."

"That sounds good, Batman. A typical Earth summer afternoon, over."

"Yes, Robin." Jeremy crouched down and whispered hotly in my ear. His breath was sweet and chocolatey. I wanted to hold him for a moment. The water was making me think of the lungfish. I kept seeing the doctor's face, wrinkling in concern for me. He would have stroked my hand. I didn't want to think about that. I just wanted to hold my little brother. Jeremy would never stand still long enough. He always wriggled away to get on with the game, dropping a kiss or a smile as an offering, the way a lizard drops a bit of his tail.

"I'm not being Batman now, okay?" said Jeremy breathlessly. "Because Batman knows everything, see. I'm Jeremy just while I ask this, and then I'll be Batman again, right? Well—" He drew a deep breath and his eyebrows furrowed so that he looked quite old and tired, as if he'd been carrying a very heavy package around. "Well, the sun is shining now, that's for sure, but how can it keep burning? You said it's always losing weight. Grandma said it uses four million tons of hydrogen in just one second." His voice broke. "What will happen when it's all burnt up? Imagine, Cally, the world all dark forever."

He squinched up his eyes, trying to feel what it would be like. He stood up and walked with his arms stretched out in front like a sleepwalker. People were looking at him. He fell over a rubbish bin and came back. "Could we go and live on

Mars? Do you think there'll be civilization there by then? Would Mum come?"

I put my arm around him. He let me. "Four million tons is nothing, Jeremy. That sun is one big ball of fire. There's enough fuel to keep burning for another five billion years."

Jeremy breathed out and grinned. "That's even older than Grandma, isn't it? So, you could practically say that the sun will shine forever, just about."

"Just about."

"Good." Jeremy stood up and stretched. "Now I'm Batman again, and you're Robin. Or maybe, I'll be Poison Ivy. She's really bad. She's got green fingers and she grows deadly nightshade, too. If she just touches you, you get a rash. Ooh, watch out, my hand nearly got you, look out!"

I made a terrified face and began to scratch wildly. "I need the anti-rash, the anti-rash!" I cried in agony.

A young lifesaver hurried over to us. "Do you need any help? Is there anything wrong?"

Jeremy looked at the young man huffily. "I'm saving her already, scumbuggit. I got here first." He bent down to me and whispered, "I'm Batman now, okay?"

"Okay," I whispered back, "but don't be rude." I blushed madly and tried to smile politely at the lifesaver. Then I turned to help Batman, who was slathering anti-rash cream all over my legs.

*W*e played Batman at the pool until six o'clock. Normally I find superhero games have a use-by date of about ten minutes. But that afternoon I really got into my character. I was

Poison Ivy—Jeremy wistfully gave her to me, acknowledging that she's a girl and so am I. But he loves her "long orange hair" and he does a wicked sexy walk. I personally think he can be Poison Ivy as long as he wants, but he says he's a big boy now and he can't be her in public.

I flicked back my long orange hair with dangerous allure and wiggled along the deserted concrete. Jeremy whistled and flexed his steely biceps. I only hoped the lifesaver had gone home. I cowered before the biceps of Batman. I smiled wickedly at him. I didn't want to think about anything nasty. I wanted to be Poison Ivy, who was green, not pregnant, and whose biggest problem was an antisocial rash.

On the long walk up the hill toward home, we watched the sun spilling its radiation all over the rooftops. Jeremy was still chattering away, but I could only hear the doctor's voice. It was smooth and warm, like freshly planed wood. I polished it over and over in my mind until it became silky and thin, but it wouldn't stop. Oh, why won't your mind do what you want it to do?

After dinner I read Jeremy a story. It was about space rangers who discovered life on Mars. There were alien bacteria and amoeba with teeth, but Jeremy got stuck on the poor astronauts needing oxygen tanks on their backs. "What if they get a hole in the tank? What if they run out of air? What if they float away from the spaceship?" Horrible noises of slow strangulation burst from his throat. He leapt about the kitchen, the veins in his neck standing out, rehearsing the drama of drowning in space.

"Will you keep it down in there?" Dad called out from the bedroom. "I'm trying to concentrate!"

I could just imagine it. He'd have his three suits and nine shirts laid out on the bed, pressed and perfect. Underpants and cotton undershirts would be in a separate pile, with pairs of socks folded into each other making neat colorful balls on the pillows. David May, business manager and father of two, was catching a plane to South Africa in the morning, and he wanted to have everything ready that evening.

I crept down the hall and stood outside his door, spying. Jeremy's shrieks arrived in his room like animal life from another planet.

"Place is a madhouse!" Dad muttered to himself. He set the alarm and put it on the bedside table, just near enough to reach, not so close to the edge that it would fall.

He sat down on the bed for a moment, finding a vacant spot near the pillow. He stared into space with a little smile on his face. I knew what he was thinking. He was thinking of the clean, five-star hotel that awaited him, with the soap in packets and the towels thick and soft. He'd have just one glass of French champagne after takeoff, to celebrate, as he usually did, and then he'd read through some notes. "This is the life," he'd say.

He must have remembered about earplugs then, because he sprang off the bed like a rocket and extracted them from a drawer. He placed the plugs in a little plastic box next to the socks. Hmmm, yes, there'd be time for a little snooze before Perth. Best to get some shut-eye. He smiled to himself as he decided about shoes, humming a tune that blocked out the tragedies occurring deep within the universe of the kitchen.

My father is a dealer in African art. My mother describes him as a "wheeler-dealer." She says it with a little laugh in her voice, but if you knew her well, you'd hear more suspicion than admiration in her tone. Dad makes regular trips to South Africa. He's been to Johannesburg and Soweto and the Orange Free State. He's even been to Umtata, near the Indian Ocean, where Nelson Mandela was born. Dad said the country is beautiful there, green and luxurious even in winter, with its maze of rivers and deep fertile valleys. I'd like to go one day, but I wouldn't travel the way my father does. His little comforts are like a cushiony set of blinkers around his eyes, I reckon. He travels business class. He can afford to now.

My mother sniffs at him about the business class. She looks just like Grandma when she does that. Mum says, "You must be so proud of yourself, David. You've made all that money out of people who can't even pay their electricity bills."

I hate to think of that. I hope it isn't true. Dad gets furious with her. He shouts, and his face goes all mottled and red like salami. It makes you want to squish him. "With all the money we give them," he yells, "those artists can now *afford* to pay their electricity bills."

"And I suppose they go for holidays by the sea and stay in the best hotels, too," she adds. "Just like you." She glances at him quickly, inching away. She is puffed up with daring and anger. She's panting slightly, frightened she's gone too far, but she can't resist spitting out the sharp little splinters of words in her mouth.

What I can't understand is, why did someone like my father, Mr. Organization and Control, pick something so messy to deal with as art? I could imagine him more happily fiddling with numbers, with tax breaks or bank loans, making calculations with elements that stayed where you put them. Sometimes he brings home a sculpture or a painting he's bought for the gallery. He tells me about the artist, the village rituals and the practice of magic, about the singing and dancing, the carving of wood. As he speaks his face looks quite different. His eyes are lit with those African valleys; he looks younger.

While I leant against the wall, watching him, I wondered if you could ever truly know your parents. Maybe David May, father of two, was really going to meet a gorgeous black woman in Johannesburg. Perhaps he let his thinning hair down over there and danced wildly to the beat of jungle drums. How would I know? I went back to inspect the situation in the kitchen.

Mum was washing up and Jeremy was wearing his helmet. The astronaut theme must have set him off again. I decided to take that book straight back to the library. I picked up the tea towel. As I wiped I thought about the lifesaver at the pool. I didn't want to think about the other thing. I'd noticed that the lifesaver had nice eyes—he was attractive, in that eager, athletic sort of style. A bit like Tim. I wondered what he'd thought of me. I'd seen his eyes move rapidly down my body, so he'd probably dismissed me after he'd seen the emptiness of my bikini top. If you really want to know, I hate wearing a bathing suit. I loathe and detest the treacherous way the cloth collapses into little folds when the bikini gets wet. Those swimsuit manufacturers should know that—why, thousands of women could sue them for false advertising. Or maybe it's just me whose distribution of fatty tissue in the bra area is so disappointing.

Thinking of the lifesaver, I suddenly heard the last part of Jeremy's question. The part I didn't answer. "Would Mum come to Mars?" he'd asked. He hadn't even bothered to ask about Dad.

I watched something on TV after Jeremy had gone to sleep, but I can't remember what it was. Sometimes the television is an excuse to sit like a rotting vegetable and decompose silently while you stare into space. Our family does that often. Sometimes we talk to each other in the breaks. That night I couldn't concentrate on anything—I didn't know who was shooting who, or why. I could only hear my own doctor dialogue inside.

I gave in and went to bed. There was an ancient-history exam the next day, and I had to read a chapter about that weird emperor Caligula. Did you know he made his horse a senator? I got out my books, but I couldn't concentrate on old Caligula, either. Each time I turned a page or stretched up, my arm would brush against my breasts. They tingled, as if electrified.

I touched my nipples gingerly. It felt like I'd had a terrible accident and suffered gravel rash. I felt wounded there.

Before, my breasts had been as dead as Jeremy's modeling clay. This new sensitivity was a symptom of pregnancy, the doctor had said. My disappointing breasts would swell, grow to new proud heights! That is, if the pregnancy continued.

It was so hard to believe. I couldn't believe it. My mind kept skipping over the facts, like a stone skipping on water. You think you know your body, every single crushing deficiency. And then, this.

My periods have never been regular, if you really want to know. I remember being so proud when the blood first came. I was a woman now. Eagerly I waited for the next. I had to wait a long time. Everyone else was stocking up on tampons and sanitary napkins and new pairs of knickers. For them the bathroom became a special place—secret, softly pink, filled with flowery packaging and locks on the doors. It seemed all the girls were gliding into another world—they flowed together, damp with their animal nature, fertile and generous as wild moss growing in a cave.

I was as dry as an old stick. I stood outside the circle. Six weeks apart, eight weeks, the blood came. I'd watch the moon waxing and waning every twenty-eight days. My moon. Why couldn't I keep up with it? Some women sang to the moon during their cycle. They'd join hands on a hill, the full moon blessing their faces. My mother once belonged to a group like that. The moon seemed to pull their bodies toward it, just as it pulled at the tides. I longed to let go and dissolve into that ocean, drawn this way and that by the sky. I took books out of the library to research this phenomenon. Perhaps just a little crumb of information could change my whole view of it all. But the books only pushed me further away. I was always standing outside the circle.

"For most women, the menstrual cycle is every twenty-eight days," the book *About Women* said. So what was I, a hyena? I just wanted to be normal, for God's sake, and keep time with the rhythm of the universe. Was that so much to ask? The world kept dancing away from me.

I closed the history book and picked up my diary. I kept my recent menstrual dates in this small blue book. I riffled through the pages. The black numbers glared at me, all askew and irregular, like the wrong ingredients in a spell. My last period, the book said, was seven weeks ago.

I remembered my last period. Jeremy had come rushing into the bathroom without knocking and seen the blood running down my leg. His eyes had widened and he'd flung his arms around me. "Where's your cut? Was it a flying meteor?" When I told him that I had my "woman's time," he nodded wisely, relieved. "You should wear a nappy, then, like Mum," he advised. "I don't need one anymore," he added proudly, "not even at nighttime. I've got excellent control."

Good old Jeremy. Once I tried to talk to Mum about my abnormalities, and she just said I should eat more yin (or was it yang?) food. I wanted her to see my faint mustache and the excessive hairiness of my arms. But she didn't look properly. "Don't be silly," she said. "I'm sure your cycle will settle down soon. You can be too obsessive about appearances. Feed your soul, Cally, instead—your beauty will shine through."

Well, I know I'm obsessive, I know that. I wish I did think more about abstract art, or all those poor people starving in India and the war in Afghanistan. And I do, sometimes. I worry about them as well, all right? But I can't help returning to my estrogen deficiency. Mum stands there with her hands on her hips, shaking her head at me. It's all very well for her. She has beautiful ripe breasts that move under her shirt like luscious fruit. I feel like I belong to another species when I look at her. It's hard to believe I'm her daughter. There's a silence between our two bodies in space. Sometimes I want to lay my head in the hollow between her breasts. I want to burrow in.

*W*hat the hell was I going to do? Maybe I could lie here on my bed for nine months and my family could pass food in under the door. Mashed avocado through a straw. I could lie here in eternal procrastination. That word sounds rude, antisocial, like something you do alone under the covers. I suppose it is.

Have you ever considered how much the ingredient of time has to do with decision making? If you put in two tablespoons of time instead of one, perhaps the flavor of the decision would be different. Imagine if you only put a quarter of a teaspoon in, the way Tim does.

My grandma was telling me, just before she went away, about the idea that time freezes at the event horizon. We're talking black holes here. It's almost impossible to imagine, isn't it? But frozen time—it must be paradise for the procrastinator. A black hole, some say, is a collapsed star with an escape velocity faster than light. The curvature of space-time becomes infinite inside the hole, and if you fell in, you'd never get out. You'd stretch into something as skinny as an elastic band. Well, space-time inside this hole loses its timelike qualities, and what you get is space-time *foam*——can you believe it?——where time has no real direction.

Of course it's all theory, and you couldn't see any of this, on account of the tidal effects in the black hole stretching you into those weird shapes. But it's something to think about. Sometimes I wonder if I fell into a black hole many years ago (maybe there's one lurking at the bottom of the garden) and that's why I have a problem with time and a body like a rubber band.

Anyway, what I couldn't understand, lying on my bed and looking at the dates in my diary, is this: How did I get into this trouble when I decided long ago that my body was a desert in which nothing would grow? Sparse periods like grudging oases, breasts that wouldn't keep a beetle alive. And now this. It was a terrible shock. I couldn't get past the shock waves.

It was very hard to think through this whole thing alone. There was just dark matter in my head, and tides of panic that blurred the facts. It was like being on drugs that wouldn't wear off.

I hadn't told Tim yet. I felt so far away from him. My situation seemed to have nothing to do with him. This bubbling nausea, these feverish nipples, the image of a little fish swimming in warm waters. The fear. It was all so personal. I'd plunged into a strange interior world, and Tim was an extraterrestrial.

I remember when I told Jeremy about the earth for the first time. How we are always moving on our own axis, on our long journey around the sun. "Nothing ever stays still," I'd said with excitement. "Things are always changing. The universe is expanding and galaxies of stars are flying away with it!"

I'd brought out this piece of news, delivered by Grandma, like a valuable treasure. For me, this evidence of change, of ours being a rebellious, restless world, was a sign of hope. Just because you were born into a certain family, a certain pattern, it didn't mean you had to stay there. Why, families of stars were changing all the time, breaking up, swelling into powerful red giants, cooling into white dwarfs, transforming into neutron stars that could spin more than a thousand times per second. It was the way of the universe!

But Jeremy's lip had trembled. "I don't *want* everything to change," he'd protested. "I want us always to be here, together, with those sad ladies in the living room, and our trips to Manly pool, and my Batman videos and ice creams when I'm good."

At the time I hadn't seen why he'd been so upset. Especially the bit about the sad ladies. But now I understood. Just then those sad ladies on Wednesday seemed comforting rather than irritating. I wanted to wallow in the luxury of yesterday—I longed to be bored again and to feel superior.

Like when my mother was watching some old soapie on TV and I nagged to see *Quantum,* or Dad gave us a lecture on mess. It seemed like a suburban paradise, looking back. Life unfolded at a strolling pace, wearing sensible shoes of Hush Puppies brown. The main event at night was selection of the garbage taker-outer. Just a few weeks ago, nothing in the family landscape stood so much taller than anything else. The garbage, the TV programs, homework, what's for dinner?—all those things were so reassuringly familiar, like rosary beads you could rub together between your fingers for comfort.

I thought about Dad's trips away, and how we'd relax at home then and watch television with our dinners on our laps. I thought about Grandma's astronomy lectures in our garden, with the grass curling round our toes. There were talks with Mum in the kitchen as we washed up and argued about the afterlife and my homework. We knew what came next.

Maybe when you look back from the cliff of disaster, everything appears cozier than it really was.

Now there was a subtext to everything. A dark running undertow that dragged me along. *What will I do? What will I do?* it whispered on and on. It pulled me, obsessed me, took the color out of everything. Every time I thought of something else, laughed, ran, lay on my bed, it pulled me under—*think about me, worry about me, solve me, don't forget about me!*

I wanted my old life back. Me, Callisto—tail-wagging, overeager, estrogen-deficient old me.

I wanted it back, the time before my breasts changed and the blood stopped and I became inhabited.

*A*t eleven o'clock my mother, Caroline, came in to say goodnight. That's a lovely name, isn't it? Caroline. I've always thought it sounded very feminine. You couldn't mistake it for a boy's name, the way you could with mine. Anyway, there she was, drifting in across the carpet. She squinted at the light as if it hurt. Lines sprang up around her eyes like pulled threads. Under her arm was a thick book. I glanced at the title. *Meditation—Discover the Real You.* She'd probably been lying in the dark as usual with her eyes closed, intoning a new mantra.

"Can't sleep?" Mum asked. She didn't wait for a reply. "I've got a letter here from your grandmother." She rolled her eyes. "From Venice, of course."

She had her old cardigan on, and as she bent over, I smelled the familiar odor of avocado and pears. Ever since I could remember, my mother had made her own moisturizer with "only natural ingredients." My father said she smelled like a vegetable garden. "More appealing than a chemical factory," she'd snorted.

When my mother bent over to kiss me, I felt a sudden urge to put my arms around her. I'd breathe in great wafts of peace and avocado; I'd lie down in silence and meditate among the grass and vegetables.

But I lay there, inert. I only moved my hand to cover up the dates in my notebook. A hug wouldn't mean anything, anyway, because a hug is worthwhile only if you share the same knowledge. And my mother didn't know something very important about me. A hug now would be a surface thing, like a white lie. My mother would be embracing the old skin, before the secret.

Mum straightened up and walked briskly over to the window to pull the curtains.

"No, leave them," I called out.

"But the moonlight will keep you awake. You've got a history test tomorrow and you need your sleep."

That old history test. I'd had a far more significant test today. Didn't Mum ever see anything? She always read the contents of jars at the supermarket so carefully. But that was food. When it came to her family, she was quite content to just recognize the label.

She paused at the window, her hand raised uncertainly for the curtain cord. Her hair was silver with moonlight, and she was standing so intently it was as if she were awaiting a celestial blessing. Her eyes seemed fixed on something very far away. Or perhaps she was still listening to her mantra. She could have been an object in a still life, leaving the shell of her body here for appearance's sake while her soul flew gratefully away.

She shook herself momentarily, as if awakening from a dream. Her hand dropped from the curtain cord as if she'd forgotten why it was there. She focused back on me and smiled. "Don't read too long, then, Cally," she said. It was like a nursery rhyme, that phrase, repeated over and over through my childhood. When you said the same thing often, I suppose your mouth could move on automatic while your brain was busy thinking something else for yourself. Mothers probably perfect that technique over the years.

But as I watched her walk to the door, glancing back and blowing a kiss, I wanted to shout, "Look! Look at me properly! Don't you see how pale my face is? How red my eyes are? Don't you want to know why I'm so quiet?" I thought of Jeremy, and how incessant were his daily cries of "Look at me, look at me jump! Look at me dive! See, I can do a handstand!"

"Well, sleep well, Cally, sweet dreams," she murmured as she stood at the door.

I looked at the dark square of carpet between us. I was standing on the bank of a river, and my mother was on the other side. The river flowed between us, familiar, chilly, always there. My mother hovered, studying the moon shadows on the water. I tried to catch her eye, but she turned just then and went through the door. As I watched her go, I saw the river slow and ice over, just a long dead gap between us.

When Mum had gone, I thought about getting up and making hot milk. But I didn't want to joggle the anxiety, set off the alarm. Moonlight drenched the bed, blanching my toes. I wriggled them. I wished I could vanish like a dust particle into nothingness. At a certain altitude I would dissolve, just like that, as easily as sugar in black tea.

One thing you ought to know, if you are going to understand my family, is that Grandma is passionate about cosmology. It was her profession. Mum said it was her life. Grandma Ruth thrived on the unknown and delighted in scientific confusion. It gave her breathing space, she said, to risk and theorize. Science gave her the tools to imagine the world. Confusion gave her the chance to prove everyone else wrong.

Grandma was a hotshot astrophysicist at the university. Professor Ruth Cook. I always listened to Grandma Ruth. I hung on her words, like Jeremy does with his glue ear. I learnt the tiniest details about her life. Sometimes I pretended I was her. As I listened to Grandma there were blazing moments of discovery when I understood something for the first time. It was like falling in love.

It was Grandma who told me that space is not empty. At least ninety percent of the universe consists of dark matter, and no one is sure what this matter is made of. "Maybe WIMPs," said Grandma. "That's weakly interacting massive particles!" She said these particles tended to roam about, not sticking to atoms and molecules like the more familiar stuff of the universe. I added WIMPs to my vocabulary, and found it extremely useful in describing certain people I knew.

And it was Grandma who introduced me to the language of the universe.

*T*he truth—as Grandma tells it—was that she was born with "eyes for the skies." She was labeled from the beginning, as clearly as if she'd shot from the sky, stellar wind in her hair, plasma swirling from her feet. When she was a small baby, just a few months old, the only way to quiet her was to take her out to the garden and place her on her back in the grass. There she would lie, motionless, silent, watching the theater of the stars.

When she began to talk, she could say "moon" before she said "Mummy," and was more interested in experiments with gravity than in hide-and-seek. She never did sleep very much. Later, when she could justify her behavior, she said that sleeping was dumb, because you missed out on the sky's best performance.

Grandma Ruth joined the library when she was very young, and was allowed to take twelve books out at a time. Soon she knew about electromagnetic forces and elliptical galaxies; she could describe the impact of meteorites and theorize about why the dinosaurs died out. She was breathless with information and dying to use it. She couldn't wait to add herself to the map of the universe, like a new star.

At university Ruth was not popular with other students. She wore the wrong clothes and argued with everybody. But Ruth says she didn't care. She was far more interested in the color of Mars than the color of lipstick. Once when she'd been reading through breakfast and was late for class, she raced out in her pajama top, and when she realized, she wasn't even embarrassed. Can you imagine?

At university Grandma Ruth irritated people terribly. She admits it with a laugh. She developed a particular sneer—the left corner of her lip rising almost to her nostril—when any of her colleagues held forth about the absolute truth of some new theory. She often quoted the astronomer Fritz Zwicky on the subject—he was a prickly individual, just like her. "Absolute beliefs are nearly always absolutely *wrong!*" she'd declare with that lift of her lip. She prided herself on her scientific flexibility.

At lunch she usually ate her sandwich alone. But this

didn't worry her, as she always had a book in her bag. Her constellation of friends sat in her heart, continually talking, exploding, transforming hydrogen into helium and lighting up her dark.

Grandma told me once that she found the cosmos far less complicated than the human mind.

Grandma Ruth met Granddad at university. He was studying humanities. He probably had no absolute beliefs, so he was safe. Humanities people, Grandma said, were like washing in the wind. They went wherever it blew them. She admitted to me that secretly she rather admired this flexibility. But she sneered at the way "they" weren't interested in facts, only feelings. Granddad said imagination was greater than knowledge. "Only a scientist could think of that," Grandma retorted. She was right—the quote was from Einstein—so she had the last word.

Strangely enough, when *she* holds forth, she always expects other people to listen and believe. This is one of the things that Mum seems to find most enraging about her. I just sit back and soak her in.

*I*t was the Christmas when I was twelve years old that Grandma said the thing about space. I'd just finished unwrapping my mother's present and it had been a long process because it had been clumsily done, with too much sticky tape, to make up for lack of ribbon. Under the wrapping I found a small square cardboard box. I took the lid off. It was empty.

I peered into the box. I dug my finger into the four corners, tracing the smooth flat base. A false bottom, like a drug runner's suitcase? No, just empty space, framed.

That was when my grandmother leaned toward me and we looked together into the box.

"That box is full, not empty," said Grandma Ruth. "It's brimming with a rich, gaseous mixture of oxygen—twenty-one percent *vital* for life on Earth, my dear—and other amounts of nitrogen, argon and carbon. Without the contents of that box, we would not be here having Christmas!" She gave a great crow of triumph and took out a packet of cigarettes. "Remember, space is mostly matter and matter is mostly space!"

It wasn't until months later that I began to understand about matter—that the atoms inside it were like galaxies, holding huge valleys of space. It was a great discovery, and I looked at ordinary old tabletops and rocks with wonder for weeks afterward.

But in that moment, at Christmas, it was hard to concentrate. There was the dreadful disappointment about the present. And yet through the fog something penetrated. The sounds of Grandma's words were sharp and delicious—like new tangy fruits you'd love to put in your mouth. The possibilities of meaning I folded carefully away into a pleat in my mind.

There was a shift in the way I saw the world. It was as if I'd walked through a wall and come out on the other side. I was standing close to my grandmother in this new place, so near I could smell the layers of her. There were the fumes of Christmas sherry, thick as petrol, the peppermint of toothpaste, and underneath, the eternal menthol cigarettes. I saw my grandmother's quick black eyes darting like fish, and the iron gray hair whirling out of its pins like roving electrons. In this new world my mother was very far away, a diminishing speck, almost imagined.

I was learning a new language, and I was going to make it my own.

That Christmas, Grandma Ruth's words gave me something else to think about, right when I needed it.

"Oh, damn it!" my mother cried when she registered the empty box. "Where is the ring? I put a mood ring in there for you, Cally. You know, it changes colors according to how you feel." She'd grabbed the box from me and tipped it upside down. "It's a beautiful ring, it reveals your innermost feelings. Even if you have developed a hard shell"—and she stopped staring at the box and stared at my father instead—"it can show you and others the true state of your heart. *Damn,* it must have dropped out when I was wrapping it. It'll be here somewhere."

I said nothing. I was thinking about my grandmother's words. The thing about space. "It's a paradox," she'd said. "You'll find a lot of those in astronomy!" It was as if she had given me a present instead. She'd filled the box with an idea so rich it was impossible to put the lid back on.

My father sighed heavily.

The family had then gone on a search for the ring, led by my frantic mother. We picked up rugs and pushed back sofas. Beds were flung apart and cabinets as heavy as elephants were inched out from the walls. Dust fluttered up in clouds. Grandma Ruth sneezed and her eyes streamed.

Mum, I saw, had begun to enjoy it. She had closed her eyes and was using her mental energy to tap the secrets of the house. Her face was feverish with excitement. "Come on, everybody! Let's look on this as a symbolic journey!" she cried, clowning, one foot balanced precariously on the windowsill and the other on the kitchen table. (As if it could possibly be there.) "We are looking for a ring, a mood diviner—buried under all the weight of material possessions!"

I stared at my mother. It's strange how people like her seem to feel every quiver of their own hearts as if they were earthquakes, but are deaf to anyone else's. (Unless you are a sad lady of forty or over, of course.)

"This is ridiculous," my father said. He detached himself from the search party and began to wipe a thin gray coverlet of dust from the leather sofa. He sank down heavily with his paper like a ship throwing down anchor.

Just then Jeremy, who was only a few months old, slid off the cushion where someone had put him, and onto the floor. He wasn't hurt, but like a cricket on its back, he couldn't turn over. His howls were like sirens.

Dad sighed loudly. "Who's going to get him?" he asked, just as if the baby were a kettle screaming. "Go on, Cally, there's a good girl. I've just got comfortable."

You should have seen him, sitting on that sofa. He was like a well-manicured mountain, immovable and unruffled. A baby's cries were supposed to make the milk start in a mother's breast. What should it do to fathers? I walked stonily toward Jeremy, wondering why some people *had* children.

I scooped the baby up and cuddled him into me. His cries stopped as suddenly as if a cork had been popped in his mouth. He smiled at me and dribbled enthusiastically onto my new Christmas dress. I smiled back. I breathed in the warm earthy smell of his head and promised him then, as I looked at the back of my father's newspaper, that I would teach him the language, too. He would grow up with the universe, and the names of the planets would be as familiar to him as apples and oranges. Maybe he could become a star, one of the lucky ones who make their own light. And Grandma Ruth could help.

I looked around the room, at the wrapping paper washing up at my feet like debris at the beach, my grandmother sticking strands of steel-wool hair back into its pins, the shape of my mother's legs as she bent to look under the piano. I felt piercingly empty and full at the same time. Just like the cardboard box I still held in my hand.

After Christmas lunch, when Dad and Jeremy were asleep and Mum was clearing up, Grandma Ruth led me outside into the garden. The sun was sinking behind the rooftops and power lines, and rising in front, like an actor coming onto the stage too soon, was the moon.

"Why does the moon shine while the sun is still in the sky?" I asked. I sat down in the grass and crossed my legs. I looked at my grandmother expectantly, hoping to hear more of the universe. But suddenly I saw the long thin shape wrapped in black canvas, tucked behind the clothesline. It was standing on a tripod that looked to me like the claws of a giant prehistoric bird. I jumped up.

"What is it? A rocket?" I tugged at the canvas, believing in the magic of my grandmother.

Grandma Ruth smiled. "Well, it's nearly as good as a rocket." She took my hand away from the canvas. "Guess! Come on, Cal. How can you go to the moon and stay on the earth at the same time?"

I frowned. I desperately wanted to win in this first test with the universe. But I could only see my grandmother's face, only feel how vital it was to hear her say, "Yes, you're right, that's my clever girl!" Why couldn't I *think*?

"Well? Well?" Grandma Ruth tapped ash into the grass.

How can you go somewhere and stay home? Can you divide yourself in two? I thought of when I read my books—lying there on the bed, I felt nothing of the blue cotton coverlet or my chilly feet. I'd be far away in the story. Or what about Mum lying in the dark, off in some other daylight world of her imagining?

"You can *imagine* the moon, and live there, in your mind!"

"Hmmm, yes, imagination is very important in science," Grandma Ruth agreed vaguely. But she snorted with impatience, blowing smoke through her nose. "Before you imagine anything, Callisto, you need to have a framework—you need to see a bit of the world before you make up the rest. Look at the shape of this thing—how do astronomers see the stars?"

"With a telescope," I said dully.

"Yes!" crowed Ruth, and she began to peel back the Velcro flaps of the canvas. I was trying not to cry. My throat ached. It was so constricted I couldn't utter a sound. The canvas fell to the ground like a magic cloak, revealing the silver-and-glass elegance of the telescope.

"This will be your eye," said Grandma Ruth in heroic tones. "Keep your eye on the universe, Callisto!"

The beauty of the instrument worked its way past my tears and loosened my throat. I walked all around the telescope as Grandma Ruth explained about the lenses and mirrors, how they were arranged to gather light. She showed me how to scrunch up one eye and look through the lens with the other. A light-gatherer, this instrument was, and I had it in my very own back garden.

At eight o'clock Ruth announced that it was Jupiter Night, and the family came out to investigate. They stood around in the grass, Mum holding sleepy Jeremy, Dad with his hands in his pockets.

"Jupiter is the largest of the planets in our solar system," Grandma told me. "And tonight it is in position for us to see it." I moved toward the telescope, but she clicked her tongue. "Listen first, and you'll know what you're looking at."

"Well, don't go on too long, then," my mother said, looking at Jeremy, who whimpered in his sleep.

Ruth ignored her. "So," she breathed expansively, "did you know, Callisto, that Jupiter is a giant world, the brightest planet after Venus?"

"What is it made of?" I asked, proud of my question.

"Green cheese and puppy dogs' tails," said Dad with a grin, and tweaked my ear. I scowled at him.

"On the contrary, the core of Jupiter," replied Ruth loudly, "is composed of melted rock, and is even hotter than Earth's core. There's a shell of ice around the core and over that an atmosphere of hydrogen that is thousands of kilometers thick."

My father began to pull up weeds. He hummed the *Star Trek* theme under his breath. Soon a bundle of limp dandelions lay in his arms, so he excused himself and wandered off to Mum's compost heap.

I began to finger the telescope. It was growing harder to wait.

"Through the telescope," Ruth went on, "you may see the poison clouds around Jupiter—they look like bands of different colors. They rush around at vast speeds—and on one band there is the Great Red Spot." Ruth brought out this last phrase with relish, like a chocolate she'd been saving for me.

"What's that?" I asked. I imagined a giant leak of blood, unstoppable.

"A storm that has been raging for over three hundred years," Mum answered quickly, before Grandma could open her mouth.

"Is that true?" I looked from my mother to my grandmother in amazement.

Caroline gave a short bark of laughter. "Well, I am the encyclopedia's daughter, am I not?"

Ruth smiled happily. "Yes, the Great Red Spot was discovered by Galileo, the first man to point his telescope in its direction. Thanks to him, we've been able to see the storm raging ever since."

I stored that piece of information away. It made me shudder; it was fascinating and horrifying, the idea of a storm continuing forever. All that lashing rage and fury, with no horizon of forgiveness at the end. I looked at my mother, who was looking at *her* mother, and wondered why Caroline had never told me anything about this.

"Before the telescope was invented, no one knew that Jupiter was the mightiest of the planets," Grandma Ruth went on. "But it is named after the most powerful of the Roman gods. And you know, Jupiter's gravity is so strong"—here Ruth lowered her voice to a whisper, so that I had to stop fingering the telescope and lean closer—"it keeps other members of the solar system *captive*!"

"Oh, Mother, for heaven's sake!" cried Caroline. "Why do you have to put it that way?"

"Who's captured?" I asked.

"Asteroids, dark matter, moons—your namesake, of course!"

"What?"

Ruth looked at Caroline, her eyebrows raised in surprise. "There are sixteen known moons that spin around Jupiter." Ruth turned to me. "Four of these you'll be able to see with the telescope, and one of them is called—*Callisto*!" Ruth stood back to gaze at me, like a painter who stands back to see the effect of her last brushstroke.

"You knew that, silly," said Mum, shifting Jeremy to the other shoulder. "I told you about it years ago, but you were never very interested."

I blushed red. I didn't want Grandma Ruth to think I was so out of tune with the universe, such a dull stone. Once I'd seen my name in a science book at school, but it had seemed like a coincidence, nothing to do with me. When I'd asked Mum about it, I remembered her saying dismissively, "I don't know, I heard the name from your grandma, and I thought it sounded musical, like *calypso,* or *castanets*— something with a Spanish flavor, exotic." And she'd gone on preparing the table for her ladies' meeting.

I looked at Mum. She was staring fixedly at an insect crawling on her shoe. It was my mother who wasn't interested, I thought, not me, and I kicked at a paving stone with venom.

"The Jovian moons are ice palaces," Grandma Ruth said into the silence. "Callisto has a twin, called Ganymede, which is the largest moon in the solar system. You'll see it up there—it is even bigger than the planets Mercury and Pluto."

I heard a sharp intake of breath. My mother was standing rigid, like a tree struck by lightning. She moaned, and the movement of her mouth was terrible against the stillness of her body. The sound woke Jeremy, and as if in sympathy, he began to wail. She clutched him tightly and stumbled away, moving over the dark grass like someone who couldn't see the path.

Grandma Ruth shook her head. She turned, as if to go after her, but then stopped.

"What, *what?*" I cried. "What's up with Mum?"

Ruth looked at me. Then she looked back at the telescope. She took another cigarette out of the pack. "So, do you want to have a look at the universe? Come on," she said briskly, "stand here and close that eye, that's right. No, don't hold on there, it's fragile."

I hesitated. My pulse was still hammering with the sight of Mum, her face all broken up like a shipwreck. I kept remembering her mouth. I had never seen her like that. She was like a stranger. But Grandma Ruth was *tsk*ing impatiently, and the lure of the universe was strong.

At first I could see nothing, just a black surface, opaque, like canvas. I felt a leap of alarm—*Oh, I can't even see through a telescope, I'll have to make it up for Grandma!* But then Ruth twisted the lens position slightly. Suddenly a round silver ball came into view. It had four smaller beads strung around it like a perfect necklace. I felt shock spread like a current through my body.

I was seeing it, another world spinning in the universe. I could hardly breathe. I turned for a second to gasp at Grandma. She laughed and gave me a thumbs-up sign. I swung back again. The telescope was a living nerve attached to my eye, and I was traveling along it into space. Those shining spheres, fixed in motion, were like balls thrown up by a juggler. They were so near, I could almost catch them.

To see pictures of something in a book and then see the real thing in the world is heart-stopping. It's like your favorite wish jumping out in front of you. I shifted my weight onto the other leg. I had a cramp. It didn't matter. To think that this other world had always been there, orbiting, storming, fighting with meteors while I went to school and played with Jeremy and ate my sandwiches. All those huge transforming things were going on and I never knew. The sky was suddenly different, inhabited by ice palaces and beads of silver.

As I gazed I was aware of the blades of grass on my ankle-bones and the smell of Grandma Ruth's cigarette on the breeze. But these things were muffled, more like memories of things familiar.

"Can you see the four moons?" Grandma's voice was eager. "The Galilean moons? Now you can imagine how Galileo felt when he discovered them!"

I managed to nod and keep my eye glued to the lens at the same time. Grandma's voice was like background music for the theater I was watching.

"Galileo, you know, made his own telescope. At that time everyone believed the earth stood still while all the stars and planets traveled around it. Galileo expected to prove everyone wrong." Grandma chuckled. She obviously liked that bit. "Just think, Cally—until then everyone believed that our moon was the only one. But when Galileo focused on Jupiter, what did he see? Three strange dots of light in line with it!"

Galileo, I thought, couldn't have been more excited than me. Even though four centuries separated us, I felt intimately close to him, as if our souls lay side by side, somewhere up there between the moons.

"Well, soon he had proof that the dots were moving around Jupiter. He could prove that some objects in the sky don't circle the Earth. Would the telescope lie?"

"No!" I cried.

"No!" echoed Grandma Ruth.

"So what happened to Galileo then?"

"He was put in jail like a common criminal." Grandma spat out the words angrily. She began to pace around the garden, as if she were still trying to work off the rage caused by the infamy of human beings four hundred years ago.

"But no one could destroy the moons of Jupiter," she concluded when she came back.

"Tell me about them," I said. "Tell me about *mine*."

Grandma Ruth smiled. "Callisto—it comes from the Greek, *kallisto* or *kallistos,* meaning 'the most beautiful.' "

I made a face, but I looked at Callisto again.

"Gosh, I'm everywhere!" I said. I hugged the knowledge to myself. Somehow having my name up in the sky, in that precious place, strengthened my claim there, making it more complete. My name was like the flag that mountaineers put up on the summit after a long climb. It made the language of the universe seem peculiarly my own.

Then another thought fell like a shadow. "Did Mum know all this?"

At that moment the porch door slammed like a pistol shot and Caroline came out of the house. We heard only her footsteps in the darkness, and then she emerged so suddenly, her face swimming up to us out of the deep, that we both jumped back, startled.

"Jeremy's asleep," she said. Her mouth was calm now, and composed. "You'd better be getting to bed, Cally."

Grandma Ruth looked at her watch. "Heavens, it's ten o'clock. I didn't know it was so late." She ruffled my hair. "You're all right then, Caroline?" Ruth's voice was soft and she reached out to touch my mother's hand.

Caroline folded her arms. "Fine," she said.

I heard the full stop that came after it. Mum still hovered there, tense, like a rubber band stretched tight. The night was silent out in the clipped, smooth garden, but I could feel the swarm of words buzzing in my mother's head. She seemed electric with feelings. She was staring at Grandma Ruth, but she said to me, "So, did you thank Grandma for her present, Cally? Do you think you will enjoy exploring the skies?"

"Yes, Mum. Thank you, Grandma, it was lovely, it was all . . . great."

"Good," Caroline said briskly. "Your grandmother always spent more time looking at the sky than she did at me. It's a very nice telescope, Cally, top of the range, so make sure you look after it." And she nodded at her mother as impersonally as if she were saluting the postman, and went back inside.

I stared at the swinging porch door.

"She's just tired," said Ruth, peering through the mulberry leaves at the moon. "You get very emotional when you're sleep-deprived, you know. Jeremy wakes her up all through the night. Caroline will have to stop breast-feeding soon."

"Why?"

"He's not getting enough milk, in my opinion. And if he's hungry, he won't sleep well. The bottle would make things more regular. This family needs a bit more order in it." She sighed and shrugged. "But try telling any of that to Caroline. . . ."

I glanced back at the wire door. It had stopped swinging, but I could feel a presence, "a spirit," as Caroline would say, that was as strong as my mother's real flesh. Clinging in the gaps of the wire was another Caroline, almost speechless, hardly there. I could just catch her outline if I joined the dots of her words, rough in the soft night air.

Ruth and I looked back at the moon. It was round and full tonight, a circle of silver. Grandma breathed out with pleasure and smiled. "The Greek philosopher Plato said that the sphere is the most perfect geometric shape because it contains the largest possible volume within a given surface area."

I gazed at perfection. It was a relief. I agreed with Plato.

Grandma gave a sudden chuckle. "Did you hear the one about getting fat? Well, a scientist once said that you shouldn't worry about becoming rotund, because it means you're approaching a more perfect shape!" And she patted the gentle hill of her stomach. For someone who was so taken by the skies, she didn't look very ephemeral. Her two legs were planted firmly on the grass, as solid as tree trunks. Only her hair looked a little wild, the way it sprang out of its pins as if pulled furiously by some invisible alien force.

I grinned politely at her joke. But I didn't want to think about human flesh right now. I wanted to stay on the moon. It was like watching a movie that you never wanted to end. Up there, I'd have a different address, different parents. They'd be powerful and perfect, without flesh or gravity. Tomorrow night I'd point my telescope at the moon and have a good look at it. I'd fly toward that cool shining place, unstained by earthly words or mysteries of feeling. I knew that no matter how long I looked, no matter what storms or explosions occurred around it, the moon would remain itself, untouched.

And that was something to rely on.

We drew the black canvas over the eye of the universe and walked back into the sleeping house together.

It was years later that I remembered my mother's words that night. *Your grandmother always spent more time looking at the sky than she did at me.* When I found her diary and sneaked into her bedroom to read it, that remark was like a footnote, helping me to make sense of things.

*Y*ou needed footnotes, or maybe *A Guide to the Living Dead,* if you wanted to understand my mother. She told me once I was just young and cynical, and if I focused on my spiritual life, I'd understand. I told her that if she thinks *I'm* cynical, she should meet old Caligula. I got the dead-bird gaze, so I quit.

Luckily, I had my own language. When I was fifteen, I decided that Caroline was made up of dark matter. She was no longer a moon. The particles of her skin and heart were derived from foreign substances that were unable to absorb or emit light. She held up a shadow to the world.

On the Friday night following my discovery at the doctor's, I decided not to go out. I felt so sick. Just the thought of green ginger wine could make me vomit. I remembered when we were kids we'd sometimes chant "greasy pork chops" fifty times and see if it would make anyone throw up. The nausea was worse at night, strangely enough. Weren't you supposed to have morning sickness? It figured, though—of course I'd be different from most women, wouldn't I?

The other reason I didn't go out was that if a quiet moment came, I thought I might tell my mother. It was only a strand of a thought, but the urge to tell someone was becoming overwhelming. The roar of the undertow was deafening—*What will I do? What will I do?*—and I wanted someone else to hear it, this awful thing, and tell me everything would be all right.

But Mum had a friend over to dinner. Beth. They were huddled up on the sofa, deep in conversation, for most of the night. Beth cried over coffee. Mum patted her hand. At around midnight I came out of my room to speak to Mum. She shooed me away with a finger on her lips. "But I need to talk to you," I said. "I've just had a terrible dream. I saw a ghost." I thought that would get her in. The friend began to cry again. My mother looked at me in a scathing way and said, "Go back to bed, Cally. I'll come in later." But she never did.

That Friday night it was very hard saying no to Tim (borrowers *never* say no). But I just couldn't face going out. I said I was coming down with bronchitis again. I was so anxious anyway, it was quite easy to sound breathless. He looked annoyed, and some of the light cooled in his eyes. I almost changed my mind then. It was terrible to see him look away from me with that disapproving frown. I knew he was wondering who else he could take to the dance. His mind was flicking over girls at our school. He was standing there in front of me but he was absent. Far away. I couldn't bear it. I felt like I was dying. I grabbed his hand and told him I'd see him on Saturday night, and weren't his parents going out again? I managed to smile provocatively, my lips promising a banquet of sensual delights.

He kissed me then and I saw that his eyes were lit up and warm. I was so relieved. I felt like someone who'd had a reprieve from the gallows.

I didn't know what my mother thought about sex. I didn't know what she thought about a lot of things, I suppose. I have always collected most of my information about life from books. Like my grandma, I've usually borrowed twelve (the maximum amount) each fortnight from the library. I learnt about the mechanics of sex from a book when I was seven. In the photos I saw toads and birds and rabbits humping. Around that time my uncle Dan came down to visit us from up north. He told us they were having a terrible time there with tropical pests—they multiply like nobody's business. Take the case of the cane toad, he said, spreading his hands. He gave a wicked grin and told us how every night, around eleven o'clock, he'd take his bow and arrow out into the garden to hunt cane toads. "Jackpot!" he'd yell if he got two cane toads mating. They'd be stuck together like glue, and the arrow would go straight through them. "Two for the price of one!"

My mother made a ghastly face at this story and changed the subject. Mating always seemed to me such a dangerous thing to do after that. Especially if you were a cane toad.

When I was ten, Uncle Dan's daughters came down to stay for a week. They were a lot older than me, and at night I would listen to them talking about boys. Lisa, the blond one, had let a boy "do" it to her. She said it was "beautiful," and he'd loved her so much that he'd kissed her all night. In the morning her lips were all puffed up to twice the size.

Alone in the shadows, I shuddered. I didn't want to have puffy lips. It seemed that this sex business always had some scary consequence. But I rather liked the thought of being held all night. Like someone's precious jewel.

The first time I made love with Tim was like that. He held me tightly, kissing every inch of my skin, as if he wanted to lap me up. We were slow like treacle, our tongues tasting each other, gentle as kittens. Minutes were drugged; we flowed into some other time, into each other.

It wasn't like that at all, actually. I make up a lot of things, lying on my bed. It was all over in about five minutes. It was a terrible disappointment, if you really want to know. I felt empty afterward, like I did on that Christmas Day without the present.

We'd only gone out together twice. On our first date we went to a movie. It was full of big-breasted women with startling cleavage. He kept gawking and digging me in the ribs. But afterward we kissed in his car. It was lovely, the kissing, all wet and soft and generous. He kissed my hair and my nostrils and my chin and my neck, and everywhere he kissed, I felt alive. I wanted that part to go on forever. That's all I wanted to do.

But you're not allowed to do that. If you kiss that way, then you have to go further. Otherwise the boy suffers terribly. That's what Tim said. When it was time to go, he groaned a lot and acted as if he were in pain.

On the second date, we went back to his place. His parents were asleep. We tiptoed into his room. The comforter on his bed was a startling white. I wondered how his mother got it so sparkling. She must have been very organized. On a small square sofa on the other side of the room, the cushions were lined up one after the other like soldiers. There were surfing posters on the walls, with blue-eyed bronzed gods looking out of them, just like Tim. My heart lifted a little—after all, here I was, picked out of the masses by one such god. I smiled at him and sat down on the bed.

"No, not there," he said.

He pointed to the polished timber floor, where there was today's newspaper spread out. He took my hand and pulled me down. "If it's your first time," he explained kindly, "you might make a bit of a mess."

He began to take off my jeans. I helped him with the zip. I felt like a puppy he'd decided to train. Maybe I'd get a nice bowl of meaty bites if I performed well.

He didn't kiss me first. He put two fingers straight inside me. I hoped I didn't smell down there. His nail scraped against me. I winced. I was so dry. "Sorry," I whispered. He said nothing and took them out.

I didn't know how he would get anything else in there. I was clamped shut like the Reserve Bank.

He persisted. Our bodies moved against the newspaper, which crackled like nobody's business. I thought of Uncle Dan's cane toads and wondered if Tim's mum, so efficient with her washing, could get both of us with one arrow. Over Tim's shoulder I kept my eyes on the door. I was sure at any moment she'd hear this tremendous crackling and burst in.

When it was finished I stood up and put my jeans back on. I looked at the newspaper. There was only one drop of blood, like a fingerprick. It made me think of Snow White.

Maybe some girls bled hugely. They might have covered all the newspaper, dripping over the weather section and into sports. You could hardly even see where I'd been.

He could have told his mum he had a nosebleed. He could have washed the spot himself. I could have told him cold water takes bloodstains out. It could have all been different. But it wasn't. That is how it was, if you really want to know.

*W*hen I arrived home after that first time with Tim, I went straight to the bathroom to look in the mirror. I looked into my eyes, at my mouth, I ran my fingers down the sharp bones of my rib cage. I looked at all the places that had been touched. I bit my lip in disappointment. Nothing looked any different. I was still the same.

In bed, I hugged my arms. I touched my nipples, the softest circles on my body. Pushing my breasts together, I forced a faint line of cleavage in between. Invisible ink. I kept searching for signs of change, my entry into woman-hood. But there was nothing.

After a few more outings I decided that after all, I was relieved. Seeing as I felt so little with Tim, it seemed only natural that it had no lasting effect on me. We progressed from the floor to the soldier sofa. I never did get to lie on the bed. It frightened me now anyway, all that saintly white. It was a marital bed, I thought, suitable for grown women with big busts who felt something.

When I took off my clothes with Tim, I settled into wait-ing mode. It was like being at the dentist's, reading about other women in magazines who were having glamorous sex. Women with breasts. Those women had wild cleavage, the kind of deep cleft between valleys that could hold a pencil, a diamond, something useful.

When Tim put his hand on my breast, I always felt a hot flame of shame. What must I feel like to him, the kitchen table? Empty space? Grandma Ruth would have reminded me that space is not empty at all, but I couldn't imagine Grandma had ever spent much time agonizing over what men thought of her.

I read once that the human female had breasts purely for sexual attraction. They were for the man. All other females of the animal species had tiny teats, just for their babies. It made me feel ungenerous, that piece of information, like coming empty-handed to a birthday party.

Tim never did much with my breasts, anyway. He tweaked my nipple, a bit like a shopper at the greengro-cer's, testing for ripeness. But he always passed over that half of my body, as if I were not yet juicy enough. It wasn't his fault, I knew, because I lay there straight and clenched like a post, waiting till that part of the examination was over. Often I'd whisper words from the language of the universe to myself, words like *isotropy,* or *inertia,* or *cosmic microwave background.* The words were a comfort, like a soft toy or a piece of silk.

What I did like was the attention. During that brief time on the sofa, Tim was thinking about nothing but me. I knew it. He looked at me with such hunger, as if he could eat me, as if he could stuff all the flesh on my bones into his mouth. I'd have done anything for him then. It made me feel so important, lit up like gold, the way he looked at me.

"I adore you," he whispered as he unzipped my skirt.

"Really?" I'd whisper into his shoulder.

I couldn't understand why I wasn't hungry, like him. I wondered if I ever would be.

I began to think of it as a kind of contraception, this peculiar lack of excitement I had. It was like a world without sound, or smell. Like a planet with no atmosphere—everything floated, nothing made an impression. I supposed that was how moons like me had sex. All reflected heat, nothing of your own. There was no atmosphere on the moon, either. I decided the only benefit about being a moon in this situation was that it allowed all kinds of things to happen to you without any consequences occurring. Nothing was left behind after these surface episodes, nothing moved, as if I were a sailing boat becalmed on a windless sea.

I imagined that all my life I would be trapped on this same sea, without the weather. Other people had weather in bed, I didn't. It was as immutable, I decided, as having brown eyes or crooked toes.

But it seemed now you couldn't even rely on the weather.

I did as I was told, that Friday night, and went back to bed. But I couldn't close my eyes. For three nights now I hadn't slept. Anxiety must be a stimulant, like speed or cocaine. I felt as if there were liquid caffeine running through my veins. I was trying to think, really I was. The trouble was that I just still couldn't believe it.

Maybe if someone else knew, it would seem more real. But there was no one to tell. Maybe the doctor was wrong. I'd read about those "hysterical" pregnancies, where women blew up like puffer fish and bought maternity clothes and everything, and then suddenly their bellies went down like balloons at the end of a birthday party. I felt a sudden lift of the heart. That'd be right—I could just imagine my mixed-up body doing something crazy like that. Maybe I'd go back to that doctor and ask him to consider this. We could consider it together while we waved compassionately at the lungfish.

I felt almost excited by this idea—better than I'd felt for days. I noticed that if I was really firm with it, the nausea seemed to fade now, too. Perhaps the whole thing was in my mind.

I snapped the light on with new energy. Lying on the bedside table was Grandma's letter from Venice. I hadn't even opened it. I shook my head at myself and smiled indulgently. All this worry over something that was only in my mind.

I plumped up the pillows, settling back for a good read. I loved getting Grandma's letters. The stamp showed one of those delicate Renaissance men with the long nose and chiseled jaw. The wavy black postal lines ran through the stamp, smudging it slightly. Pity, I'd have liked it perfect.

"Venice is *magnifico,* as always," Grandma Ruth wrote. "But I don't have much time to wander the streets. There's so much going on at the conference, and so many hotheads! The Moscow gang are still arguing that the neutrino has mass, and the Swiss deny it. Look up Enrico Fermi, Callisto, and we'll talk about it when I get back. Oh, the Italians—they know their stars, and their coffee! Every time there's an interval, you can't resist one of those short blacks—tepid, so's you can taste it, bitter and sweet at the same time. I sip liters of the stuff, watching the gondolas drift along the canals, then race back for the next lecture. Heaven on earth, Cal!"

God, it would have been great to be there with Grandma. I could listen to her argue, watch the caffeine and excitement shine in her face. It would be like visiting another planet.

She was in Italy for two months, to attend La Conferenza di Galileo. Every five years astronomers met in Venice, the city where Galileo worked for most of his life. They discussed the latest discoveries in cosmology, and this year the theme was dark matter in the universe, the name coined by the scientist Zwicky back in the 1930s.

Grandma went to all the conferences, even though she

was retired from the university now. She said that just because the skies no longer kept her in menthols, it didn't mean she'd stop looking up. My grandmother arrived at the peak of her career only a few years ago. She'd been one of the astronomers who discovered thousands of previously unknown galaxies in the cloud-veiled skies of the Milky Way.

I had already written to Ruth in Venice. My letter was probably waiting for her when she first set foot in her hotel. I liked writing out the address, using Galileo's name—it was as if some of the light anointing the heads of those conference stars might rub off on me, just on contact.

With my letter I'd included an essay I'd written in English at school. I thought she might appreciate it. We'd been asked to examine the use of the moon as a symbol in literature. I'd spent hours over it, studying the celestial facts, quotes from poetry, my own private feelings. Even though I had learned everything from my science manuals, I still preferred to see the moon as a perfect place, invulnerable and remote (like me). "The moon is an island of perfection," I wrote, "a silver jewel on a black sea. Nothing touches it, but the moon touches everything here on Earth."

I'd been quite proud of this essay, and I'd pinned a photo of myself at the telescope to it as well.

I scanned Grandma's letter. I swallowed in anticipation. I had to read all about the coffee and the gondolas and the dark matter before I saw any mention of my essay.

"Fiddle!" wrote Grandma. "How can you write all this drivel about the moon, as if you'd never heard anything I said! 'So remote, so self-sufficient, floating up there alone on stellar winds . . .' Well, that's just romantic nonsense.

The moon is not self-sufficient, nothing in our universe is. Haven't you heard of gravity—the phenomenon of attraction between bodies? Why didn't you put that in? Don't tell me you're becoming all fanciful like your mother! The moon is wired gravitationally to this planet, without which it would sling off into space like a stone from a catapult. Don't you remember that experiment we did with the bucket and the rope? Can you describe any object in our solar system without reference to its relationships to other bodies? Come on, Callisto!"

I could feel my cheeks burning as I read. I slammed the letter facedown on the bed. *Shut up!* I wanted to shout. *Shut up and let me talk! I know all that. What do you think I am, a member of the Flat Earth Society? This is just the way I see it, right, it's my own world, it's a fantasy, get it? And I'm not anything like* my mother. I winced. I had a sudden picture of Mum sitting round the living-room table at her ladies' meeting, talking to dead spirits.

I picked up the letter again. I wanted to cut my grandmother off, like scissors to paper. But the letter had its own magnetic field, and my eyes raced down the page. "I know, I know," I kept chanting as I read.

The language of the universe had never been like this. I could feel tears burning my lids. Since I was twelve the cosmos had been a world of infinite space, permissive, elastic, consisting of exotic materials, wild chemicals. Suddenly it had boundaries of brick, and they were shutting me out. Or maybe it was just my grandma. Why did she have to be so damn rigid?

"There is even some evidence, Callisto, that the moon is made from the same stuff as Earth," she wrote in her deafening scrawl. "When the earth was very young, it was hit by another mighty planet, and the vapor created by the heat of the collision spurted out into space, settling into orbit and condensing as the moon."

"I know, I know," I chanted to myself. *But Einstein said that imagination was more important than knowledge, remember?*

"Practically speaking, the moon isn't so remote, so unearthly, so angelically different, my dear. Its face is pocked with craters, like someone suffering from acne. I'm sure you've seen them with your telescope."

I groaned. I tried to remember the bold A+ that Mrs. Graham had marked in red on the last page of my essay. "And really, Cally, how can a satellite with no wind, no water and no air be invulnerable? Every trace of history remains like a scar on its landscape."

I stopped chanting. I held my breath, as if to hear better. "Just think, the footprints left by astronauts will never be worn away! Isn't that remarkable?"

Yes, it was. I didn't know that. Or at least I hadn't thought that far. I was not good on consequences. I closed my eyes. I saw tracks left by birds in wet sand, tire marks in dusty roads. I saw myself lying still on Tim's floor, out of the weather. There was silence in my head, like the moment after lightning, when you're waiting for thunder. I pulled up my T-shirt and looked at the white lunar landscape of my stomach. No atmosphere meant no protection. Inside, there were footprints.

I believed it now. My mind stopped skipping and the thought dropped like a stone into my body. I was heavy with gravity, and I lumbered into the bathroom to throw up.

PART
2

Callisto doesn't like me anymore. I don't know what I've done. When I go into her room she says, "I'm busy, Jeremy." Yesterday was so hot, but she wouldn't take me to the pool.

"It's the only place we'll be safe," I said. "The man on the radio told us we're having a heat shave."

"I'm busy," she said.

What I want to know is, how can she be so busy lying on her bed? Maybe she doesn't like me because I wear a helmet. Sam Underwood at school said I should be locked up. Why? Only bad robbers are locked up. I haven't hurt anyone. I told Sam that helmets protect you against flying objects, but he wouldn't listen. No one listens to me. They're all too busy.

I feel sorry for Sam Underwood, really. If he only knew what I know, he'd wear protection gear, too. Before Callisto stopped liking me, she told me something. She said the earth is growing all the time. Every second, thousands of little pieces of iron and stone called meteors fall onto our planet. She said the pieces are no bigger than pinheads. But I think some of them must be ginormous, otherwise why do they make the earth so much heavier every day?

Mum says, "Stop filling the boy's head with scary facts, Callisto."

Cally says, "At least they're facts and not spirits from the other side." When she says "other side," she makes her voice go all low and shivery, and Mum gets mad.

Another reason I feel sorry for Sam Underwood is that everyone calls him Sam Underwear. He pretends he doesn't care. When I say "underwear" to myself, it makes me laugh, too. But I only do it under my breath. There was a man on telly last night, and his name was Bob Bottom. Even Cally laughed at that. We laughed together for about five hundred hours right there on the black sofa. I kept making myself think of "bottom" and "underwear" so I could keep going.

But then Cally hopped up and went back to her bed.

I asked Mum why my sister is always lying on her bed now.

"She's got the teenage blues, Jeremy," said Mum. "It makes her cranky. Don't take any notice of her."

Is it catching, this teenage disease? Will she turn blue? My lips went blue at Manly pool once, when I stayed in the water too long. Cally said my lips gave her the creeps, and she made me put my sweater on. She said only dead people went blue. I hope Cally isn't dying, with her teenage blues.

If Cally dies, I'll never have anyone to play with. I might as well go out into Belmore Park, the one with no trees, and wait for a meteorite to get me. I wouldn't even wear my helmet.

Sam Underwood is always asking if he can come over to my house. "Do you live in a tent?" he asked me last week. "Do you live in a zoo?"

Mum never lets me have anyone over to play. She says we'd make too much noise. She's always got sad ladies in the living room. Cally says we may as well go and live in a funeral parlor. When you're dead, you get a funeral. I know that much.

Dad says, "Why don't you go and play rugby? I'll take you on Saturday mornings." A boy in our class, I saw him, got his whole top row of teeth knocked out. You have to wear a mouth guard to rugby, as if you're in a war. I said, "No thanks, Dad."

Dad would miss a lot of Saturday mornings, anyway. He goes away all the time, mostly to South Africa. He does business there. Mum is always putting newspaper clippings about South Africa up on the fridge. She says it's terrible what goes on there. Dad takes them down when she isn't looking. He says those things don't happen anymore, not since Mr. Mandela, and doesn't she live in the modern world? I don't like her pictures. There are children with no arms and men with angry faces. There are women crying over small boxes with dead children in them. I lose my appetite, looking at the fridge. I prefer things in packets, from the pantry.

I wonder when you're dead, if you can still think.

Grandma says you can't, that it's like being asleep. That must be nice, in a way. Mum says it's not true, and that silly old Grandma doesn't believe in the spirit. I don't like her calling Grandma "silly." Mum says when we die our bodies change, but our spirits are still there.

"What does it look like?" I asked her.

"You can't see it," she said, "it's so light and free, it wafts around like a breath of wind."

I want to ask her about gravity, but she gets this look in her eyes and I know she's gone away somewhere. No one ever asks me to come with them.

My sister lay on her bed for about twelve hundred hours yesterday. When I went to bed I had a bad dream. Batman lost his space suit and fell off the moon. He was choking, there was no air. Cally didn't come when I called, so I went into her room. She was lying on her back. There was a bucket on the floor with some sick in it. She was so still, I was scared. Batman couldn't breathe. Nor could I. There was a pocket mirror on her bedside table—she uses it to look at her pimples up close. I put it next to her mouth, to see if she was dead. The mirror clouded up every two seconds. She was okay.

Mum came in then to see if Cally was all right. She felt Cally's forehead.

"What are you doing?" she whispered to me.

I told her. She smiled and patted my head. "I used to do

that when you were a baby," she said. "When you slept for more than an hour at a time, it made me nervous—it was so unusual!"

I made her tell me the story a second time. When I was in bed, I said I'd go to sleep only if she told it a third time. I liked thinking of her coming in to see my breath making little clouds on her mirror.

*T*here's never anything much to do in the afternoons now, so I thought I'd make a bunker. There's a good spot under the house. No one goes there because there's just a lot of old dirt and a nest of cockroaches. They all run away when they see me. I found a shovel in the garage, which is excellent for this sort of digging. It's quite a big shovel, because it's for grown-ups, but if I put both my feet on it and stab it into the earth, I can get a good scoop.

Dad won't miss his shovel because he never does any gardening anymore. He says it makes his nails black, and anyway, Mum is the expert on plants. She's always trying different ones for her aches and pains. She grinds them up with a little hammer thing. Sometimes she puts onion juice in my ear. I hate that. It itches like mad and then burns. And I still can't hear much, anyway.

Maybe Sam could come and help me dig. Under the house, no one would hear us. They wouldn't even know we were there. That way Sam would have protection, too. Even though he says he doesn't need it. But hey, like Batman says, protection is my racket!

If a meteorite hits this house, we'll be goners. And no one can really tell when they're going to fall. They could just fall out of the sky at any moment. They could come like bad dreams, when you're asleep. If that happened, then it wouldn't matter anymore that Cally is always lying on her bed, or that I can't have friends over, or that there are little children lying in boxes over there in South Africa. We'd all be dead. Only our spirits might make little breaths of wind on a mirror.

So I'm making a bunker for us all. And Sam can help.

On Saturday night I told Tim. He said nothing for ages. We were at Miranda Blair's house, out in the garden. The music was loud, even out there, because she had speakers dotted like garden gnomes in among the potted plants.

"I'm pregnant," I said again more loudly, in case he hadn't heard. I looked nervously around, to make sure no one was listening. "But don't tell anybody," I added.

We were sitting on those canvas director chairs. I took a slug of green ginger wine. Something sour rose up in my throat.

"Jesus," said Tim. He took my hands and wobbled the ring from Franklin's back and forth on my finger. He coughed.

"Cally," he said, and squeezed my hand. "Don't worry, Cal, I'll look after you."

It was almost worth it, all of it, to hear him say that. All the sickness and the anxiety and the newspaper and everything. His face was shining with concern. There were little crinkles of worry at the corners of his blue eyes. He made me think of the doctor. I know it's not cool for a woman entering the new millennium, but I'd have given everything to be looked after. I started to imagine us in a little flat, with carpet (not timber floors) and our own dining room table. We'd have people over for dinner, and a stock of green ginger wine. It would be just the two of us. Tim would go to work, and he'd come home to delicious smells of roast. I couldn't quite get to the baby bit, but I just needed more time to imagine it.

I started to feel breathless, as if I'd just run a mile. Our little flat was becoming so clear in my mind. I could see the guests around the new dining table—there was Miranda Blair in her black lipstick, and there was her tribe. They were all laughing at something I didn't hear. They kept drinking our wine and breaking our glasses, and the house was filled with people, surfers and lifesavers and others I didn't know. The floor was littered with surfing magazines. There were no issues of *New Scientist* anywhere. No one had heard of black holes or inertia. When I went into our bedroom there was still the noise and the music. There was nowhere to go. Nowhere that was mine. The comforter was too white. I put my hands over my ears, but it didn't do any good. I wanted my father's earplugs. God, I even wanted my father. I wanted to go home.

"Are you all right?" Tim asked. "You probably shouldn't be drinking that." He took my glass away from me and put it on the wooden table, out of reach. I'd done that kind of thing with Jeremy when he was four.

If I lived with Tim, I couldn't keep wearing this bad disguise. Eventually I'd have to take it off. Then he'd see me in the nude, with all my bones and my tail wagging and my estrogen deficiency. And then we'd both die. It would be like one of Jeremy's meteorites hitting the earth. The end of life as we know it.

But I didn't have to worry, as it turned out. It wasn't that kind of "taking care" that he had in mind.

"Listen, Cally," he said. "I know this guy in the Cross, he's a friend of my brother's. He's an expert with herbs and plants that cure you of all kinds of things. He's at the cutting edge of this stuff. I'll talk to him and see if he can give you something to make your period come on. He helped one of my brother's girlfriends once."

I looked up at him. "Really?" I said. I thought of my mother with her onion juice.

He nodded. "We could go, say, Tuesday night? Monday night I've got swimming training."

I beamed at him, showing that I understood.

"We could go out to dinner afterward, Cal. I know this nice little place in Kellet Street. We could go there, just the two of us, after the cure."

I told him that sounded lovely.

I went and rescued my glass from the wooden table, and someone filled it up for me. I took a swig. It was sickly sweet—marsala. I could see it lying in my stomach, a red band of liquid on top of the green ginger. It would be like that oil-and-water experiment I did with Jeremy. The two substances never mixed, no matter how much he shook the test tube. I felt the two wines staring at each other in a hostile manner in my intestine. One of them tried to climb back up my throat.

We didn't stay at the party much longer, because Tim wanted us to go back to his place. I didn't like to say no. My head was spinning as we walked into his room. I told Tim about my head and he spread Saturday's newspaper out on the floor in case I was sick. We lay down and I don't remember much until the last part. I turned over and threw up all over the Leunig cartoon on the back page. We both sat up in horror. I must have drunk quite a bit of marsala, because the vomit was a stunning color, quite scarlet and swirly. It lay in bands across the headings on the newspaper, like the Great Red Spot around Jupiter. We watched the red spread and stain the paper, seeping onto the polished timber floors, and out into the universe.

Tim jumped up and ran to fetch a rag. I just sat there, leaning against the bed. I felt almost satisfied, watching my Great Red Spot. I don't know why.

Tuesday, January 27

Callisto started high school today. Nearly twelve years old. She's growing up so fast. Poor Cally, she was nervous this morning. She talks nonstop when she's anxious. "My uniform is too long, Mum," she wailed. "Everyone will think I'm a nerd. First impressions are really important." And she embarked on a long diatribe, following me into the bathroom.

"Take the case of ducks and imprinting," she said to me in the mirror. "A duckling stumbles out of his egg and thinks the first animal he sees is his mother. He'll go on all his life expecting some green tree frog to teach him to dive. It's tragic, and now all those Meadow High kids will form the impression that I'm a dork, no matter what I wear tomorrow."

To cheer her up, I told her she's so good at arguing, she should become a lawyer. She said she couldn't convince me to take up a lousy hem, so how could she persuade a jury? She folded her arms then in a gloomy fashion and went into her cone of silence. I wished I *had* taken up the hem last night. I meant to, but Naomi rang up in a dreadful state. Lost her job!

I wish, too, that she wouldn't worry so much about appearances. She's always puzzling over what other people think of her. It makes her so vulnerable. I want to grab the people she likes and put a spell on them so they all rush to be her friend. Find a love potion.

I used to be just like her. My mother laughed at me about it. She thought it was idiotic to worry about other people's opinions. I never let her know how much time I spent in front of the mirror.

At forty the state of your face is the least of your worries.

In the car, on the way to school, Cally fiddled with the catch on her bag. Open close, open close, snap, snap, snap. She was holding her breath while she fiddled, and letting it out in great gusty sighs. Snap, sigh. So irritating. But I was sick with anxiety for her. I know what it's like. All those new faces, kids making mysterious instant decisions about you. "I've got a purple bag and so have you, let's be twins."

Cally never had the right bag when she was little. Now I think she has, because she's done the research. She takes it very seriously, this watching of other kids. Notes what they're wearing, and the words they use. She does a far better job of camouflage than I ever did.

I never had many friends at high school. Kids didn't come to our house much, because my mother was always working. She had to—how different would my life have been if Dad had lived longer? Mother says he could put a smile on anyone's face. He told long, complicated jokes, more like stories, really, and he never forgot the punch line. He was like a good long drink after a tiring day, my mother said.

When Cally was in kindergarten, I used to wait for her in the afternoons with the other mothers under the big oak tree in the playground. I'd listen to them talk about what they put in the children's lunches, what toys they bought them for birthdays, which friends they were having over to play. It made me so depressed. They were Professional Mothers. They knew what special packets of crisps children liked, where to get those biscuits shaped like teddies, how to pack the drink bottle in the lunch to keep it cold. They seem like small details, but there were so many of them, and I didn't know how they learnt them all and remembered them. Cally would run out to meet me but I could barely smile at her. I used to wonder if she would rather go home with Sharon or Melanie. I wondered if she pretended that their mothers were hers.

Sometimes I wished they were, too. Then I wouldn't have to worry like this, all day, every day. And I'd know someone was looking after her better than I could.

It's hard to believe my baby Cally is almost a teenager!

I never thought she'd get there, that I'd be able to do it. Every day is such a mountain to climb. In the early dawn, that wattlebird wakes me up. It has a squawk like a scream. My heart sinks. I think of all the things I have to do by eight o'clock. Lunches, clean clothes, library books, polished shoes. I remember I forgot to buy the bread. Maybe there are no sprouts for the sandwiches. I hate myself.

Today I drove Cally to school. I normally do, unless David is around. Even if he is, he usually leaves for work at sunrise. He misses the traffic that way (and family breakfast disputes). He's good at avoidance techniques. My husband, the empty space.

Today we got all the green lights. It made my spirits rise. We seemed to fly through the traffic, with nothing stopping us. I thought that was a good sign for Cally's first day. I told her that, but she just sniffed.

Well, it was a good sign. Maybe Cally will blossom in her teens, she'll go straight ahead like a green light. With any luck she'll be better than me; she won't be pulled back by every little snag in the world.

I'm like a jinx, the way I think everything will go wrong. She'd be better off without me.

Wednesday

Naomi rang again tonight—still upset. Perhaps we went too far with the hypnosis. But she did want to explore the notion of double consciousness. There is the possibility of reaching a secondary personality through neurohypnotism. When Naomi was in the trance, she said things that were completely out of character. I made some notes about it in the red book, but must put more detail in. There was a lot of anger, and her voice changed—it was rougher, more masculine. I told her that, and she was amazed. Next time I'll put the tape recorder on. It's as if these two personalities, these two halves, have no knowledge of each other. Someone said once that "perhaps we are also—preponderantly—what we forget."

I can't forget, that's my trouble. People so often dismiss that other personality—the one we experience in dreams—but I think it rules our lives. A nightmare will influence your decisions the next day, whether you know it or not.

David says that's a lot of rot. But he never remembers his dreams, anyway. The past for him is a confusing landscape he wipes clean with turps each day. He says we have to look toward the future, that every day is a new day, and why do you have to rummage around in the back streets of history when you can be making it?

We don't "make it" much anymore, anyway.

My mother would probably agree with David. About history, I mean. She says that there is so much to see out there in the universe—"It is continually expanding, Caroline, do you realize?—Why bother staring at your puny navel all day?" She says it with that sneer of her nostril.

I think that is very superficial of her. Even scientific theory supports my argument. When we look up at the night sky and see all those stars and planets shining, we are looking back in time, at the past. It takes all that time for the light to reach us. *Jupiter's light takes thirty-three minutes to arrive, Ruth, do you realize?* If we had no past, we'd have no light. Every crumb of matter and energy holds traces of its history, if only we can learn to read it there.

My mother spends all her time looking outward. I suppose I look more inward. But it isn't puny, the interior world. It is continually expanding, the more you look. Inside each cell there are atoms and inside the atoms are protons and neutrons, and they hold traces of your father and the ape you once were and the talent for music your great-grandfather once had. The more you travel into the past in your mind, the more there is. It's like a treasury of Russian dolls.

I just hope tomorrow is a better day for Cally. For me, too.

I must try to act positive, be encouraging. She must never know how it really is for me.

I found a hidden stash of these diaries in my mother's room. They were in a row of shoe boxes she keeps at the bottom of her wardrobe. I felt like telling her she'd be a lot better off if she kept shoes down there, like any other normal person, instead of private weird notes that her daughter can find. But I couldn't say anything, because I wasn't supposed to see them.

Funny, isn't it, because I remember my first day of high

school, too, and I thought we caught every red light. We were late, as usual. Mum had to drive like a madwoman with wings just to get there on time.

That first year of high school I was put into the top class. I was sure there was some mistake. I sat at my new desk and studied the letters chiseled into the wood. Whoever made those deep gouges must have used something very sharp, like a penknife, or maybe a dagger. It made me tremble. Even the graffiti was difficult to understand.

Melanie, Sharon and Morgan weren't in this class. We'd known each other ever since we were five. In high school they were put into a lower class. They'd be sitting together now, all cozy and giggling at someone else. They'd be well camouflaged. Company gives you that. When I dared to raise my head from the desk, my heart pounded even faster.

The kids around me looked sharp as foxes. They were A-class people, with pointy chins and high foreheads. They were buzzing with talk, and they threw insults at each other, back and forth, like bombs. Even their insults were complicated and sharp with geometry. They had algebra stuffed up their sleeves, arithmetic multiplying in their jumpers. I dreaded arithmetic and geometry and algebra. Kids who could do that seemed like another species. They worked in gangs, firing answers to math puzzles like pistol shots.

It was terrifying.

It was like entering a war zone, with no soldiers on your side. And no ammunition.

The A people were carnivores, with their sharp brains and dagger teeth. Melanie, Sharon, Morgan and I had always been herbivores. All through primary school we grazed gently in the valleys of noncompetition. We learnt to share and we let each other win. We said things like "It's only fair." We knew about the cutthroat world of carnivores. We watched it at a safe distance, shuddering at all that tooth and claw. It was like being cozy and safe in the movies, holding hands in the dark while people did brave, scary things on the screen.

In Year 7 they threw me into the lion pit. I was so scared, I couldn't think. In science I was frozen. In English I stuttered. People sniggered. A group of male carnivores made spitballs and chucked them at me. A missile got me in the eye one day, and it scraped my cornea.

"How did that happen?" my mother asked me.

"Glen Gill threw his ballpoint at me."

"Did you tell the teacher?"

I rolled my eyes. It hurt. "If you rat, you get into even worse trouble. Leave it alone." Mum sat there frowning. Her mouth opened and closed like a fish gasping. She didn't know what to do. She's not very good in social situations.

I sat there squinting. My eye felt as if it had grit in it, a crumb of sand.

"Well," Mum said finally, "let's bathe it and apply some drops of comfrey. That's an herb for quick healing."

I jumped up. This was an event I could do something about. "No," I said. "I'm not having comfrey or hocus-pocus or anything else. I'm not going to lose the sight of one eye just because of some old carnivore called Glen Gill. I'm going to the eye doctor. A proper one with letters after his name."

Mum just said, "Oh, all right." She looked depressed, slumped there on the sofa. I felt sorry for her, as if she were the one with the sore eye going into battle each day. Obviously her daughter wasn't going ahead in life like a green light. "You don't have to come with me if you don't want to," I told her. She cheered up for a second at that.

While I put on my shoes she dithered about, wringing her hands. She disappeared into her room and returned with her bag, saying she was coming. I know she hates doctors' waiting rooms. They give her the creeps. She never even reads those interesting pamphlets, for heaven's sake. So I said, "Thanks, Mum," and gave her a hug.

By the time we came home from the doctor's, I wished I'd taken the comfrey drops instead. He'd put a black patch on me and said I had to wear it to school tomorrow.

You can imagine the carnivore reaction to that. There was feasting for days.

*H*ave you ever noticed the wall between adults and kids? It just seems to grow higher when there's a problem. "Don't worry, it will be all right," adults say, when there's absolutely no evidence for this whatsoever.

When you're a little kid and have a nightmare, they tell you that monsters with ten arms and slimy heads don't exist—it's okay, go back to sleep. But the picture is still real in your head. You can see its slavering tongue, the bloodshot eyes, the claws red with blood. You look at the adults sitting calmly on your bed, their feet in slippers, their faces sleepy, and you realize that they live in another world from yours.

They don't see the things you see, they don't have the feelings you have. So how can you trust them? The wall between you both is thin but strong, like a spiderweb.

I wanted to go and sleep in their bed. But there was the wall.

I felt terribly alone the year I turned twelve. My father was very angry when he heard about the ballpoint incident. That was rather nice. He said some rude things about the ballpoint shooter and he stroked my eye patch. He said I made a very handsome pirate. I soaked it up. I wished he were home more often. But when he said he'd go and see Glen Gill's father, I lost it.

"No, no, no!" I screeched. "That will just make it worse. Don't you see? He'll tell everyone that I ratted. Everyone will know I'm spineless as a slug. They'll just gobble me up and spit nothing out!"

"Oh, Callisto, you're gabbling!" my father yelled back. "Take a deep breath and count to ten."

"I *hate* arithmetic!" I screamed hysterically.

"This place is a madhouse!" my father concluded, and looked sharply at my mother.

"What's that look for?" she retorted, instantly flaring up. "My fault, is it? My fault Cally got shot in the eye and is upset? What should we all be, robots like you?"

Mum and Dad got into the combat zone then, so I retreated. Funny how often that happens.

Looking back, I don't know what Mum or Dad could have done, really. On account of the wall. Dad suggested I get a math coach. It would make me feel more secure. So a teenage girl came to our house every Thursday afternoon. Her name was Valerie. She was kind and explained everything in a soft white voice like feathers. She politely ignored the sighing and murmuring of the meditation class in the next room. But I couldn't hear anything over the roaring of my heart.

My heart told me to go to the principal and ask to be put back into the lower class. I made an appointment for after school. I packed sunglasses and a long coat in my bag so I could go in disguise. But in the end I came up with the cunning idea of saying I was in trouble. "They caught me putting firecrackers in the garbage bins," I told the others. "So I've got detention with the head. Maybe I'll be suspended." That earned me some points with the carnivores and got me there safely as well.

The principal was a short man with bandy legs. You couldn't really tell about the legs while he was in long pants—there was just the suspicion, until the swimming carnival. He turned up in a safari suit, with shorts. When he stood up straight, cheering on the team, the space between his hairy legs made a kind of elongated O. You could see the grassy bank through the space. The bandy legs made me feel closer to him, as if he were really a little child who hadn't grown up. He pretended all day that he was a big man doing a big job, but you only had to glance down at his legs and you could see how he'd waddled along when he was two.

I deliberately thought about his legs when he showed me into his office and gestured grandly to the leather chair. He sat behind his desk and shuffled some papers into a pile.

"Well, well," he said, clearing his throat. He had to look down at his papers to check the name. "Callisto. What can I do for you?"

I told him I had a hole in my heart. My medical condition gave me palpitations and arrhythmia. I was known to pass out if I became stressed. "I happen to be very stressed at the moment because I'm in the wrong class," I said. "There was some kind of administrative mix-up." (I didn't tell him that all the animals in my class eat meat, and you can't put a sheep in with the wolves. I just kept to the medical facts.)

He fiddled with his tie and shuffled some more papers. He raised an eyebrow. I just kept on talking. I was very nervous. But I was fighting for my life. It was almost exhilarating, being in the battle. I told him I could give him a medical certificate if he needed it. I'd forge it if necessary, I thought desperately.

When I got up to leave, he still hadn't said if he'd put me back in the right class. "Just one class lower, if you don't mind," I repeated. "Where the stress isn't so great." He cleared his throat and shook his head and nodded. What can you make of that?

But the next day I was put into the lower class. It was official. I breathed a sigh of relief and my palpitations stopped. At least for half an hour.

At recess I realized that it was all too late. Melanie, Sharon and Morgan had made other friends. They sat with Sally and Jo on the benches and shared their biscuits. They made a couple of remarks about the "brainy bunch" in the top class, the "snobs." They inched away from me. I looked at them closely. Hadn't their teeth grown a little? Didn't their nails look sharper? Perhaps they'd changed into *omnivores*. This thought was confusing and threatened to break down my whole classification system.

My temporary move to the higher realms had created another invisible wall. When they looked at me, I could tell the image was blurred, as if they were looking through tracing paper.

I ate my sandwiches alone in the shade. My uniform was still too long, but it didn't matter anymore. Other girls had pert little skirts. They sat in the sun and rolled their socks down so their legs would get tanned. They ate Vegemite or ham sandwiches or sausage rolls. I had tofu and sprouts and avocado on lumpy bread bursting with seeds. I felt like a budgerigar. But I grew a lot that year, and I began to tower over my mother. I hated being so visible. I hunched my shoulders and drooped my neck forward. My bones seemed too big. I felt more and more awkward with all those bones—huge and angular like a giant cassowary. Head down, I went blundering through the bushes.

(I once saw a documentary about cassowaries, actually. I was surprised to hear that they can be very aggressive. Even if you try not to look at them, they charge ahead and attack you. In the documentary we saw a man with twenty stitches just under his rib cage from a cassowary kick.)

That Christmas, when the school year was over and I had turned twelve, Grandma Ruth gave me the telescope.

It was like a ripe fruit dropping to the ground. I caught it just in time.

My herbivore/carnivore classification was in tatters. There was no viable escape from Earth—until Grandma led me out into the garden and read the skies. Then I flew up into a world so powerful that Glen Gill and his ballpoints looked about as big as bull ants.

Over the next year I used the telescope constantly. During the day at school I'd be like a nocturnal animal, only barely awake. I was waiting for the night. I began to visit the observatory that sat on a big hill right in the middle of the city. I saw Saturn there for the first time. It was thrilling. Those rings around the planet are the most beautiful things I've ever seen. The guide told us that the rings are made up of millions of tiny particles circling the planet. The light they give off comes from the sun, but it's reflected like sunlight off particles of ice. So astronomers think Saturn's rings may be made of little pieces of ice.

I came home from the observatory that night, bursting with Saturn. Mum was still up, and I told her about the ice and the rings. She was very tired. She smiled at me and said that when you looked at the sky you were looking at the past. I was quite intrigued by that idea and asked her to go on. But Jeremy started crying then, and she had to haul herself up to go to him.

Sometimes I think Mum really does belong to the past. Maybe she's the reincarnation of some nineteenth-century medium. When I was in Year 8, soaking up the heavens, Mum was absorbing the Victorians. She read about the spiritualists and their meditative trances, and researched their ideas on amnesia and hysteria. She believed the ghosts of the past flowed about our world—they were as common as clouds. You just had to be in the right "state" to see them.

A sprinkling of women started coming to our house, and they did experiments together, mostly in the dark. They set up a Ouija table. It has a smooth surface strewn with letters and digits set all around in a circle. In amongst them are YES and NO and certain other symbols. A glass is placed in the middle, and everyone puts a finger on it. When I've peeped through the crack in the sliding door, I've seen the glass move wildly between the letters, spelling out names and messages. It is truly creepy. The living room seems to be inhabited by invisible guests, all rushing around like the wind. My science teacher, Mr. West, said that the involuntary spasms of the muscles in the finger are responsible for the glass's movement. But he hadn't seen the speed of that glass or the shock in those women's faces.

Mr. West was the one person I looked forward to seeing at school. Sometimes after a science lesson I'd stop and tell him about my visit to the observatory and what I'd seen. He was always interested. He'd put down his chalk and draw up a stool, encouraging me to go on. Then he'd tell me things that I could talk about with Grandma when we stood with our bare feet tucked into the earth, reading the night sky.

When I was fourteen, Jeremy went to preschool. The kindergarten was practically next door to my school, so sometimes I picked him up in the afternoons. I liked doing that. He would run to me with a whoop, his arms full of the paintings and crafts he'd done. "Look at this, it's a submarine!" he'd yell, and hold up a tissue box plastered with bits of material and a toilet roll for a funnel and cotton wool for smoke. Then the other kids would run up, too. They'd climb all over me as if I were a sofa and show me their boats and airplanes or how fast they could run. It lifted me up, all that joy and welcome. They were so twanging with life, those little ones, and they wouldn't notice if your skin was black or white or your hem was down to your feet.

One afternoon I had a surprise for Jeremy. We'd been talking about chemicals and how they react to one another. For his birthday I'd given him a science kit. It included a good instruction booklet that told you how to make a volcano. All you needed was a little flour to make the mountain, and something acid to react with something alkaline to sprinkle on top. The fizzing result flowed down the mountain like boiling lava. Just add a drop of red food dye for drama.

"Why can't we do the volcano experiment *now*?" he'd been protesting for days. So I'd asked Mr. West if I could use the science room after school.

"I see we've got another science enthusiast in the family." He smiled. "Your grandmother must be pleased. I'd like to see your little brother again—I'll be present, of course, to supervise."

I hoped Jeremy wouldn't get carried away and fling bicarbonate of soda all around the desks. (That was the alkaline part, you know.)

Anyway, I went to pick up Jeremy and told him about the surprise. He hardly let me finish before he went scampering off. "Guess *what*!" he yelled to his mates. "I'm going to big school to do an experiment!" He could hardly contain himself. He kept giving little squeals of excitement all the way down the hall. He leapfrogged over the submarines and went to find his teacher so she would know exactly how fabulous life could be. When he'd told her and everyone else on the premises, including the caretaker who'd come to fix a leaking toilet, we were able to go.

As we skipped to the corner, I worried about his excitement. How can reality match such enormous expectations? Wouldn't disappointment be inevitable? I tried to tell him that science experiments don't always work, but it's okay because that is how you learn.

"Yeah, yeah, are we nearly there yet?"

When we stepped into the science room, Mr. West shook Jeremy's hand. Jeremy was suddenly shy and hid behind my legs.

I got out the ingredients for the volcano. Mr. West found a big green tray and told Jeremy he could make the mountain of flour. We made a yellow plasticine crater and nestled that into a small hollow at the top. Mr. West was lovely with Jeremy. He gave him clear, simple instructions, then stood back and let Jeremy try. He told him how clever he was with making the crater. I could have hugged him.

The alkali and acid reaction was very successful. Bleeding with red dye, the mixture fizzed and flowed over the side of the mountain like the deadly lava of Pompeii. Jeremy sprayed his packet of plastic dinosaurs all around the base of the mountain. He laid them in horrifying positions, jaws down in red lava. He made their ghoulish voices as the lava gushed down. Mr. West laughed and laughed.

After about six or seven volcanoes I needed to go to the toilet. Jeremy said he'd be okay with Mr. West. Strolling down the asphalt quadrangle, I kicked a stone happily along. Good old science, I thought. I shouldn't have worried about Jeremy being disappointed. You could rely on the miracles of science, which is more than you can say for most miracles.

As I entered the toilet block, I could smell burning. The hair rose on the back of my neck. Cigarettes. I stood in the doorway, wondering if my bladder could hold on until I got home. Or maybe I'd duck into the boys' toilets. But a cubicle door slammed and out strode Miranda Blair.

She was followed by two of her tribe.

"Well, if it isn't little Miss Science," said Miranda in a singsong voice.

"Sucking up to old Westie," said Amanda, her first mate. Amanda was drawing on a cigarette. She took such a deep drag that her cheeks collapsed into hollows. Under her eyes were dark circles of smudged mascara. She looked as if she were dying of diphtheria. She blew smoke rings into the stale air like a professional. They reminded me of Saturn's rings, and I tried to think about them, all shimmering with ice. Amanda stepped closer and blew smoke in my face.

I coughed. I couldn't help it.

"Oh, she's so pure," sang Amanda, "there's just no cure." The three girls did a little dance on the dirty concrete floor. The smell of old urine mixed with the smoke. My heart was pounding so hard that my head began to feel light and floaty.

"Teacher's little pet," said Miranda, and ground the butt of her cigarette into the concrete. "Do you do it with old Westie? Hmmm? What's he like?"

Her voice was black as Vegemite. She smeared it all over me.

Just then Amanda gave an excited grunt and pulled out her lighter. There was a moment when I could have run. But I didn't. I've always wondered why. I couldn't take my eyes off those girls. A powerful force field throbbed around them. I was like a captured asteroid in their belt. Amanda swung out, past Miranda, and flicked her lighter at me. It was yellow. I can still see it.

She set my hair on fire.

The girls ran. I could hear their black school shoes pounding up the asphalt. I slapped at my hair. I pulled my long uniform up over my shoulders and tried to smother it. I leapt about with the skirt wrapped tight over my head. I screamed a lot. I kept wishing that person would stop screaming because the noise scared me more than anything else.

After a few minutes I stopped. The smell of burnt hair was putrid. I crept over to the cracked mirror above the sink. I kept my eyes down, studying the gray porcelain of the bowl, the brown stain around the plug. Then I looked up into my face.

I had been very lucky, really. The right side of my hair at the front was a good four centimeters shorter than the left. But the line was quite neat, except for the wiggly frizzed ends that had gone a yellowy brown. At least I wasn't bald. I sang that out into the mirror: "I'm not bald, I'm not bald! I'm still alive!" I felt a sudden rush of elation, as if I'd been saved from the jaws of death. I wasn't scarred or mutilated. I even felt a glow of gratitude—those girls could have killed me, and they didn't! I wasn't in my right mind. Or, as my mother would have said, I was in the second half of my personality—the one we don't normally meet.

I put my hair back in a ponytail so it wouldn't show so much.

As I trudged back to the science room, I tried to work out why those girls hated me. They were older than me—they weren't even in my year. I hardly ever saw them. I just didn't understand it. Perhaps my height annoyed them. Or maybe I was just so naturally irritating I could annoy people even at a distance.

Whatever it was, it was scary, because if you don't know what it is about you that annoys people, then you can't fix it up.

*T*hat was when I decided that if this was war, then I'd better get serious about camouflage. I didn't stop and chat with Mr. West anymore after school. In science I pretended that I hadn't done my homework and I wouldn't know Jupiter from Pluto. I said "Wot?" every time a teacher asked me a question, and they sent me to the school nurse to have my hearing checked. I finally took my uniform up myself. It was so short that every time I bent over, you could see my bum.

I was getting ready to become a borrower. But you have to be in the right state before you can attract the light. You have to be reduced to a cinder, have nothing left. Then the light-givers take you up, making you their creature. They flick you off into space, watching you glow with gratitude.

I remember a new girl coming to our school. She was Finnish, and she couldn't speak much English. She was plump and white and tender-looking, like a new egg. She smiled and said yes to everything, just in case. She wouldn't have hurt a fly.

Minna was put into my math class. I could have been her friend. I explained a little about numbers being to the nth power. She nodded eagerly and touched my hand, thanking me.

One day, on the playground, Miranda Blair sat down next to her on the benches. Minna turned to her with a smile. Miranda swiped Minna's lunch, just like that, and doled it out to her friends. She was chief wolf feeding her pack. Minna sat there waiting. She kept that smile on her face for ten minutes, I don't know how. She looked frozen, like a wax model. Her jaws must have been aching. But Miranda didn't give back the lunch or offer any of hers. She and her pack ate every crumb, smacking their lips.

I stood on the opposite side of the quadrangle, watching. I could have helped. I could have gone over and snatched back the lunch. I could have told Miranda what a nasty bitch she was. I could have walked over and taken Minna's hand. Comforted her. But I didn't. I just watched. Standing there, like some creepy voyeur, I felt so ashamed of myself. I wondered what Minna must think of this country, where people step on each other like ants. I had a bitter taste in my mouth all day.

But I couldn't afford to annoy anyone again.

One afternoon Mr. West asked me to wait after class. He asked me at the beginning of the lesson and I was so anxious, I couldn't hear anything he said after that. I fooled around on my desk afterward so that people would think I was just being slack tidying up. When everyone had gone I looked at Mr. West.

I hadn't really seen his face properly for weeks. I felt a wave of affection. Then guilt.

"Are you all right, Callisto?" he said gently. His tone was so kind. His voice lay on the air like a soft blanket. You could sink into that voice and be wrapped up, safe.

He asked me if I was on drugs. My attitude had changed, he said. I was so thin. I never said a word anymore. Could he help?

I remembered the way he'd been with Jeremy. How he'd put down his chalk whenever I dropped in. I wanted to tell him about the war, and explain that sometimes you just have to choose sides, and that it was nothing personal. But I knew he would question me and ask for enemy names and it would just mean suicide. So I said nothing.

I kept looking down at the floor so I wouldn't have to see his face. But at the end, when I heard him stand up and scrape back the chair, I caught the disappointment in his eyes. They weren't warm and understanding anymore. I wanted to tell him that what he offered was very kind, but what I needed was twenty-four-hour protection. And a man in his position couldn't possibly provide it.

When he left the room I felt lonelier than ever.

I wish you could live in brackets. You could take whomever you want inside with you, and the rest of life would wait outside, politely looking the other way. When you popped out of the brackets, life would go on as before. There'd be no consequences, and the walls would be where you needed them for once. Easy peasy. If only.

When the doctor told me I was pregnant, I did consider talking to Mr. West. He wasn't family, and he wasn't too close. He might still care about me. I knew he had a son, so he probably understood about kids. I thought he might also show an unemotional, scientific approach to the problem—being a scientist and all. It could be comforting to step inside a bracket with him.

But when I mentioned this to Tim, he went into a total spin. "Are you crazy?" he whispered, too shocked to even raise his voice. "Tell a teacher? No, he'd go and tell the principal and your parents. Think, Callisto! You know how the world works!"

I supposed he was right. There were no brackets except in books. And the world spins on consequences.

February 10
Caroline Herschel Cook
    Caroline Cook
   Herschel Cook
Caz Cook, Hersh or Hish?
No matter where you put *Herschel*, it ruins everything. It sounds like something hairy, masculine. I think Mother would have preferred a boy.
Twinkle twinkle Mamma Cook, how I wish you'd close that book.

I didn't know my mother's middle name was Herschel. God, how dreadful. That entry was very old, judging by the yellowed paper in the diary. There was no year. The paper was all dimpled with fingerprints. I was so interested, I tried to find a way to talk to Mum about it. She wouldn't elaborate. Her mouth went all dried-pearish again, so I didn't insist. Herschel. It made me think of Hershey chocolate bars, and I had a sudden urge to go down the street and buy one.

I had developed quite a few strange food urges lately. I always thought that was a myth about pregnant women asking their husbands to go and buy beetroot or something at three o'clock in the morning. But me—I had an obsession with parsley. I couldn't get enough of it.

I observed these symptoms with a kind of detached fascination, as if it were all happening to someone else. It had been a week since I'd known for sure, but there was still the numbness, like at the doctor's. Whenever I forced myself to sit down (on my bed) and think through my problem—list my options, the consequences of those options and so on— a fermenting panic crept along my skin. I got as far as imagining my father's reaction: instant shock and horror, and an epilogue of eternal judgment. He would dismiss me forever as "that" kind of girl—a chaotic sluttish female, devoid of moral backbone. Nothing I did after that would bend the bars.

Sometimes, sitting on my bed (I didn't actually *lie* on it anymore because sluttish girls don't deserve to be comfortable), I imagined being hugged by my father. I saw his eyes smiling warmly at me, open wide, listening to my torrent of words. His eyes didn't change as I talked—they stayed open and uncritical like a blue lake in the sunshine.

After that, everything would seem worse than ever. I was a moron as well as a sluttish girl without moral backbone, because all I could do was daydream. I wasn't even capable of thinking properly. I was a total failure as a human being. My shoulders slumped and my spine rounded, and I looked like the hunchback of Notre Dame.

Blankness descended, like being in a mist with earplugs. The world went away for a while.

But by Tuesday night it would all be over, wouldn't it? Tim had said it would. He was older than me and probably he'd had experience with this kind of thing before. I bet hundreds of girls would lie down for him anywhere.

On Tuesday night I planned to devour a kilo of parsley and a Hershey bar to celebrate. And then I would lie on my bed again.

While I was waiting for Tuesday, I went over to Grandma Ruth's house. She gives us a key when she is away, so that we can collect her mail and put it in a neat pile on the kitchen table. When Jeremy comes with me he always checks under the bed and in the wardrobes, in case there is a very slim robber hiding there, sucking in his belly.

I went alone on Sunday, because Jeremy said he was busy. I found him under the house. He sounded a bit angry, and

I'm sure he said "scumbuggit" under his breath. He said he was busy doing nothing, like me.

At Grandma's I prowled around in the quiet. The lounge and armchairs were all draped in white sheets, to protect them from dust. The blinds were down and only thin tiger stripes of light lay across the carpet. It was almost pitch dark in the corners of the lounge room, and there wasn't even the whirr of the fridge. This would have been a perfect place for Mum's séances, I thought.

I put Friday's mail on the kitchen table. Then I went into Grandma's study. She has hundreds of books. You could browse in there for weeks. I found *A History of Astronomy* and looked up *Herschel*. There were William and Caroline. Caroline was in the "Hidden from History" section.

Caroline Herschel was born in Hanover in 1750. She was gifted in music and became a solo performer, but just as she was beginning to achieve some measure of success, she was forced to give up her career and go to England. Her brother, William, required assistance with his scientific work, and a housekeeper as well.

William was an astronomer. At night Caroline took notes on her brother's observations, and during the morning she recopied the notes, made calculations and organized the work. In order to accomplish all that was expected of her, she taught herself math. She also helped in constructing William's telescopes, making models and grinding and polishing the reflectors. In addition to all this she ran William's household even after he was married.

While her brother and his family vacationed during the summers, Herschel did her own astronomical work. She was the first woman to discover a comet, finding eight in all. In 1798 the Royal Astronomical Society published two catalogues of stars she compiled, and in 1825 she completed her own (and her brother's) work by presenting a star catalogue of 2,500 nebulae and clusters to the Royal Society.

The society made her an "honorary" member, for women, of course, were not allowed regular membership. The highlight of her life, however, was receiving a small salary from the king. Despite the fact that this was one-quarter the money paid to her brother, she had achieved her modest goal of earning her own keep.

I shut the book and put it in my bag. I was sure Grandma wouldn't mind if I borrowed it for a while.

As I stood up to leave, I saw a little gray statue on the bookshelf. I'd never noticed it before, but it had probably always been there because it was scuffed and old-looking. It was a small plump man with an elephant head. He had a ridiculously long trunk. You felt if you looked away for a moment, he'd burst into giggles. He was perched on a wooden stand that was inscribed with gold writing. "Ganesha," it said, "the Hindu god of overcoming obstacles."

I loved that. I laughed aloud in the dark room, with the dust motes dancing along the tiger stripes. I kept looking at Ganesha, and I'd have sworn he was chuckling with me.

I bet old Caroline Herschel knew about Ganesha. Maybe she prayed to him every night, and he helped her with her obstacles and the vacuuming. I wished I had someone like Ganesha on my side. It was very hard to walk away from him. I wondered if Grandma would mind if I borrowed him for a while, too. She wasn't using him at the moment, was she? I scooped him up and put him in the bag with Caroline.

BIRTHDAY!!!

My baby. My baby. My baby was born today. He weighed 3.4 kilograms. Healthy and normal, said the pediatrician. I could have kissed him. Normal is the best word in the English language!

"Caroline Herschel Cook?" said Dr. Campbell when he strode into the ward. He peered around. For once I called out with pride, "Here I am!" He held my baby up in the air and tickled him. He wrote down all my baby's details on that piece of yellow cardboard. Head measurement, weight, results of his blood test. I kept that piece of cardboard on my chest when the nurses took my baby away for rest time. I was supposed to be sleeping, but I couldn't stop thinking about him. His black hair, thick as wool on the crown of his head. His little furled fists. His

bottom, soft and smooth and compact as two apples. I
just wanted him back with me, curled under my arm. I
missed him after five minutes!

It is so nice being able to lie here, with people bringing
you meals. I don't even read. I just lie among the
crisp white sheets in my pretty maternity nightie and
feel clever. Brilliant, in fact! I think this joy is about to explode. I've never felt like this. I love my little baby. I love
him.

David is over the moon, too. He keeps calling his partner in Johannesburg, telling him how the baby slept, how
he fed. He says he can delay his next trip. Such a relief.

David wants to call the baby Jeremy, after his father,
but I'm not very fond of David's father. He's cold and distant, and he's always criticizing everything. I see him in
David sometimes. Whenever David gets really annoyed
about something, he withdraws, just like his father. He
makes a judgment and puts it up like a wall that he glow-
ers behind. Takes ages to coax him out of it.

When we first met, he said he loved how I was so easy
to please. I could find beauty in anything, he said, and he
had a kind of awe in his voice. I must have been so different from his father.

I feel like drawing hearts all over the wall, and arrows
through it with my name and my baby's. Only I don't
want to think about names yet. I just want to enjoy him
and me without labels for a while. Maybe he will help me
to be myself. I don't have to prove anything anymore; I
don't have to talk astronomy with Mother or wear the
right clothes and cook the right business meal—at least

for a while. I'm a mother, and I'm going to be a damned good one!

Saturday
Tonight the baby didn't feed so well. Seems to be having difficulty latching on. The night nurse said even though sucking is an instinctive behavior, we mothers need to learn how to offer the nipple. I loved it when she said "we." It encouraged me to keep trying.

Mother came in to see me today. As soon as she heard there was a problem with feeding, she pounced on it.

"Well, you don't have to breast-feed, Caroline," she said. "These days women want to get back to work as quickly as possible. Bottles are probably more efficient, and they free you up."

"I don't want to be free!" I said. "And I want to breast-feed. I want to give my baby everything." I saw her face go all disapproving, with those thick eyebrows of hers knotting in the middle. My heart started to beat fast, I was so agitated. Why is it that as soon as my mother walks into the room, all my calm and happiness fly out the window? She looks at me with that cynical smile, and suddenly I feel like some silly actress in a soapie.

Mother didn't look at the baby very long. She stroked his cheek for a minute and we both gazed at him to-gether. That was good. But then she looked back at me with that frown and started on about I should organize the house, and where the cot would be and if I had to use bottles, the Milton sterilizing kit would be the best.

David came in then, and he and Mother had a long earnest discussion about the advantages of Milton as opposed to the old boiling techniques.

I just looked back at the baby and tried to block them out. It took me a long time to find the joy and the calm again.

I don't know if I'll keep reading these diaries. They make me feel a bit sick. My stomach gets all stirred up. There wasn't one mention of me in that entry. It was as if this were her first baby! But I know I went to visit her. Dad picked me up after school one afternoon and took me to the hospital. I remember seeing Jeremy for the first time. He was so small. His little nails were like those translucent slivers of shell you find at the beach. I didn't feel jealous, I just wanted to hold him. I couldn't wait for my turn.

Obviously my visit in hospital wasn't as important as anyone else's. Not worth mentioning.

I kept that diary under my pillow over the weekend. I sat on my bed a lot. I thought about my grandmother. How would she react if she knew about me? I could see her face, disapproving like she'd been with my mother. I knew what Mum meant about the eyebrows. "You silly girl," Grandma Ruth would say, "how could you be so stupid when you have all the biological information? Carried away by romance—of all the empty-headed things to do. What about school? What about university? What about all your plans?" I don't know if she'd suggest the other thing. About not having the baby. I don't think Ruth is that modern, for all her science. And if she did think of it, she wouldn't suggest it because it would mean too much emotion and ambivalence. I love and admire Grandma. But I know that she prefers facts.

By late Sunday night I got around to thinking about Mum. What would she say? Really. It was three o'clock in the morning when I gave up. I just didn't know.

Jeremy woke up with a nightmare. I tucked him back into bed. Usually he snuggles into me, even when he's asleep. But he turned away and pushed his forehead against the wall. I'm worried about Jeremy. He spends so much time alone. But I can't think about him now. There's no room since the undertow. Mum should take over. Why doesn't she ever take over?

When I thought about telling Mum, I just felt this matted dark dread come over me, like a cloud. It was as if this cloud were her feelings. She seeped into me, and the dark was something intangible, nothing you could chew over, like words. She wouldn't say it, there'd only be sadness and disappointment. My news would confirm all her sorrowful pictures of the world. I would no longer be a daughter shooting ahead like a green light. She would have to help me bring up the child. I'd be tied to her forever, watching her fumble with my child, the way she had with me. She'd hold the baby at a distance. My child would grow up surrounded by ghosts and crying.

But I didn't really know what she'd say, because I didn't know her well enough.

There was a gusty southerly wind that Sunday night, and it blew the branches of the mulberry tree against the window. They made a regular tapping noise, like fingers on the glass. It was eerie, as if all the orphans in the world were trying to get in. I went over to the window and watched the bare branches snake in the wind. Rags of cloud raked over the rooftops. There was hardly any moon, just a whisker.

Maybe, I thought, pressing my face against the window, maybe your background isn't everything. Maybe you can rise above the wasteland you came from, and light up its darkest corner. Could my little fish do that? I thought about molecular clouds being among the coldest things in the universe. They are made of inhuman things like formaldehyde and carbon monoxide. But they are star-making machines. When stars form, they heat up their bit of icy cloud, brushing it clean and transforming the remaining gas into glowing light.

I always thought Jeremy would do that. I'm not sure anymore. Could anyone, really?

Tuesday

Fed left breast 2:20 A.M.

    right 4:50 A.M.

    left 8 A.M. (only 2 minutes, then cried)

    right 10:20 A.M.

    sleep 2 ¼ hrs.

    very runny/liquid poo

    Why won't he sleep? Cries on the breast. Does he have wind, colic? Is breast milk drying up? Does anxiety reduce it? Must ask clinic nurse. Clinic nurse says alternate breasts—so they can fill up. But left breast is always empty.

Doesn't sleep. Desperate.

I'm scared of the crying. I want him to be happy. Why isn't he happy? Poor little baby, poor little baby. Why can't I do it right? What should I do?

Wed.

Fed right 2 A.M.

Left 4:30 A.M. very sleepy, sucked only a little. Fell asleep on breast. I couldn't sleep for fear I'd roll on him.

House is in a mess. Can't get dressed to go shopping. Can't do anything else. David says I should vacuum when he's asleep. But what if it wakes him? David doesn't know what it's like. He doesn't feel terrible when the baby cries. But I do. He says to let the baby cry. It's called the control crying method. It teaches the baby control. David is a stranger.

He seems like a different person. Or he's so far away I can't see what he's made of anymore. Straw. He comes home so late at night. He asks, "Can I do anything?" It's 9 P.M. and I'm trying to sleep. He goes into the kitchen and opens the oven door. I can hear his sigh from the bedroom. Poor Mr. Hubbard went to the cupboard. Well, why doesn't he cook dinner for me sometimes? Why doesn't he get up in the night? Why doesn't he help me?

Yesterday I rang up his office. He came on the phone startled. When he heard that it wasn't an emergency— well, not one he could understand—he got so impatient.

I said I was panicking. All the leaves on the tree outside were going funny colors. I couldn't see anything properly. He said to go outside again and see what a beautiful day it was. The sun is shining, the leaves are a funny color because it is autumn, darling. Find the beauty in things, Caroline, you're always so good at that.

I wanted to tell him that I'm not his Caroline anymore. I'm different. Hadn't he noticed? Don't call me Caroline because I'm not.

"Listen," he said softly, because there were people in the office, "listen, you have a beautiful son who is healthy and normal, you have a husband with a job, you have a lovely home. Doesn't that make you happy?"

I put down the phone. I laid my head on the big wooden table. The tears wouldn't stop, there was an ocean behind my eyes. It poured out, all salty and warm, I saw it wash over the table, trickling into the wood until it was sodden, the table would disintegrate into splinters, sodden splinters lying on the carpet.

I rang back. I said into the phone, "Have mercy, I don't know why the world is ending. I know I should be grateful. I don't know why I feel so bad, I don't know."

He said we'd talk about it when he got home. I was asleep by then. I have to sleep whenever I can. It builds up my milk.

May 22
STERILIZE BOTTLES AND UTENSILS—use Milton instructions on fridge. Mother says cold sterilization is

best. She said I'd be sure to knock over the saucepan and burn someone if I used the boiling method. I didn't say anything. Maybe she's right. She went out and bought the Milton sterilizing unit. Showed me how to do it. She bought the milk formula, too. Said the baby was starving.

Maybe she's right about that, too. But he still doesn't sleep. He still cries and fusses. I know he's not happy. Even with cold sterilization and fake milk. The doctors say there's nothing wrong with him.

When you measure the dried milk formula out, you have to get it exactly right. Mother said to use a knife to scrape the level flat on the spoon.

I wish I could just lie in bed with the baby sleeping on my chest. I wouldn't ever get up, only to wee and get glasses of milk. We'd lie together and make a tent with the sheets. But when I do that, just for a while, and take the phone off the hook, I can't help seeing the little spirals of dust whirl up as a breeze blows in, and the egg I didn't have for breakfast cementing on the plate. I worry that the utensils won't be sterilized in time, and the formula won't be made up. If I don't look after things, who will?

Tuesday
Fed 6 A.M.—160 ml.

Baby doesn't ever drink enough. I have to walk around jiggling him in my arms, showing him the fans, switching the lights on and off while I put the teat in his mouth. This morning I couldn't stand the cold empty house, so I took him to a café. It was only 6:30 A.M.! Andiamo, the café's called. David and I used to go there before we were married. We used to order cappuccinos and read the Saturday papers. Sometimes we'd just talk.

"Andiamo, bambino!" I said in a cheerful way. I do quite a good Italian accent. The baby looked at me as if I were mad, and he laughed. God, it was good to see him laugh. I chattered away to him in a big loud voice, doing my brilliant Italian accent, and he soaked up my silliness like a little sponge.

Outside, it was so early that the streetlights were still on. The café was full of cigar smoke. Only taxi drivers and truckies were there, munching rolls and sipping scalding coffee. It was freezing. The air was blue in the café and I knew this wasn't the healthiest place for a baby. But it was so good to see smiling faces—come in, get out of the cold, what a cute little baby, how old is he, look at him smile—and I ordered a cappuccino and then I thought I'd really throw money around (didn't I deserve it?) and have raisin toast as well.

I jiggled the baby on my knee as I drank my coffee. I thought of Mother saying I'd knock over the scalding water, and I held the cup far from me. A truckie with a thick blue sweater came over and tickled the baby under the chin. He said, "Can I hold him a minute?" My heart leapt in alarm, but his face was so friendly, with these two big lines around his mouth like commas when he smiled, so I said yes. He held the baby tenderly and talked to him as if he'd known him all his life and threw him up in the air a couple of times just as if he were a sturdy soccer ball. Then he gave him back to me and winked. "He's still in one piece," he said. "I've got two of them at home— twins. Haven't had a decent meal since they were born."

I felt sad when he paid his bill and walked out of the café. He knew about things. He seemed to miss his babies. I supposed he worked long hours. He probably drove his truck at night, as well as the day. It made me think about David. I wondered if he missed his baby too, when he went on his trips. I wondered if he missed me.

On Tuesday morning I dreamt about the herb cure. In my dream the leaves of the herb were huge, shooting out from the trunk like a giant's fingers. I didn't know how I was going to swallow them. I woke up with a bitter taste in my mouth.

I didn't really understand how the plant cure worked. None of Mum's books referred to it. Tim said this Jim Shepherd was at "the cutting edge." Of what? I hoped that didn't mean I was going to be his guinea pig. Or frog. In Year 7 we'd cut one open in science.

I had a shower and put on my uniform. Mum called me for breakfast. Homemade muesli. As Jeremy said, you took about five hundred hours to chew your way through it. We had this kind of breakfast more often when Dad was away. He called it "birdseed."

Only Jeremy would laugh. He liked the way Dad flapped his wings.

Mum had the radio on. I opened my mouth to say something and she put her fingers to her lips. "Listen," she mouthed. They were doing a story on the Aboriginal stolen children. Mum turned up the volume in the kitchen. She brought her coffee over to the table. They were playing a tape of a grandmother meeting her grown daughter for the first time.

You should have heard their voices. The daughter said when she was little she was taken to a girls' home. It was hundreds of miles away. She was two years old. Girls were groomed there to start work as domestic servants at fifteen. In the beginning, she kept climbing over the fence to look for her mother. After a while she didn't look anymore. The silence between the women made you wait, holding your breath. The loss lay between them, a drowning substance. "We are strangers with the same blood," the grandmother said. She was weeping.

A government minister came on next. "They're a lot of wimps," he declared. "All those people saying sorry, falling about crying. They're in the crying game. We weren't responsible for those policies. We must put the past behind us." His voice was as bland as a yellow plastic toy in the sun.

"Did he mean weakly interacting massive particles?" I asked Mum. "Was he using the acronym?"

She just said, "Shhh!" She looked annoyed. Well, if anyone was interacting weakly, I reckoned it was him.

The reporter said there was going to be a national Sorry Day. You could write "sorry" in a book, and give it to the Aborigines.

"It's about understanding," an Aboriginal man said. "For our people, saying sorry is simply a way of recognizing another person's feelings."

Sports news came on then. There was hardly time to hear the *s* in *feelings*.

I heard Mum telling Jeremy about the stolen children when he was going to clean his teeth. She was following him down the hallway. He said, "Well, I'm not saying sorry because I didn't do it." Mum told him he sounded just like the government. Only Jeremy is five. When you're five you don't know about history and how pain is handed down. You don't know about facing stuff before you go on to the next thing. Jeremy thinks you can just live in brackets, and events that happened in the past are all closed off, like air in a balloon when you tie the knot.

Mum came back to the kitchen and poured me a cup of coffee. Our fingertips met as she handed me the mug. We were both tearful. For a moment we were cocooned together in the same feeling. She stroked my hair. When the program finished, it was like coming back to earth. It had been so riveting, I'd forgotten everything else. The thought of the present, of this day, was like an alarm switching on. Tim was to pick me up at five o'clock. We were going to buy the herb cure.

It was hard to find other things to think about for ten hours.

But I managed. So did Tim. On the way, in his father's Ford Laser, I tried to tell him about the stolen children report.

"It's a damn shame," he said, shaking his head. But his

fingers started to drum impatiently on the steering wheel. I told him about the silence—how terrible those pauses were on the radio. "You know, radio is noise and entertainment," I said, "with no gaps for reflection. The silence was dreadful, almost shameful, like wearing only your knickers to a black-tie function. I mean, you're not performing like you're supposed to. You're being yourself instead of someone else. It was all so naked somehow. All that inexpressible feeling. I think sometimes it's the nakedness of things that people can't deal with. Why do we have to spend so much time painting over things, pretending?"

"Never mind, you've got enough to worry about right now," Tim said kindly, patting my knee.

So we talked about swimming training instead. Tim stopped drumming and his face lit up. The other guys who trained with him were awesome, he said.

"Bob and José shave their legs. They're that serious, Cal. Even that tiny friction of hairs in the water can slow you down. Do you think I should?"

I nodded. "Maybe you could shave your head, too."

He practically ran us off the road. "Are you crazy?" He says that often. He shook his long golden mane, tucking a piece behind his ear protectively. "I wear a cap," he explained. "That keeps it out of my eyes and stops the friction. That's what the coach says."

He looked so worried, I squeezed his arm. "You've got to keep these things in perspective," I said.

But I knew what he meant. I worried like that about my estrogen deficiency.

The subject of hair kept us involved for the next twenty minutes. We arrived at the office in Kings Cross ten minutes early, but we went in anyway.

"Good evening, won't you sit down?"

I was relieved to see a plump, clean-looking man of around thirty. He wore a white coat and a courteous smile. The people in the main drag of the Cross hadn't looked nearly so polite. I wondered why we had to go to a red-light district to do this thing. All the way along the street there'd been men in bow ties and greased-down hair standing in the doorways of strip joints. They'd glared at us, flicking their cigarette butts onto the pavement like hand grenades, demanding we come in and "see the hottest girls in the Southern Hemisphere."

"The rent is cheap," said the clean-looking man with a shrug, seeing our faces. He was as bald as an egg. Tim flicked back his hair and we shared a quick smile. "Jim Shepherd," the man said, extending his hand energetically. I saw that he'd shaved his head. There was a bluish gray shadow around his crown. I wondered if he swam. He had a small silver stud in one ear.

"Callisto May," I whispered.

Mr. Shepherd walked over to the desk. He eased himself up onto it and sat there cheerfully, swinging his legs. I hoped he wouldn't swing them too high and break all those little glass jars of herb cures beside him.

"I'll just be outside, will I?" Tim said in a rush. He didn't wait for an answer. He closed the door behind him. I began to sweat all over my top lip.

"Well, Callisto, what a far-out name you have! Where's it from? Mongolia, Poland, Tibet?"

"Galileo," I murmured. "I'm named after one of his moons." I had a weird sinking feeling in my stomach. I wanted to go to the toilet.

"Cool." He nodded, looking puzzled. "So, how pregnant are you?"

"Not very," I said hopefully. I told him the date of my last period, and how sick I'd been and my obsession with parsley. I suppose I talked a lot; I do that when I'm nervous. As I talked, I looked all around the room for a plaque. There should have been some sort of certificate with Mr. Shepherd's name on it, followed by some important-looking capitals. A Diploma of Something. There was only a Japanese print and a primitive wood carving of a man with huge dilated nostrils and impossible genitals. I hurriedly looked away.

Mr. Shepherd sprang up off the desk, clutching one of the glass bottles in his hand. "So, Callisto, I don't know what Tim's told you, but I've been working with herbs for years, well, many months anyway, and I've had some remarkable successes. You can feel safe with me. Arthritis, schizophrenia, back pain—you name it, I've dealt with it. I've been all around the world. Next year I'm going to the States to continue my research." He held up the glass triumphantly. "This particular mixture stimulates female hormones and brings on a period. I can't guarantee it will stop the pregnancy, but you never know."

"I'm willing to try anything," I said eagerly. I smiled at him nicely, to show I wasn't disappointed.

He poured the herbs into a small bowl and began grinding them up with a pestle. He put a lot of muscle into it, humming as he pounded. He obviously loved his work. I closed my eyes, picturing my mother making her mixtures in the kitchen. I wondered why I'd come all the way to the Cross to see a deluded stranger without a diploma when I had one at home.

When he'd finished grinding, he poured some of the fine powder into a glass and filled it with water from the sink. "Drink that now," he advised, "and I'll give you a packet for tomorrow. It's best to take it less than twelve hours after the first dose."

I took a sip. The grains stuck to the roof of my mouth. It was like eating sand. They hadn't dissolved at all. I started to gag.

"Drink it all in one gulp," Mr. Shepherd said. "It's easier that way."

I smiled at him, to show that I was grateful, even if my body was heaving.

"Do you have any orange juice or Pepsi?" I ventured.

He frowned.

"Oh, it doesn't matter," I said quickly, "it was just to disguise the taste. I'll swallow it now, it'll be fine." I opened my throat and poured the revolting stuff down.

"Thank you," I said, and smiled again. I could feel the olive green sand gritting between my teeth. But I didn't like to ask for more water. In fact, I didn't want to open my mouth again, in case I was sick all over his diplomaless office.

"Good luck!" he called as I went out.

I made an enthusiastic noise and waggled my eyebrows at him to show goodwill.

Outside, perched on a chair in the hallway, I found Tim reading a surfing magazine. "Look at these tubes, Cal," he said, pointing to the long glossy waves on the page. "That's Bob Jamison in the corner; he's from Hawaii. Man, is he hot."

"Mmm," I said, and started going down the steps.

"Hey, wait," called Tim. I heard him ask Mr. Shepherd if he could take the magazine. Then his feet came clumping down the wooden steps after mine.

The air was warm and smelled of hamburgers. Next to the strip shows were fast-food shops. Men with sweaty hairlines were frying chips and stewing coffee. There were crowds of people on the street now. Some of them looked as if they'd just swallowed Mr. Shepherd's wilder herbs. Others were dressed up like expensive sweets, all shiny and delicious-looking in their wrappings. The women's high heels clacked along the pavement.

"The restaurant is just around the corner," said Tim, taking my elbow. A man in a dirty coat asked me for fifty cents. We wove through the crowd, dodging the drunks, the bow ties' cigarette butts and the swinging handbags.

Around the corner it was different. The pavements were spacious and elegant, with soft lights streaming subtly out of the cafés. Tim steered me into one of the nicest.

There was a candle on our table, and a single rose in a vase. Tim handed the rose to me. I pressed his hand. I didn't really know what to do with the rose, so I laid it on the table next to my fork. We gazed at each other for a while, until it became embarrassing. We couldn't keep staring, not saying anything, and my nose was excruciatingly itchy. We both looked away at the same time, which was a relief, and glanced around the room.

The restaurant was almost full. A man and a woman near us leaned toward each other over the starched tablecloth. Their laced hands, pointed skyward, perched like a small cathedral on the white lawn of cloth. The couple murmured together, their lips very close, as if they were praying. It was hard to drag my eyes away from them. I wondered what they had to talk about for so long. Their faces were so close, breathing in each other's air, hearing each other's thoughts. The distance between thinking and saying would be nothing over there on that white lawn.

At the long tables people were celebrating. They made the most noise. I decided that the long-table people must work together—maybe after being cooped up all day saying polite things to the boss, they needed to go out and roar like tigers for a while. They were pouring wine into fat glasses and laughing helplessly, clutching onto their neighbors' arms, shouting into their ears. Tim said something I couldn't hear. Voices broke like waves against the walls. I smiled and nodded anyway. He pointed to the menu with a questioning glance. I nodded; yes, please, anything. I still didn't want to open my mouth very wide. I had to swallow a lot.

I suppose I should have told Tim I wasn't hungry. I knew I wouldn't be able to eat, and it wasn't as if he had much money. It would be such a waste, me sitting there deaf and dumb with a piled plate costing fifteen dollars. But I couldn't bring myself to say it. I felt like a black cloud hovering there among all that hilarity. I wished I could remember a good joke to tell. But I only thought of Jeremy and me laughing at Bob Bottom on the TV.

Still, it made my lips twitch. Bob *Bottom*.

"That's better!" Tim shouted across the table. He was smiling at me, turning his knife over and over on the crisp white tablecloth. I felt better for a minute, with Tim smiling and approving of me. I watched him fiddling with the knife. He was probably nervous, too, poor thing. He was probably too shy to ask how it had gone with Mr. Shepherd. Even when Tim said "period" he always went red. So did I, for that matter. Well, I'd tell him all about it now, without him having to ask. I'd make it light and funny, show what a woman of the world I was, like those dazzling girls with the loud voices at the next table.

"That mixture was evil," I began, raising my voice over the noise. "It was made with snake oil from the deserts of Arizona, a pinch of bat's blood and a leg of cockroach—"

"Oh, no," Tim cut in quickly, "don't be silly. Jim's a friend of my brother's. He wouldn't give you anything poisonous."

"I was just joking," I said, but he didn't hear. He looked preoccupied. I wished our meal would arrive. After that we could go. Maybe when we were walking, arm in arm, it would be easier to talk. When we didn't have to eyeball each other.

Tim started in on the knife again. Over and over. "Listen, Cally," he said. He paused, testing the point of the knife. I wished he wouldn't do that. "Next week—"

"Yeah, it's a long weekend, isn't it? That's great!" I thought of all the time I'd have to lie on my bed. I sneaked another look at the couple. Their dinner had arrived—crabs in their shells, with a biscuity cheese sauce. You could smell it. The woman was picking at the crab delicately. She giggled as the man took one of her fingers and put it in his mouth, together with the crab leg. She licked the sauce off his lip. I figured that must be something you do when you're at least twenty-five and confident. I looked at the woman again. Her breasts made a soft billowing shelf on the tablecloth. Just as I expected.

"Yes." Tim nodded eagerly. "So, the guys are going up north—you know, Bob, José, Phil Jones—there's a surfing comp on, up at Byron Bay. I said I'd go, ages ago. The guys are counting on me. I hope you don't mind—you know, after tonight and all . . ." His voice trailed away like smoke.

I could smell his eagerness to escape. It drifted out of his skin, burning, acrid. It made the candle glow more brightly. A surfing trip up north—it was his idea of paradise.

"Do you know about escape velocities?" I said.

"What?"

"Well, every massive object has an escape velocity. It measures how fast you have to go to escape the gravitational pull of that object. For instance, to escape from Earth in a rocket you have to travel at forty thousand kilometers an hour. Now, let's see, I wonder what my escape velocity is?"

"What are you raving on about?"

"I'd say it's minimal—only about a hundred kilometers an hour, about the speed limit on the Pacific Highway going north. Nah, you won't need a rocket to get away from little old me."

Tim grinned doubtfully. He shook his head. "You're such a crazy lady," he said, "that's why I like you."

But he didn't look convinced. He was fiddling with his glass now, until the waitress came over and filled it up. Some sort of claret—at least it wasn't green ginger. We picked up our glasses and clinked them together. I don't think anyone ever looked less festive than we did.

Over the chicken cacciatore, I listened to Tim's plans for his surfing holiday. He was more relaxed now. I wasn't sure if it was the allure of the surf or the effect of the wine, but he was chewing and talking with gusto. His blue eyes were sparkling, whipped wild with excitement. He flicked back his hair, burnished in the candlelight. He looked like a Greek god sitting there—one of those awesome, athletic types, god of the waves or something. I knew then, poking the grit around my gums with my tongue, that Tim had always been out of reach. He had done what he could for me. Now he was on to the next thing. I could see him surfing way out deep, where the waves are born. He was moving up and down with the swell, always moving, always further away. I was stuck on the shore like a clam.

I picked at a few olives on my plate. My mother would have been disgusted at the waste. All that good food, and so many children in the world were starving. It was true. But I could still taste the grit.

As I sat gazing at Tim, I realized old Shepherd could have given me chopped-up cow pats and I'd have swallowed them. "Thank you, they're delicious," I'd have said. It's a terrible thing to conclude about yourself. Borrowers are the pits. We make ourselves sick.

I began to wonder if being a borrower is hereditary, like dark hair or how tall you are. Or perhaps it's your background that decides these things. My little fish was doomed, no matter which way. Because I didn't know how to stop being a borrower, even if I wanted to.

"These herbs may not work, you know, Tim," I said. I saw that I'd cut into his lecture on southerly winds and their lethal effect on the surf. His face fell. You could almost hear the clang.

"Did Shepherd say that?"

"Yes, but then again he said it *could* work, just that there were no guarantees."

"Well," said Tim, his beautiful mouth curving upward again, "let's be optimistic, then."

"Yes, let's," I agreed. "They say that cancer patients who are optimistic usually have a much better recovery rate than pessimists."

"Well, there you are, then!" He smiled uncertainly, and held up his wine to toast me. "Here's to our good luck."

Here's to a good fuck, I heard him say. There was a lot of noise in the restaurant. It was hard to smile back. Tim and I were like two foreigners meeting in a neutral country. We didn't share a common language, so we simply gestured to each other in a friendly way. We meant well. But we never knew *what* we meant.

Tim was looking forward to next week. He was looking forward to his life. He'd done what he could for me. And now he was on to the next thing.

*W*hen I got home, I went to lie on my bed. I slipped off my shoes, but that was all. I didn't bother taking off my dress or my earrings. I didn't even wash my makeup off. I'd have dirty pores and blackheads the next day, but I didn't care. I didn't see the point of caring anymore. Even when you did, nothing happened the way you wanted.

I scratched my leg and felt nothing. I was numb, like a plastic bag.

I remembered watching a documentary on spinal injuries, and how the doctor had pricked the patient in her leg with a needle. Again and again he stuck the needle in. Each time you'd be holding your breath, hoping the woman would cry out. But there was nothing. The woman looked so disappointed. Afterward Jeremy and I kept wondering how it would be to have no sensation in your body. He said you would feel heavy, like a piece of wood. Because gravity's heavy, he said. But Jeremy's got a thing about gravity. He thinks God is gravity. Me, I think you'd feel like a plastic bag with nothing in it.

Some animals roll over and play dead to protect themselves. Maybe that's what my skin does—play dead, I mean. I think sex is overrated. I think living is overrated. What on earth is everyone going on about all the time?

I got up from the bed to rummage around in my bag. I found the packet with tomorrow's herbs. I poured them down the toilet. Who needs gritty gums on top of everything else?

Monday, June 2
I think the baby has something wrong with his digestion. I took him to the doctor yesterday—the local GP. He's

sympathetic, but he really didn't examine Gany for very long.

"That's an interesting name," he said, as he stuck his auroscope into the baby's ear. Gany started crying; the point of the instrument must have been cold and sharp. The doctor kept talking as if there were no noise in the room. I can't stand it when people do that. They think a child's pain is nothing.

"It's short for Ganymede," I said, and looked away. People often stare at me when I say that. I hope I haven't done the wrong thing. David wanted Jeremy. But he said, "Oh, anything to make you happy." I did it for Mother, really. I thought she'd be impressed. Ganymede is the largest moon of the solar system, after all. It was discovered by her precious Galileo. At least there was nothing to live up to. I mean, it's just a shining moon in the sky. You can't even see it without a telescope. Caroline Herschel was impossible to live up to. Every time people said my full name I felt guilty. Like a miniature model of the real thing. It's strange how so much of your own childhood surfaces when you have a child of your own. I'd forgotten, until now, how Mother used to read to me about CH's life. She was Mother's heroine, and mine. Other children had Wonder Woman and Superman. I had Caroline Herschel.

Mother says there's nothing wrong with Gany. He's just an intelligent, wide-awake boy. Hope she's right.

In any case, I'll take him to the pediatrician tomorrow. Just to make sure. Might still change his name to Jeremy. Maybe it would be for the best.

Friday Doctor 4 P.M.

I'm still worried about Gany. Hasn't put much weight on. Pediatrician said to add one more feed a day and put him on solids early. Why can't I stop panicking?

David home today. I tried to talk to him but he's too preoccupied. Business not going so well. He tells long stories about the difficulties of working with government agencies and the people, but I can't concentrate. I hear the baby crying, or my mind drifts off somewhere else. How can he work in such a racist country, anyway? He says at least he's trying to do something in the world, and pay his family's bills. Then he nags on about money again. Keeps telling me to shop at the supermarket, not the local deli. He's right. But I only bought bocconcini last time to celebrate when he came home. He thinks I eat it all the time.

Wrong time for talking. Should have waited until after dinner. There actually was dinner tonight. Chili con carne. I was quite proud of it. And it was minced meat, at just eight dollars a kilo. David said not enough chili. Still, the carpet was vacuumed and the sink was wiped down. I'd even managed to put away the washing.

I followed him into the bedroom as he put away his suits.

"How's Gany?" he asked. He was peering into the wardrobe.

"Still not drinking much. I'm so worried about him."

David sat down next to me. He took my hand. I laid

my head on his chest and listened to his breathing. It was deep and healthy and reliable.

"Look, women have been raising babies for a long time, you know."

"Well, I know that!" I jerked my head away. "So what? So I shouldn't be worried? I should just have that whole collective experience in my head?"

"Look." That *here-she-goes-again* sigh. "There's a problem, okay, so let's find a solution. You've asked the doctors—"

"Yes, but I feel—"

"Talk about your feelings later, let's find a solution now. I have problems all day in my line of work, and I've developed systems to solve them. Maybe Gany needs a different kind of formula. Maybe he's lactose-intolerant. Ask the doctors, take their advice, and decide what works for you."

He makes me think of Mother. She deals in formulas too, like $E=mc_2$. Those equations are so neat and tidy. Cause and effect. They make a thud, like bricks dropping. No light or space underneath. Mother says, think logically and you'll find the right answer. As if feelings are an irritating by-product, just "noise" in one of her experiments.

But how can you find a solution without including feelings? Like having a bath without the water.

Look at him, sitting there with that fancy suitcase, always on the verge of running away. Look at his spotless shirt and polished shoes. Look at me, Goddammit, look at me. I've lost ten kilos, you blind man, I've got enough circles under my eyes to look like an Olympics logo, and you don't even notice. You wrap yourself up like a present, but no one can undo you.

I'm going to invite Sam Underwood over to play. Mum said I could. It'll have to be on a Wednesday, because Sam's really busy on all the other days. He's got soccer on Monday, gymnastics on Tuesday, and Mike is coming to his house on Thursday.

Mum said Wednesday would be all right if we didn't make any noise. Maybe we can have some of her special pancakes. Sam said that when he went to Mike's house, he had ice cream cake and Coca-Cola. We never have Coke at our place. Mum says it puts artificial conservatives in your body and rots your teeth. I hope Sam likes pancakes. And filtered water.

Sam really wants to come home with me because he can't wait to see my bunker. No one else he knows is building a bunker. He said he'd help me dig. Then, when a meteor falls, he'll be able to come in with my family.

Sam understands about meteors now. His father heard a program on the radio that said scientists are tracking a giant meteor orbiting around our galaxy. There's a one-in-twenty chance that it will crash on Earth. Sam says we'd better get a move on with our digging. He's trying to be super nice to me because he wants his dog, Simba, to be invited in, too. Simba is very big and he slobbers a lot.

Sam said he'll be my partner for gym. It's really good having a friend. The problem is, ice cream is about fifteen hundred times yummier than pancakes, I think. But Mike doesn't have a bunker.

Cally keeps her door closed all the time. Sometimes I don't even know if she's home. Once I ran in without knocking, because my magnifying glass was on her desk and I needed it. She was sitting on the bed.

"Why aren't you lying down?" I asked. She just shrugged. I told her about Sam coming over and she was really pleased. "Good on you, Jem!" she said, and her face actually went happy for a minute. I asked her if she'd make us afternoon tea when Sam comes. I mentioned about Mum's ladies and all, and how maybe we could sneak a few pancakes.

"I'll tell you a secret," Cally said. "I'll buy a lovely chocolate cake and we'll have that out in the garden."

"With filtered water," I said, "in case we get thirsty."

"I think my budget can stretch to orange juice."

I jumped onto the bed and gave Cally one of my best hugs. She held on to me for ages. My nose was squashed and I had to breathe through my mouth. I wriggled a bit and she let go. Her face was all wet.

"What is it, did I hug you too hard?"

"Yes, Batman, your muscles are like iron. You should be more careful with us delicate girls."

We had a really good game then. Cally was Poison Ivy and I was Batman. I actually prefer being Robin. He gets more interesting things to say, like the time when Batman goes out to capture Tony Zucco—that terrible man who killed Robin's parents. Batman won't tell Robin where he's going, because it's too dangerous. So Robin says, "Aw, don't shut me out, man, don't treat me like a kid!" I *love* that part! I rewind it on video all the time. It's the best. You should see the way Batman looks at Robin. He gives this sort of crooked smile and says, "Okay then, little buddy, it's just you and me!" I love that bit.

I can't wait till Wednesday.

All this waiting was driving me mad. I was just one big twisted knot. I knew the herbs wouldn't work, really, but I thought I'd give them four days to do something. You could be lucky, couldn't you? Every time I thought of that idiot, Jim Shepherd, the knot in my stomach pulled tighter. I saw myself sitting there in his "office" with that grit all over my gums, smiling away while Tim gave him fifty bucks. Jim Shepherd was a crook. He was like those old-fashioned quacks who used to travel with circuses, selling magical potions. Schizophrenia, arthritis, my ass!

It made me so angry I sat there biting the sheet. I wanted to scream with rage.

But I still hoped. As Tim said, I was a crazy lady.

On Thursday and Friday I found it hard to concentrate in class. Every half hour I'd feel a twinge in my belly—was that a cramp? Now *that* was a dull sort of ache—maybe my period had started. I'd shoot up my hand and excuse myself. I'd steam down to the toilet block, hardly waiting for the door to bang shut before I'd tear down my pants to see. Nothing.

"Cally's got the runs! Cally's got the ru-uns!" The kids in

the class were chanting like kindergarteners. Mrs. Graham let me go early on Friday. I think she was afraid I might have an accident.

By Friday night I wasn't really hoping anymore. I was exhausted.

Some people might be lucky, but not me. I'd thought that if by some miraculous chance the blood did start, it would mean there was such a thing as luck in the world.

Over the weekend I looked at the phone book a lot. I threw up my lunch. On Sunday I found my doctor's after-hours number. I asked him for a referral to a clinic. He suggested a place with an excellent reputation that offered family-planning advice and terminations. I didn't know whether I preferred the word *termination* or *abortion*. *Termination* was softer, but it made me think of that ghastly movie with Arnold Schwarzenegger, *The Terminator*.

Is that what I was?

See, you're not going to read this anymore now, are you? Well, are you? You won't approve of me, I bet. You might say—well, what a creature, a sluttish girl with no moral backbone. Would you? In the olden days girls went ahead and had the baby because anything else was impossible. Many wounded themselves irreparably with knitting needles, others drank gin in scalding baths. Girls killed themselves with cures.

I swallowed some herbs. If they worked, or if I had a miscarriage, I wouldn't have to make a decision. I wished like hell I didn't have to. Jeremy got his finger stuck in the plughole once. When we got it out it was torn and bleeding and he wailed at what he'd done to himself. I could see him feeling so sorry for his finger. "Oh, why didn't I know not to do that?" he cried.

Sometimes we just don't know. People can tell us what it's like for them—that if you do A, then B will happen; if you have sex, then you could get pregnant—so whatever you do, be careful. But we're each encased in our own little bags of skin, so tight and separate that even the facts of life can't get through. At least that's how it was for me.

On the phone the doctor started to ask how I was feeling, and did I have anyone to talk to, but I just said I was fine, adding that full stop the way my mother does. I couldn't begin relying on anyone else right now.

When I got off the phone a scene came into my mind of a grown woman—at least twenty-five—with a house and a job and a dog and breasts and all, rushing to meet her husband with the news. The two of them would be overjoyed, hugging and cavorting all over the flower beds. Their little fish would be welcomed. She would spend her nine months stroking it into being with her mind. He would pat her belly each night and put his ear over her gentle rise.

It made me cry, that vision, if you really want to know. I kept seeing it, like a rerun of a movie. Over and over they kept leaping over the flower beds. But the man didn't have Tim's face. I was sixteen. I wasn't ready to have a baby alone.

Do you understand? I need you to hear my side of this. When I think of you out there disapproving of me, shaking your head or quickly flicking over the page, it fills me with shame. I grow so hot I think I'm going to burst.

Some girls, I knew, had babies when they were as young as

me. They didn't have husbands or jobs. But I couldn't imagine how they did it. Or what the rest of their lives would be like.

I only knew what *I* was like. And I wasn't ready to have a baby. I had to make a decision. And I had to do it fast. And to tell you the truth, I just wanted to get it over with. The undertow was drowning me—*What will I do, solve me, think about me, do something about me!*

I wanted a second chance. I was only sixteen.

*M*y appointment at the clinic was for next Thursday week, in the afternoon. There would be counseling first, and then if I wanted to go ahead, I could have the operation. The woman on the phone was so patient and helpful, even when I kept getting the address wrong and mixing up the times. "That's all right, just take your time," she said. I would need to wait for a couple of hours after the operation, she reminded me, just to make sure there were no complications. Would there be someone to take me home?

I panicked for a moment. Then something stirred in my head, some new voice that seemed to have awakened in there, and it said, "Oh, yes, I'll take care of that."

I could get a taxi. I'd been putting my pocket money for house cleaning in the bank for years now, and I'd managed to save quite a bit. If I needed a new dress or a pair of jeans, I always agonized so long, making up my mind, that in the end someone else bought the thing. Procrastination was good for my bank balance, if nothing else.

When I put down the phone, I felt a small surge of energy. It had a voice, the one that said, "I'll take care of that."

Now it said, with a little upbeat tone, "You'll be all right, Cally, I'll look after you. We're doing this, all by ourselves!"

It was true. Maybe you don't approve, but for once it was me, Callisto May, who was organizing everything. I'd found the clinic, I'd made the time and appointment, I was taking care of business. And with no help or light or warmth from a single other human being. It mightn't seem much to be proud of, it might seem pretty miserable to you, but for me it was something.

Then an alarming thought struck me. Thursday—Mum didn't have to go out anywhere, did she? No, she had her meditation class that day. Jeremy could just play in his room while the meeting was on. He often did that. But I thought I'd better check, just to make sure.

"Thursday the fifteenth?" echoed Mum. She was standing in the kitchen, peeling potatoes for a roast. The chicken lay in the baking dish. Skin wrinkled and flabbed all around its feet. I kept my eyes on the white kitchen cupboards to avoid being sick. The sight or smell of food was enough to set off the nausea. Especially raw chicken, with its neck still on.

Next to the baking dish was a book opened on the bench. It looked like a recipe book, the pages all spotted with grease. I peered closer and saw the first few words. "Double consciousness is a concept not easily measured by science."

"Oh, Mum," I snorted. "How can you cook and read at the same time? Why don't you just concentrate on one thing at a time? And I hope that's not a library book." Sometimes I wondered who the parent was around here.

Mum stuck out her lip like Jeremy does when he gets caught. "I just want to finish the chapter, that's all." She gave the chicken leg an angry prod. "I hate meat, anyway," she muttered. "Those hens are stuffed so full of chemicals, trapped in their airless cages all day. When they die, we eat all their anguish. It's repulsive."

"You should write the ads for the Vegetarian Society, Mum. You'd win over even the most hardened carnivores."

Mum smiled for a moment. A strange light came into her eyes.

"No, no," I said in a rush, "I was only joking." She was busy enough with her séances and hypnosis and meditation and herbal remedies. I couldn't stand another cause.

"Thursday afternoon," I reminded her. "I have to go out. I probably won't be home until nineish. You'll be here to look after Jeremy, won't you?"

"Hmmm," said Mum, giving my question all her attention. She was raking out the insides of the chicken.

"You can buy them with their innards already cleaned, you know," I said.

"I know that, but I don't trust them. When I do it myself, I can see how healthy the chicken was. Get a good look at the state of its insides."

I went back to staring at the kitchen cupboards.

"There's a meditation class on Thursdays, as you know, Cal," said Mum. "Jeremy's too young to join in."

Heaven forbid! "Yes, Mum, but he can just stay in his room. He often does that."

Mum looked up. "You usually take him out. It's easier that way, and it's better for Jeremy. I don't want him cooped up all afternoon in his room."

So many protests sprang to mind that I didn't know where to begin. This new voice of mine was becoming quite loud inside me. It made me jiggle with irritation.

"What is it? Don't jiggle about just where I'm working, Cally."

My new voice wanted to say: *If you cared so much about the quality of Jeremy's life, you'd take him out yourself.* My new voice wanted to say: *Have you ever noticed how much time I spend looking after your son?*

Standing there, fuming at Mum, I also wanted to ask what on earth had happened to that name of "Gany." It would have been a terrible name to give anybody—much worse than Callisto—and I was very glad for Jeremy's sake that she'd changed it. But I would have liked to know *who* made her change it—Dad or Grandma Ruth?

I just jiggled there for a few more minutes, saying nothing.

She didn't even ask me where I was going on Thursday afternoon. Can you believe it? I imagined the scenario of other teenage girls who had to sneak out of their houses, inventing elaborate excuses of homework at a friend's house and arranging it with the friend in case the parents rang up to check, and so on, and so on, forever, amen.

The peeled potato skidded out of her hand and bumped

the book off the bench. "Now I've lost my place!" Mum scowled, bending down.

"Look, Mum, I'm going out on Thursday, and you'll have to take care of your son for the afternoon, okay? I've got something to do."

"There's no need for that tone of voice, Callisto," said Mum, straightening up. "I don't *have* to do anything." I could imagine her adding, "And you're not the boss of me!" just like Jeremy. But her shoulders caved in a little.

"All right." She sighed and opened the oven door. The chicken slid around in olive oil on its way to the oven. She put the dish in and banged the door shut.

I went back to my room and lay on the bed for a while. I felt bad about Jeremy. Fancy his mother sighing about "having" to take care of him for an afternoon. What was wrong with her? Dark matter in the head, that's what. Impenetrable substances. How can she have been so obsessed with him as a baby and so neglectful now? Sometimes I almost hated her.

I churned around on my bed. I felt so angry, I didn't know what to do with myself. Everything was so unfair. No one helped you with anything, no one cared about anything but themselves.

I turned on the radio. There was an interview with a woman who had just been made the new head of DOCS—that's the department where they look after orphans and abused children. It was so depressing. Budgets and staff had been slashed, and 136 children had died in suspicious circumstances that year. The woman sounded a bit defeated already. You couldn't blame her. She said sometimes parents just can't cope with the demands of children. They need support themselves. She said she'd just visited one single mother who had smashed her twins together. One baby was dead and the other had brain damage. I slapped my hands over my ears, but it was too late. Sometimes you don't need to hear things like that. I wondered if that single mother had wanted to be pregnant in the first place.

I lay there numbly until dinnertime. I kept thinking of the baby who was still alive, the one with brain damage. I sucked my pillow. Could the child be aware of the loss? She'd never be able to express it. She'd be left lying near this icy draft, unable to move, and the wind would keep blowing. I changed the station and tried to concentrate. But when you have a mountainous obsession, you can't hear anything else. "Abortion laws in Western Australia challenged," said one station. "Doctors striking over legal issues concerning abortion in Tasmania," said another station. The bigger and heavier your problem is, I reckon, the more gravity it possesses. It attracts little bits of matter, crumbs of information that come flying in from all over the universe, and the stuff sticks to it, confirming its mass, adding to its weight. Or maybe it's just selective hearing, as Grandma would say.

Jeremy knocked on my door and called, "Hey, Cally, dinner's ready!" He gave me a big grin. I sat up and tried to grin back. He'd melt the ice off an igloo, old Jem.

He was hopping around in the doorway, shaking a piece of paper at me. When I pretended to grab it, he snatched it away and held it up high, dancing over to the table.

When Dad was away we usually had dinner on our laps, but Mum obviously thought the roast deserved a table. She'd gone to all that trouble with her anguished chicken, after all.

Next to the carving dish were two letters. Mum served our chicken and potatoes and pumpkin and we began to eat.

"Guess what, Cally!" Jeremy blurted out with his mouth full. A spray of chicken fat landed on my place mat. He was waving the paper again. "I've got something here for you!"

"Let's read these two letters first, shall we, Jeremy?" said Mum. "One is from Daddy and the other is from Grandma Ruth."

"Why should we read *their* letters first when they're not even here?" cried Jeremy.

"He's got a point there, Mum," I said.

Mum sighed again. "All right." She went on chewing her potato. I noticed she didn't give herself any chicken.

"Well," said Jeremy importantly, "at our school today the teacher handed out this notice. See, it's from the observatory. And it says that on Saturday the tenth it's Jupiter Night—children under eight can get in for free! That's *this* Saturday. Isn't that cool? We can look through these gigantic telescopes and there are guides and everything to tell you about it." He looked around the table, expecting to set our hearts on fire. I tried to look as excited as I could.

"I don't know whether I can on Saturday—" Mum began.

"No, no, it's okay, Mum, I'm talking to Cally." He leaned toward me and began whispering like a spy. "Then," he said, lowering his voice even further, "there's going to be a party afterward with chocolate biscuits and lollies and a cake in the shape of a star! Can we go, Cally, please, please, please?"

"Bees and peas." I smiled. Well, I certainly wasn't doing anything else. I didn't have a hot date or anything. "Of course we can go. It sounds fantastic."

"Hurray!" cheered Jeremy. His place mat looked like a smeary Jackson Pollock painting.

"Now that's settled," said Mum, "I'd like to read you these letters." She looked at Jeremy with an offended expression.

"What, Mum?"

"Oh, nothing."

"What?"

"Nothing. Eat your dinner."

Grunt, swallow. Everyone expresses themselves so well in our family.

"So let's hear this letter," I said.

Mum read Dad's letter first. He wrote that he'd had a "major breakthrough" with the marketing department of his business. It was a bit like an annual report, and I noticed how we all tended to play with the salt cellar or fiddle with the fringe on our mats. But I suddenly focused when he mentioned my name. "Last night I was invited to dinner at Steve's house—you know, Steve Markham, he deals with the arts council for us. I met his daughter, Julie. She's just about your age, Cally. She made me think of you. She's a pleasant girl, but she seemed so young. Not nearly as mature and capable as you. The whole evening made me homesick!"

I scrunched up my napkin. Typical. "Mature and capable"—the only things he approves of. My model-citizen and child-minder role. How "mature and capable" would he think I was if he found out about my current little problem?

Mum smiled at me. Jeremy knocked over the salt cellar. When I'd wiped it up, Mum went on reading. "Everything's gone so well, in fact, that I'll be home earlier than I thought, on Thursday the fifteenth. I'm really looking forward to seeing you all. And hearing all your news."

"Well, I hope he doesn't expect me to pick him up from the airport, because I'm busy that day," said Mum.

So am I, I thought. It was like God the Holy Father arriving home for judgment day. I wondered if *he* would ask me questions about where I was going. Oh, hell, I didn't need this.

"And then the traffic is terrible on that route out to the airport." Mum was worrying aloud.

"I'm sure he wouldn't expect you to be there," I reassured her. "You never are."

She gave an irritated snort and looked at me sharply.

I'm sure he won't expect an enthusiastic welcome from your department, either, I thought. It was amazing how just a word from my father could change the color of my mother's face. Even when he wasn't here.

"Let's hear the letter from Grandma," I said.

Mum moved her plate to the side and unfolded the thin blue airmail letter. "'I'm sitting at the Caffè d'Oro and I'm onto my second espresso,'" read Mum. She made her voice go all posh and crossed her eyes. Her eyeballs swiveled so far into the corners I thought they'd get stuck. There was no doubt, Mum had the most rubbery face in the family. Jeremy let out a shout of laughter.

"Mum's making funny faces!" he cried gleefully. "Do it again, Mum, do it again."

"Don't worry," I told Jem, "she will."

"'The conference has been *fascinating*,'" Mum went on in the voice, "'but sometimes I think you learn more over coffee, when you get the chance to chat with your colleagues. They're such an inspiring bunch, especially the physicist Ennio Bagnadentro. Have I ever mentioned him to you, Cally? I've read his papers over the years, so it was very interesting to meet him in the flesh. I'll miss them all very much when I leave. It's rare that you get the opportunity to have such stimulating conversations—'" Mum sniffed loudly.

"Look!" yelled Jeremy, pointing at Mum. "There she goes again!" He dug me in the ribs, chortling.

"Her own flesh and blood aren't interesting enough to bother with, of course," Mum was mumbling to herself.

"What?" demanded Jeremy. He still had his face all ready to laugh.

"Nothing. Do you want to hear the rest? Or maybe Cally can read it."

"No, no!" cried Jeremy. "You read it, Mum, you do it best."

Mum smiled in a gratified way and picked up the letter. She read on for a while about the conference and the art galleries and dinners. She crossed her eyes a lot for Jeremy, and her eyeballs nearly disappeared when she came to another one of Grandma's jokes. "'Ennio was telling us about that old Zwicky character—you know, Cally, the one who coined the term "dark matter."'" Mum looked up from the letter questioningly. I nodded.

Mum shrugged. "I've never heard of him."

"Me neither," said Jeremy.

"He was a scientist who liked to argue."

"Sounds like your grandma," muttered Mum. "He probably had her dreadful sense of humor, too." Her eyes ran over the page. Her lips twitched for just a second.

"What, Mum? After this, I can tell you a joke about bats," said Jeremy.

"Well," Mum read on, "'Zwicky liked to start fights, so he always took the opposite line to his colleagues. Edwin Hubble believed fervently that dwarf galaxies did not exist—Zwicky swore that they did. Funnily enough, Zwicky turned out to be right. He lashed out at his colleagues, calling them a pack of "spherical bastards"— meaning they were bastards whichever way you looked at them!'"

There was silence for a moment while Mum paused in her reading. I snorted.

"Is that the joke?" asked Jeremy.

"I suppose so," Mum said. "Side-splitting, isn't it?"

"What's sfecular?"

"It means circular," I explained.

Jeremy thought for a moment. He played with his chicken wing. A new light came into his eyes. He began to smile. "Ha ha *ha!*" he spluttered, banging down his fork. His eyes disappeared into those crescent moons. Jeremy makes very little sound when he laughs. It's as if he wants to keep all the joke inside him, like something extremely precious that could leak. It's infectious, Jeremy's laughter, and soon Mum and I couldn't stop either.

It was good to have a laugh, it really was. But the next part of the letter brought me crashing down without a parachute.

"'So I'll be leaving Monday evening, and I'll arrive home Wednesday morning. I can't wait to see you all, and tell you my adventures. *Arrivederci, cari!*'"

I pictured Grandma coming over on Thursday. She'd be rippling with news, rounding us up like her flock of sheep. She'd nip at our ankles if we were late. I'm her best audience—what an interrogation there'd be if I wasn't present to hear "all her adventures." What was so important, she'd demand, that I couldn't stay? Didn't I want to hear about the Black Taj—the shadow of the universe?

I'd have to lie. I hated lying to Grandma Ruth. She could spot whole new galaxies in the sky—imagine how quickly she'd spot a lie on Earth. And anyway, just having her in the same country while I had to do this thing made me squirm. I didn't want her to ever know. I didn't want anyone to know. Then maybe, after a while, I would forget too. I could put it in brackets and get on with the next thing. Oh, why couldn't she stay safely on the other side of the world—just for another week?

Then I had an idea. Perhaps we could visit her on Wednesday, the day she arrived home. She always goes on about her "coma"—that's her word for jet lag—but we could make it a sort of celebration. We could bring over a cake and champagne, and with all the noise and interest, she'd stay awake for sure.

I felt heartened at that thought, and helped myself to another potato.

"Arrivederci, cari!" Mum said again. She put the letter down with a flourish. Her Italian accent *was* perfect. She sounded like a different person when she spoke like that. Sort of confident and hopeful.

"The Italian language is the language of the soul," she said, and sighed. "It's so musical, don't you think? So romantic. In my first life, I think, I was born in Rome. I could almost tell you the street."

"Was I there in your first life?" asked Jeremy anxiously. "Was Cally?"

"Why don't you ever go to the conferences with Grandma, Mum?" I asked. "Then you could practice your Italian." And come home a different person. Musical, romantic. Hopeful.

Mum folded the letter into tiny squares. "She's never asked me."

Jeremy jumped up from the table. "What makes a bat flit and fly around? Can't guess? *Bat*teries!"

He whooped with laughter and began galloping around the table as if it were an obstacle course. Jeremy never waits for you to guess the punch line, in case you beat him to it. He was waving his arms like a bat as he ran, causing a severe gale to blow in our faces.

"You're batty!" I yelled at him.

"Sfecular bastard!" he yelled back.
"Jeremy!" said Mum.

Friday Clinic 3:30 P.M.

Gany watches my lips when I talk to him. His big eyes latch on, as if I'm the most fascinating person on earth. I am the first person he saw in the world. I am always here. He loves me more than anyone. Makes me ecstatic and terrified at the same time. He follows my face from side to side, and he laughs, suddenly, like a balloon bursting. I don't know what he's laughing at, but it feels wonderful when he does. I'd do anything to make him laugh. My little one, with that big dimple in his cheek.

He is almost three months old. I think he's very clever, managing to get to this great age! Sometimes he sleeps for four hours at night. I feel almost human the next day when he does that. I put him in the pouch and we march up to the shops. His chubby legs bounce against my stomach as we stride along. I feel so safe and happy when he's there—strapped to my body where I can see him, his legs tapping out our rhythm. He seems to like it, too, because he gurgles and says "awaba" only on those special days. Maybe I should wear the pouch around the house too.

Monday, July 20

Gany's skin is so smooth and clear—almost transparent. There, on his chest, that pale frond of veins. David is in the bedroom, packing. His plane leaves at nine. It's five o'clock in the morning. The sky is pearly gray, like a sheet of pewter. There is just a hint of gold seeping in, promising more.

"This is absurd, packing when I should be leaving to catch a plane!" he's complaining. He's rushing around in a frantic way, hurling socks and underpants into his suitcase. Usually he rolls them up in pairs, hard as tennis balls, and they go into the side pocket of the case, so they don't fly around and get out of order. He doesn't have time this morning.

Gany is lying on my tummy in bed. David looks at me in this accusing way, as if I'm some sort of interruption in the flow of life. But his face softens when his eyes move down to Gany. He stands there, hesitating, lost for a moment, as if an invisible thread were tying him to the bed. I wish we could stand holding the thread together.

Last night Gany cried for more than an hour, nothing would console him, and I told David to go to him. He protested, but I kept my eyes squeezed shut and didn't move, so he went. He must have fallen asleep in Gany's room. He didn't get anything done last night, he said. He meant any packing, but I said, "You let me get some rest, that's getting something done, isn't it?"

"I suppose so," he muttered in a grudging way.

He manages to smile at me and kiss Gany on his dimple before he leaves. "I'll ring you when I arrive," he calls as the taxi toots outside. "Wish me luck!"

I see him as he dashes past the mulberry tree to the gate, his coat over his shoulder, waving to the driver waiting in the street. He's running as fast as he can out into the world, like a river rushing to join the sea.

My stomach drops as I watch him. Gany begins to whimper. I stroke his head, saying something, anything, because the sudden silence of this room, this house, in which we two are all alone is frightening. I look down at his angel's face, this little baby sent to me from heaven, and I know, with this terrible knowing, that he is my responsibility. There is no one else here. There is no one else who knows, right at this moment, if we are both breathing. When David goes, there is no one else.

Sometimes I think we're in a dream of mine, Gany and I. I don't like that feeling, because in dreams you're often left stranded. Sometimes you have to scream and no sound comes out. Sometimes you have to run, and your legs are rooted to the ground.

I just can't understand why David has to set up this business now—in a country that's seventeen hours away. He has a family, a wife who never sleeps, a little baby who needs him. That other firm wanted him. Could have had a fantastic salary, come home every night, bringing take-away Chinese and maybe a video.

"I want to do something creative," he said. "You've just made a new baby," I told him. "What's more creative than that?" He just rolled his eyes. He doesn't bother explaining himself to me. He thinks he lives on another planet where the words are different.

"What's so creative about buying and selling?" I ask him.

He rolls his eyes again. I read in the *Herald* that if a couple rolls their eyes at each other more than five times a day, it means the marriage is over. Eye rolling signifies contempt and unwillingness to consider the other's point of view.

David stays in dingy little hotels when he travels. He doesn't buy and sell enough to afford rooms with reliable electricity and clean sheets. Once he found a dead rat under the pillow.

There are terrible things going on over there. At night, when I'm walking the floor with the baby, I carry the newspaper with me. I read what happens there. I read about young children being taken away from their families and never heard of again. I read about raids on houses in the middle of the night and sons being shot in front of their parents. When I cut out those articles, with pictures of children's faces pinched with fear, David crushes them up in his fist. I rush to rescue them. I smooth out the paper on the desk. I want to smooth out their hurt. I run my palm over their faces, trying to take out the creases. But they look back at me with their injuries and their creases that will never disappear. I hate him when he does that. He has no mercy.

"It's not my fault," he keeps shouting at me. "I'm trying to do something about it, in my own small way. This company I'm building is giving money to those artists, money they'd never see otherwise. But you never worry about me—your husband—only those damn children."

"Well, you're white. No one's going to arrest you in the middle of the night."

"No, but I could get mugged anytime. You think it's peaceful on the street at night in Johannesburg?"

When David goes, I have this feeling that Gany and I are on an island. The rest of the world is very far away. We can only see the top of its head.

Mother comes around sometimes. She brings provisions. She brings things from the outside.

"You get skinnier every day," she says in this disapproving tone. Her eyes run over me as if I'm a bruised peach she'd rather not handle. "Why aren't you looking after yourself? If you're not strong, you can't be a good mother for your baby, can you?"

She doesn't wait for answers. She just delivers her missile and moves on. But I think about what she says. Maybe she has no idea of the power of her bullets. I don't know why I'm no good at looking after myself. We're on this island, Gany and I, and I wish one of us were grown up enough to crawl off it.

If Mother would only come and show us what to do. She could make up Gany's Milton sterilizing mixture scientifically. She wouldn't forget how many level spoonfuls of formula she'd already put into the bottle. It would be like being in the hospital again, with meals appearing out of nowhere, and an expert always around to give advice.

But I'd never dare ask her. I couldn't.

*J*eremy woke me up on Saturday morning, jumping onto my bed like a great puppy. He licked my cheek and barked till I opened my eyes. I could smell milk and cornflakes where his tongue had been.

"Ugh!" I pushed him off me. My heart was still banging

with fright, but he looked so ridiculous hanging upside down like that, with his tongue hanging out and his hair drooping over his eyes like an offended spaniel, that I had to laugh.

"You need a haircut," I said sleepily.

"I'm Batman's dog," he announced. "Did you know Batman had a dog, Cally?"

"No, fancy that."

"Well, he does." He paused a moment, his mouth open in concentration. I closed my eyes. A tide of nausea was rising into my throat. I had to lie very still and wait for it to ebb.

"Actually," Jeremy went on, crawling further up the bed and arranging a pillow behind his back, "it's Robin who has the dog. Yes, Robin has this yappy little terrier that goes everywhere with him. And when Robin's in danger, the terrier races to get help. I can just see him, Cally, can't you? He's pulling at Batman's sleeve with these white little teeth, he's barking like a maniac, and Batman bends down and says—"

"Shut your trap, you dumb dog, or I'll shut it for you."

"No!" Jeremy thumped me on the leg. "*You're* the dummy! Batman would never say that."

Jeremy looked so outraged, I felt ashamed. "I'm sorry." I patted his head and said, "There's a good boy," and pretended to give him a dog biscuit.

"Now stop joggling me," I told him as he wriggled and panted over my knees, "and go and get me a cup of tea. Earl Grey. The tea bags are in the yellow packet by the sink, you know."

"I can't because I'm a dog. Dogs only understand certain words, like *go, fetch, sit* and *stay.*"

I sighed. Everything took so long with Jeremy. You had to have this whole story, a novel almost, surrounding every domestic event. It was very tiring, especially when you thought you might throw up at any moment.

"All right. What's your name, little doggie?"

"Grayson." Jeremy lowered his voice to a whisper. "This is just on the side, Cally, but the reason I'm calling him Grayson is because Robin's real name is Dick *Grayson*, see?"

"Okay, Grayson, come here."

Grayson came.

"Go . . . fetch . . . tea . . . kitchen."

Grayson went.

I pulled the covers up and sank back into the pillows. The buttons on my pajamas scratched my nipple. It stung savagely. Through the window I could see a shimmery blue sky weaving between the trees. It would be fine tonight at the observatory. That was a piece of luck. A mild piece, but it was something. Maybe it was a sign, as Mum would say, of good weather ahead. God, it must be catching, this superstitious stuff, especially when you're feeling fragile. I'd have to watch it.

Jeremy came back carrying the newspaper in his mouth. I told him he was a very talented dog, juggling a cup of tea in his paws as well. I didn't mention that half of it was in the saucer.

The phone rang at lunchtime. It was Tim. He was at Byron Bay, and they'd just set up their tent. The weather was fine there, too.

I got such a shock to hear from him. I don't know why, since he'd only left a couple of days ago.

"It took ages to put the tent up, because José didn't bring enough pegs," Tim said. "Can you believe that guy? He wants Tito to sleep in the tent with us—he reckons some-one might steal him otherwise. I told him, who'd want to steal a mangy old dog like Tito? He's full of fleas and he farts. He's got bowel trouble, José said, it's not his fault. So, how are you? Has your period come?"

"No," I said.

"Oh." There was a pause then, like the obligatory minute's silence we used to have at the school memorial on Anzac Day.

"It's all right, I'm going to handle it," I said briskly. It was the voice again, and I felt grateful to it. It put full stops wherever I wanted them.

"Oh, okay," Tim said. He sounded relieved. I think he liked full stops, too. He didn't ask me *how* I was going to handle it.

Jeremy kept popping into the kitchen, like annoying ad breaks in a movie. He was mouthing something to me about how I should stop twisting the cord. "Remember what the man said," he reminded me.

Once we'd had a faulty line, and we had to call in a phone man to fix it. "All that static you're getting is due to some-one twisting the cord," the man explained. When he said "someone" he'd looked at me specifically, in a suspicious, Spanish Inquisition sort of way. "Teenagers are often the culprits with this kind of thing," he told Mum. "They stay on the phone for hours and fiddle with the cord. It makes our job very hard." Mum had to give him a cup of tea to calm him down, and it turned out he had a teenager at home, too, and he was at "his wits' end." She did her comforting routine, and in the end we didn't have to pay for his visit. He went out the door whistling. I bet he would have joined her Thursday group as well if she'd invited him, only he was the wrong sex.

I felt quite unreal, sitting there on the stool in the kitchen, the telephone cord twisting in my hands. I tried to imagine Tim in his tent, with the dog and all, but it seemed like a dream. It was like talking to someone who didn't exist anymore.

"I hope you have an absolutely fabulous holiday," I told him earnestly. I really meant it. I felt sorry and guilty and regretful and determined. Maybe he did, too. I never really knew the inside of Tim Cleary.

Jeremy spent the afternoon asking me every five minutes what time it was. Why couldn't Jupiter Night be in the morning? He couldn't believe how long Saturday was taking. "Time stretches like chewing gum," he concluded at four o'clock. "It loses its flavor and gets boring in just the same way."

We had an early dinner with Mum, and she dropped us off at the ferry. "I wish I could come with you," she said in the car. She looked at us wistfully and traced the line of Jeremy's cheek with her finger.

"Why don't you?" cried Jeremy. He had it all worked out in a second. "We could go and pick up sad Beth and bring her to the observatory. Wouldn't she like that?" Jeremy couldn't understand anyone not panting to get there. It was the safest place in the world, he said, because they had all those instruments pointed at the sky. They'd know before anyone else if a meteor was coming. And tonight they had lollies as well.

Mum shook her head. "Thanks, Jeremy, but I can't. Beth's not in a fit state to go anywhere. I said I'd go and make her dinner."

Jeremy climbed out of the car. He didn't insist. He could spot a lost cause.

"Don't be too late," Mum called after us as we hurried along the wharf.

"You too!" I called back.

It was a fine, clear night. We were in plenty of time for the seven o'clock ferry, so we wandered around the boat, investigating. Jeremy decided that we should sit at the back, because he liked to watch the white water tumbling out behind.

"Oh, no," I protested, "that's where all the fumes are."

"We can just hold our breath. It's good practice if we have to swim underwater."

We settled ourselves on the seat outside. When the engine started, the sea foamed and frothed before us, leaving a path of white lace like the train of a wedding gown. It was quite spectacular. In fact, the whole evening—the glinting harbor and the black silk sky—looked like an expensive backdrop for a show. Stars glittered and the city lights dripped gold and silver into the sea. I realized I hadn't been out on the harbor for a while. You don't see these things lying on your bed. You just get a lot of lint in your pajama pockets.

The observatory is perched on top of a hill overlooking the bay. We had a long walk up from Circular Quay, and I was out of breath before we even reached the hill. Jeremy wasn't. He skipped ahead, singing something or other.

At the observatory there was a long queue. Wriggling children asked their parents the time as the queue snaked along the iron fence and down toward the bay.

The gates were due to open at 8 P.M. We stood outside under a huge old fig tree. Its roots rose from the ground like a maze of low retaining walls. I love fig trees. They are as solid and ancient-looking as elephants, their trunks looping into folds of gray skin. When I was a kid, we used to climb them. You could flip your legs over those old branches and watch the world upside down. Whenever I see the slogan Hug a Tree I always think of a fig: the mother of all trees. "Come back here, Jeremy, this is a good climbing specimen," I called.

"No way." Jeremy was already in the queue, staring viciously at the head of a boy in front of him. "If you move from here, a *scumbuggit* pushes in." The head in front didn't turn around, but a woman glared at us. I went back to looking at the tree. I laid my cheek against its smooth skin.

When the gates opened, the crowd streamed in. Children chased each other around the telescopes. I wondered if kids could ever stand still long enough to have a good look at planet Jupiter. I couldn't see Jeremy.

There were five large telescopes planted at different

167

points in the garden. Most were trained upon Jupiter. At the eastern side of the lawn I spotted the tent with the cake. Next to that was the telescope with the longest queue. My heart sank.

I peered along the queue, searching for Jeremy.

Have you ever considered how much time you've wasted in your life in a queue? At the bank, the shop, at school, even at home—that is, if you have a large family. You notice queues a lot if you're a borrower, because you're always letting people in. It's practically impossible to say no. Even if you've been waiting an hour, you smile politely when someone whirls in front and gets served before you. Once when I was standing in a cotton candy queue, a boy in front of me let nine people in—he said they were all his cousins. When the last cousin had been served, the cotton candy man put up a Closed sign. "Sorry, love," he said to me, "we've just run out."

I spied Jeremy hopping from one leg to the other as he waited. He was third from the front. He continually surprises me. Maybe he can still be a star, despite his background. I hurried toward him, making apologetic faces at the people standing in line. As I drew near, I could hear his clear, piping voice above the rumble of the crowd.

"Why is the moon as thin as a mouse's whisker?" he said, pointing away from the telescope at the western sky.

There was a titter along the queue.

The guide standing at the telescope answered him. He had his back to me, but I could hear him smiling. "That's a crescent moon you're looking at tonight. The moon travels around the earth, and at the moment we can see only a small part of the sunlit side." His voice had a deep viscous tone, sweet and giving with the smile underneath, like toffee before it has set.

The guide turned toward Jeremy, checking to see if he understood. I saw his profile. He had a long straight nose and decisive chin, rather like those Renaissance men I'd seen in Grandma's Italian stamps. His hair fell forward as he spoke to Jeremy. I suddenly wanted to push the hair back and feel the warmth of his skin. He looked younger than his voice.

I gave Jeremy's sweater a little tug. "Hi," I whispered. I felt a bit breathless.

"Hi!" said Jeremy. "It's my turn next. You can be after me."

I glanced at the guide. He was discussing Jupiter with the woman at the telescope.

"Look for the four moons," I reminded Jeremy as the woman thanked the guide and wandered off. Jeremy squeezed my hand. He gave a wriggle of excitement as he stepped up to the telescope.

The guide told him about covering one eye and looking through the eyepiece. "That's okay," Jeremy assured him, "I do this all the time. We've got a telescope in our backyard."

"And an alien in the front," someone said with a chuckle.

Jeremy lined his eye up with the telescope. "There they are! I can see them!" he yelled. "Callisto, I can see *you* up there! Oh this is great, they are bigger and clearer than at home. Wait till you see them, Cal, they're so beautiful!"

Jeremy's excitement was infectious. People began to stir restlessly. Children squirmed like worms in a jar. Jeremy stayed glued to the telescope, doing a loud running commentary on the celestial scene like a football commentator on the radio. The guide was staring at me.

"Come on, Jeremy, it's time for someone else to have a turn," I whispered to him. I was blushing hotly. I didn't dare look back at the guide.

"No!" said Jeremy.

"Yes!" said I.

I was sweating. When you blush, do you ever grow so hot that you sweat? There's nowhere to hide. Your face beams out like a torch, with these little pearls of moisture strung along your lip. You might as well announce, "I'm dying of embarrassment!" I was sweating like a madwoman. I could feel great wet patches spreading under my arms. *Don't let him make a scene now, not in front of all these people,* I prayed. *All these people he pushed ahead of. Don't let him be a brat in front of that nice guide, please.*

The guide bent down and whispered in Jeremy's ear. I heard "cake" and "chocolate" and "good boys." Jeremy relinquished the telescope, giving it a reluctant little pat.

He sidled around to stand next to the guide. He kept his eyes fixed on him as if he were the new messiah, about to do a miracle. I saw him take the guide's hand.

"Jeremy, come here now, the man has to talk to the other people in the line," I called.

The guide looked at me and smiled. You should have seen that smile. My stomach lurched. It was as if we shared a secret. My heart started hammering, and the sweating began all over again. You could have just pushed me lightly, with the feathery tips of your fingers, and I'd have fallen face forward into his orbit. My legs felt wobbly.

"Hello, Callisto. Come for the cake, have you?"

I swung round and saw a friendly familiar face. "Oh, hi, Mr. West!"

He was standing there, beaming all over his craggy old face. God, it was nice to see him. I couldn't think of anything to say. I was too surprised and I was wondering if he could see the sweat. We stood right under a lamp, sharing a pool of light like a dry patch under an umbrella. He was looking at my top lip, so I bet he noticed.

"And young Jeremy!" called Mr. West, spotting him still clasped like a limpet to the guide. "How are you?" He strode over and somehow drew us all together. We moved out of the pool of light, which was a good thing, into the soft webbed shadow of evening. "I see you've met my son, Richard," he said, clapping the guide on the shoulder.

Jeremy nodded enthusiastically. He didn't look at all astounded. He was used to the world bringing him magical connections. At five, I suppose, every day brings a surprise.

"Richard, have you met Callisto?"

"No," said Richard, "but I'd like to." He put out his hand for me to shake. It was warm and smooth, except for a Band-Aid on the little finger. I wanted to hang on to it. It was very hard to let go. I felt like Jeremy with the telescope.

I scrunched my hand up in my pocket. It was slippery with sweat. Oh, God, why was I made this way? Just a few days ago I'd thought my skin was dead.

Jeremy was tugging at Mr. West. "Let's go see the moon now," he said. "I bet it'll look like a giant banana with these monster telescopes. And the queue's only short. Please!"

Mr. West laughed. "All right, Jeremy." He turned to me. "You coming, Callisto?"

Before I could answer, Richard said, "Callisto can stay here with me and Jupiter. She'll help with the crowd." He raised his eyebrows at me. "Is that okay? These special nights with the lollies and all get really busy. I could do with some help. We can dispense scientific information left, right and center!"

Mr. West shook his head at his son and let himself be pulled away.

"I don't know enough to be a guide," I murmured.

Richard looked at me. His eyes were jade green in the shadows. "You've got a telescope in your backyard and a grandmother who's a well-known astronomer. You're named after a Galilean moon, for God's sake! Although you'd rather be called something more ordinary, like Anne."

"How do you know all that?"

"Ah"—he tapped his nose slyly—"I haf my vays and means."

"Your *father* told you about me!" I almost shouted with amazement. I'm no longer a little kid—I have my peripheral vision, and I don't expect the world to surprise me anymore. It was flabbergasting to believe that Mr. West had bothered to tell his son about this rude, ungrateful girl he knew at Meadow High.

"Dad used to tell great stories about you," Richard said

in a teasing voice. "And about Jeremy. He always wondered what happened to your hair that afternoon, when you came back from the toilets with one side shorter than the other. I did, too. It was like losing the last chapter in a book."

"He noticed?"

Richard laughed. "It would be hard not to, the way Dad described it. You were as pale as a ghost, too. And your hands were shaking." Richard frowned, and he leant forward. "There were great gaps after that. No more chapters. Dad missed you, you know. So did I!"

We looked at each other in the dark. I felt the cool trunk of a young fig tree under my hand. It was something solid to hang on to. People were working their way through the Jupiter line. Out of the corner of my eye I could see the woman who had glared at me at the gate. It was her turn at the telescope. She was looking our way and she cleared her throat impatiently.

"It's so strange seeing you here," Richard went on. "I mean, I've only ever pictured you at school—you know, in your uniform, in the daytime." He looked down at the brick paving.

The woman at the telescope coughed loudly. Richard sighed. "I'd better go and do my job. Coming?"

We walked over to the telescope. Richard's hand brushed against my arm.

"Are you really busy here, then?" I asked.

"Yeah, I guess so, but most of my time is taken up with university now—it's hard to find time to do anything else."

"Is this your first year? Are you doing a science degree?"

"Yes times two." Richard grinned. "I'm doing some psychology units and literature, too. I figured I should branch out a little—'get humanized,' as my mother says."

"It must be great having your father to help with science."

"What are all those oval spots and bands around Jupiter?" The woman with the hard face stamped her foot as she spoke. Maybe she was just squashing a cockroach (I'd seen a few on the paving), but the gesture echoed the tone of her voice. "How big is Jupiter? What is its distance from the sun?"

You'd never catch this woman letting anyone into a queue.

Richard raised his eyebrows at me.

"We think the oval features are circular currents, or cyclones, trapped by the opposing winds of the cloud bands," I said. "The largest of these currents is the Great Red Spot, which is three times the size of Earth. It's actually this spot that tells us how fast Jupiter rotates."

I glanced at Richard. He smiled at me as if I were a star pupil. I felt my cheeks glowing. He didn't think I was a crazy lady. He probably kept old copies of *New Scientist* in a special folder. Just like me.

"Well, how fast does it rotate?" the imperious voice demanded.

"At the equator the planet's surface whirls at a speed of about forty-three thousand kilometers an hour. The outward thrust due to the whirling is so great that the gases form a bulge. But they don't fly away. Jupiter's gravity is so powerful that it keeps them from escaping."

Whenever I think about that power, I get a thrill of excitement. It seems magical, the ability to keep something in thrall that way, with only an invisible force.

I went on a bit longer, warming to the theme, telling her about the three very thin rings that were discovered by the *Voyager 1* and *2* spacecraft. I forgot about the sweat patches under my arms as I described those glittering rings, which were millions of tiny dust particles coated with ice. There is nothing as gripping as astronomy, I reckon—it kidnaps you and flings you up into a giant world, so that even if you remember to look down, you can hardly see your little old beetle self anymore. It's a great relief, rather like drinking rum and Coke without the hangover. I was getting to the moons when Richard tapped me on the shoulder. The woman was edging away, toward the cake tent.

"Got more than she bargained for." Richard laughed. "You can take over my job."

"How often do you work here?"

"Oh, only on a casual basis. I help out on special nights like these, when Jupiter or Saturn or whatever is in view."

"Do they pay you in lollies?"

"Just about! This line is thinning out now. Do you want to go to the tent and get a coffee?"

But just then a group of ten people streamed in, so we had a lot more information to dispense. It was good the way it worked, with Richard giving background information, preparing people for what they were about to see, while I talked to each person at the telescope. A woman of about my mother's age was looking through the telescope for the first time. "Ravishing!" she kept saying. "It's just *ravishing!*" She had so many questions, she could hardly get them out. We talked fervently until the man behind her grew restless.

Inside the tent, the air was warm with steaming urns and chattering children. I spied Jeremy near the lolly table, taking great handfuls of fluorescent snakes. He stuffed them into his pocket and went back for the frogs. Mr. West pretended not to see. Honestly, Jeremy was like some starving child, storing up for the coming drought. The frogs practically lit up the plate with neon green preservatives. I thought of Mum with her avocado sandwiches and bushes of sprouts.

I waved to Jeremy. His hands were busy in his pockets and his mouth was full. He gave me a kind of strangled nod.

"Do you have milk in your coffee?" asked Richard. "I do here. It hides the taste."

We poured some coffee and made our way outside. I signaled our direction to Jeremy, but he'd spotted the licorice allsorts and was busy hunting for remaining storage in his shirt pocket.

Richard found a seat in the garden. From there you could see all the way down to the water, spread out like a cloak at the bottom of the hill. You could just hear it whispering against the seawall, rustling into little folds and wavelets.

"Beautiful, isn't it?" Richard said quietly as he sat down. "I come here sometimes just to sit and think. The world seems much bigger and more forgiving, somehow, in this place."

We were silent for a while. It wasn't the school-memorial kind of silence. It wasn't awkward, either. But I couldn't help wondering what Richard felt he needed to be forgiven for. Me, I could name one huge thing. I wished for the hundredth time that the undertow wasn't there. That it wasn't stuck like an ocean between us. My secret. It was so loud in that quiet place.

"So how long have you had the telescope in your garden?" Richard asked.

I jumped.

"You were far away."

"This is a dreamy place. I was twelve when Grandma gave us the telescope. We had a Jupiter Night back then, too. I can still remember how electrifying it was to see Jupiter for the first time."

I was looking at Richard, but suddenly Mum's face floated into my mind. I remembered her mouth that night. It had gone all sharp and jagged when Grandma named the moons out loud—Callisto, Ganymede, Io, Europa. I could still hear her chanting, like some celestial nursery rhyme. Mum had run away then. The porch door had slammed. *Gany*.

"What is it, Callisto?"

"Oh, nothing. I was just thinking." I smiled, but it was a rotten smile. It was one of those you put on when a photographer asks you nicely.

Gany. I didn't want to think about that now. It was like being at the edge of a dream, in that intertidal zone.

Richard looked at me, waiting. The secret was there between us, it was so noisy, nagging away, and Richard was so
close to me on that seat. It was amazing that he couldn't
hear it—*Look at me, see what I've done, I'm a bad girl, you
wouldn't like me if you knew*. I thought of that couple I'd seen
at the restaurant with Tim. Their noses had touched while
they talked. You could practically see their thoughts flowing
into each other, like fluids in osmosis. I felt such an urge to
tell Richard the secret—it was like a wave building up in
my chest. I realized then that I'd had no practice in telling
the truth. I had never really said what I meant.

"It's hard to tell your thoughts," I said in a stumbling sort
of way. "There's a distance between your head and your
mouth, filled with all these little wires and networks, and in
the unraveling along the way something gets lost. I mean,
the more you talk, the further away from the original
thought you get."

"Hmmm," said Richard, considering, "especially when
you're concentrating on how the other person will react as
you're saying it."

"Hmmm," I agreed. The dreaded blush crept up my
cheeks. It was true—how did he know that? And why did I
want to tell *him*, someone I'd met only an hour ago, when I
couldn't tell my own mother?

I wanted to close the gap between us. I wanted to get
close. I could hardly breathe with this need to show him
myself.

"There are such big gaps between people," I said. "The
more they try to close them, the bigger the gaps get." I

paused, and we watched a boat drifting across the water. "Do you know what I mean?"

He nodded but didn't say anything. He just kept looking at me with that green steady gaze. In the shadows of his eyes there was no light reflected. I was on my own.

"Well, it's strange, isn't it? Incredible, really. It's like the expanding universe."

"What is?"

"These gaps. You know the theory. Once upon a time all the ingredients of the universe were so close. Every bit of matter was tightly packed against every other bit—it was so compressed it was red-hot. There were no gaps, like lovers melting into each other, and then *bang*—"

"The big-bang theory!"

"Yes. And all those close, intimate bits of matter exploded and flew away from each other as fast as they could. They've been running ever since."

"Into the expanding universe! Hey, that's neat. And all the bits grew cooler as they ran—"

"That's right—the gaps made them cooler. So what I'm saying is, the universe began in this burning-hot state, it began in *singularity*—all places that exist today used to be the same place, right? Things used to be so cozy, without gaps."

Richard pushed back his hair. He cracked his knuckles. "So you're saying that people get close, they heat up, and then explode? Like, what's the use?"

"Well, that's a very bald way to put it." The words hung there in the night, stark as bones. I wished I didn't talk so much. Gaps—it's better if you leave some so the other person can fill you in. I bet silent types have more fun, like blondes.

"I've never thought of it all like that," Richard said. His voice had a smile in it. It was admiring, and he was looking at me intently, as if I were some new species he hadn't seen before. He seemed to be peering inside, as if he wanted to know where the words came from.

He cleared his throat. "Maybe we were all close once, like the original universe." He was frowning, bringing his words out with care. "Think about children, for instance. I have these two nephews—they're only little, one's just started preschool. It's incredible how they'll play with anyone new, without introductions, they'll chatter away about their families and their pets, tell family secrets to strangers so that their parents cringe. It's as if they think everyone is an extension of them—the grocer, the butcher, the woman next door—that we're all under the same skin, like some enormous human umbrella."

I nodded. Jeremy used to be like that. I remembered the time he told the special-delivery man that Mum couldn't come to the door because she was doing poo and she'd only just started. "She takes about fourteen hundred hours," he'd said. "But you can wait with Cally and me if you like."

"I wonder what happens to us," I said. "Later on, I mean."

"Maybe it's just growing up."

"Growing away."

"Maybe." Richard leant toward me and put his hand on my cheek. He brought my face round to his. There was a

180

sudden charge in the air. It almost crackled between us, electric. I held my breath. "I'd like to get close to you," he murmured.

I pulled away involuntarily. "Ha, the big bang, eh?" I heard myself snigger like Miranda Blair.

Richard kept his hand on my cheek. He shook his head. "No, I'd rather go slow with you. I don't want to spoil it."

Such a tingle shot up my spine when he said that, I nearly jumped out of my skin. I'd been holding my breath—it was like sitting on a bubble, and the slightest movement would cause it to burst. I *wanted* to burst, I couldn't stand it any longer. I began to burble.

"According to my classification, you, Richard West, are definitely a star. I can't imagine what you're doing with me, just a little old itty-bitty moon!"

Richard laughed and asked me what was I talking about, and I told him about my classification system and that my mother was a moon, and my father was a degenerating star, maybe a white dwarf who'd been a giant in his day. I was burbling on because I was so nervous. Or maybe I was just terribly excited. I don't know. I wasn't used to being *happy* excited, so it was hard to recognize. This feeling had always come under the "nervous" category, with those familiar symptoms of talking too much and thumping heart. Maybe I'd have to invent a whole new section if happiness was to be included.

Anyway, I'd never said any of this out loud before. It was intoxicating. (But I didn't mention the borrower bit. Borrowers can make you sick.)

"And Jeremy?"

"Yes, Jeremy. I think he's a young star."

Richard was tapping out some rhythm on the bench. He was thinking, savoring the idea. He wanted to play this game, and I couldn't believe how easy it was with him. It was like talking to Jeremy, someone with the same blood, the same language, plus there were the pheromones as well!

"My mother is the star in our family," Richard concluded after a while.

"What about Mr. West?" I protested. For me he was a kindly, warming star of the nicest kind. I felt offended for him.

"Oh, no, he's definitely in Mum's orbit."

"Is she a strong woman—is she astonishingly attractive?" I felt a prickle of anxiety for a moment.

Richard laughed. "I suppose she's attractive. I'd call her determined."

"Does she work? What does she do?"

"She's a naturopath."

"No, *really*?"

"Yes, really."

"Does she have real, live qualifications? You know, with letters after her name and all?"

Richard grinned. "Yes, she's quite successful, actually. Her practice is really busy. She often gives lectures. You should come sometime. She helps a lot of people, I think."

"She doesn't read tea leaves or throw salt over her shoulder?"

"No." Richard laughed. "Does anyone?"

"No one I know," I said quickly. I went red. "Does your father follow her diagnoses? Or is he in the grip of science—I mean, Western medicine? Do they argue about it?"

"Not about *that*. Other things, they do. There's actually a lot of science and experimentation in naturopathy. Dad's quite interested in that. Mum is always reading articles about new treatments—a different use of an herb, maybe, for some ailment, and she'll sit there on the sofa, reading little bits out to him. He always wants to hear more, but she gets immersed in the thing and goes quiet. 'Read it yourself when I'm finished,' she says. Dad gets annoyed about that because later, when she's folded it all up, he can never find the right bit. Like last night, she found something about giving up smoking—"

"Your father *smokes*? I didn't know that!"

"Yeah, he hides it well. Mum's always going on at him about it. If he smokes in the house, she walks around with a handkerchief tied over her nose like a bandit. She looks sort of dangerous, like she's going to rob a bank or something just as soon as she's finished cooking the steak."

I laughed. "But I bet he admires her just the same."

"I guess so—he says she's very talented." Richard gave a snort then. "But he still complains about dinner being late, and the way she sits up reading instead of coming to bed."

"Typical moon behavior. You whinge and salivate at the same time."

Richard grinned. Behind us we heard the clear high notes of Jeremy's voice trickling into the night air. Richard took my hand. "We'll have to go soon. Can I see you again?"

I nodded, my hands warm and folded in his.

"I like the way you think," he whispered. "You bring everything to life."

Mr. West was calling Jeremy now. Any moment they

would discover us here, clasped together on the park bench. "But I have my own classification system, you know," Richard hurried on. "It's a game, really—hide-and-seek. There are those who hide and those who seek. I think you hide behind science. Do you?"

"I've never really thought about it like that," I echoed, gaining time. "Maybe it's the only way I know to show myself."

There, that was a paradox worthy of Grandma.

Richard smiled in the dark. "Well, that's okay. I know my way around your universe. I'll find you sooner or later."

Find me after Thursday, I pleaded under my breath. *Find me then and I'll be pure and yours and uninhabited. The undertow will be gone. No more secrets.*

We heard the flat thud behind us of boots running on grass.

"Cally, I feel sick."

Jeremy loomed over the back of our seat.

"I told him not to eat that last battalion of frogs," said Mr. West, striding up after him. "But would he listen to me?"

Jeremy came and sat on my lap.

"Geez, you must be feeling bad," I said into his hair, giving him a cuddle. He curled up like a sleepy puppy on my knees. There was a loud burp, and a sickly sweet odor wafted up to my nostrils.

"I'm going to do a Technicolor vomit," murmured Jeremy.

"Right now?"

Mr. West was looking at us on the bench. "Well, Richo, I'll meet you out front. Callisto, it was great to see you here. Don't be such a stranger now, okay?"

"Okay." I smiled up at him.

"Look out for dem frogs, boy." He grinned at Jeremy.

We watched him stroll off into the dark. Jeremy leant his head back, into my neck.

"You're under May in the phone book?" asked Richard.

"Yes, D. May."

"Good." He began to stand up, but then, as if snagged by a thought, he sat down again. "Listen," he said, "about the universe thing. You know, the big bang."

"Mmm." I was going to keep my lips closed this time.

"Well, you reckon the big bang wrecks intimacy, right? But you didn't deal with the rest of the theory. The most important part. I mean, after the explosion, all those bits flew away, sure—but don't forget that once they were separate, atoms could form and life could begin." Richard looked down at his hands. "That was the only way molecules and galaxies and living creatures could exist. They had to be separate to have an identity, to have a life."

"Explosion? What explosion?" Jeremy sat bolt upright on my lap. His nose slammed into my chin. "Is it a meteor?"

"No, Jeremy, we're only talking. Go back to dreamland."

"I'm not tired," Jeremy warned. "I'm just thinking here."

Richard went on. "You can't really live in a burning-hot plasma state—not all the time. You can't evolve that way. You can only really see the other person, only really appreciate them, through the gaps between you. Otherwise if you're too close, you're only seeing yourself."

Richard ran his fingers along the slats of the seat. His ears were so sleek against his head, like twin question marks, meticulously traced.

"You can reach out across the gaps, you know. That's what they're there for."

Jeremy clambered off my lap. "Let's go home now." He started walking off toward the front gate.

"Jeremy, wait!" I called.

Richard took my hand and pulled me up. Our faces were so near, our lips brushed together. "See," whispered Richard, "you're so close you're out of focus. You're just a blur."

He kissed my lips lightly. "But I like you blurred," he murmured into my neck. His lips were like feathers on my skin. I felt my nipples tingle. I wanted him to go on kissing me. An ache started in the pit of my belly, a sort of emptiness. My legs wanted to twine around his.

"Cally, come *here*!"

"I'd better go," I said, not moving.

On the ferry, Jeremy and I sat outside at the front. I explained that the fumes at the back would surely make him vomit. "The ancient Romans used to gorge themselves like you," I told him. "Then they'd deliberately make themselves sick so that they could start all over again."

"That's really naughty," said Jeremy. "I bet they got into trouble from their mums when they got home."

"Their mums probably gorged themselves, too."

Jeremy was quiet for a while, contemplating the enormity of those mothers.

I leant over the rail and watched the water disappearing beneath us. As I moved my legs I felt the dampness between them. I smiled to myself—I couldn't help it. It felt so good, sort of slippery and easy and soft. I imagined Richard's fingers dipping into the wetness. There'd be a sucking sound, like when you pull little sea animals squelching from the rocks. It was hard to believe. I didn't believe myself.

I know what you're going to say—"How could you feel like this, when only a week ago you were lying there on the floor with Tim? You've only just met this boy. And moreover, think of the *state* you're in. You're a girl with absolutely no moral values at all."

Well, I only know that Richard makes the pit of my stomach drop. He is made of the same molecules as me. He can talk about the necessity of gaps, but I feel like we've got the same skin, the same blood. I want to crawl in there with him, under our skins, where there's atmosphere and electricity and great rushing storms of desire. I want to get buffeted around a bit in the *weather,* if it's all the same to you.

I've never felt like this before.

I've never felt like this before, if you really want to know. It's like a fairy tale, where the prince only has to bend down and kiss the lifeless princess and she awakes. He has to be the right prince, of course, with the right amount of electricity. Otherwise it won't work.

It's not very modern, is it, to compare life with fairy tales. "Life is no fairy tale," says Miranda Blair, with that sneer that could just about kill a Year 7.

Well, all I can say is that some kisses are redeeming. They can save you. They save you from the vast blank lake of deadness.

I came up to the surface, gasping for air. There was a point in breathing. I bet Sleeping Beauty felt like this. Only don't tell Miranda Blair I said so.

As soon as I opened my eyes on Sunday, I thought of Richard sitting on the park bench. I went over every word he'd said, and then every word I'd said. I remembered how he'd moved his hands when he spoke, the urgency in his tone at the end, his hopeful version of the big-bang theory. I remembered the smile in his voice.

You could tell anything to a voice like that. Well, almost anything. When I'd first heard it, I'd thought Richard was much older. You'd have to be over twenty-five at least, I thought, to sound so assured. When we were talking later, on the park bench, his voice was like a river flowing round my words, inviting me in. That voice, with its soft vowels and welcoming smile, would never harden to build walls against me, or set like concrete.

I got up and put on my white silk dressing gown. It was a bit crushed, because it had been lying stashed in the bottom cupboard under the winter sweaters. I never wear it usually, because I feel silly. Like some sort of pretend princess. Plus it looks better with cleavage.

I padded out to the kitchen. Early-morning sun streamed from the kitchen window. It made little stars of light on the white kettle. My gown was so dazzling I had to squinch up my eyes to fill the kettle. I hummed along as it warmed. The stainless-steel bench gleamed beneath, wiped clean of yesterday's traces.

When the kettle had boiled, I took my tea to the kitchen table. I ran my fingers over the wood. It glowed in the melt of marmalade sunshine. Under my hand, the wood was so warm I could almost imagine a pulse throbbing there.

I sipped my tea. I felt it trickle all the way down, along

my tongue, into my throat, warming my stomach. In that moment I could have drawn a circle around myself, and never stepped outside. I was happy there, bewitched by sunlight, hot tea and the warmth of wood.

An Indian mynah bird streaked past the sun, across the kitchen window. I watched feather shadows sweep the table.

I sat with this sense of hope—nothing solid or definite, mind you, like a plan for the day or a list of things to do. It was just a feeling of possibility, like a heat mirage shimmering in the desert.

Jeremy woke up and I poured him an orange juice.

"What'll we do today?" he asked.

"I don't know," I said breezily. "Anything could happen."

I put milk and cornflakes out on the table. Jeremy fetched the bowls. They were a rich cream color, with a thin blue line like a vein traced around the top. Dad had brought a set of six back from Africa.

"Don't they look beautiful on the dark wood?" I said, tapping my bowl where it sparkled.

Jeremy peered at me suspiciously from under his hair. "You're up early," he said.

"Amazing, isn't it?"

Jeremy nodded. "I had terrible dreams. I didn't sleep for about sixteen hundred hours."

"Must have been all those 'conservatives' in the frogs." I smiled at him. "Did you see them in your dreams, little green creatures marching around in suits?"

Jeremy was scraping the sugar off his cornflakes. It was a laborious task. "I didn't want any more sugar, Cally. My stomach still feels kind of funny. Why did you put *sugar* on them?"

His voice was whingey. He pushed away his bowl and put his head on the table. He slumped there like a jellyfish, his eyes closed.

I got up quietly and rinsed the bowls in the sink. I glanced at the telephone. No one in the civilized world would ring yet, I supposed, unless they were under the age of eight. Even so, when I'd wiped my hands I picked up the receiver, just to check the dial tone. Sometimes Jeremy left the phone off the hook in the other room.

I stared at the telephone. It was white, with greasy fingerprints on the dial panel. But it suddenly had such a weighty significance. In comic books, phones appear with frantic lines waving around them. Their ringing is deafening on the page. Often there is a girl waiting beside it, with long blond hair and ten-out-of-ten bosoms.

I put the receiver back and wiped down the sink. I noticed I was holding my breath. This phone thing—the possibility that it might ring—gave everything another dimension, like slipping on those special glasses in a 3D cinema. It's as if we were all waiting—me, sleepy Jeremy, the particles of air, the dust motes suspended in that shaft of sunshine. We were all charged, transformed, holding our breaths. There was someone behind the curtain, watching us, maybe waiting, too, fiddling around until nine o'clock when he'd suddenly dial our number and blare onto the stage, making the entrance of a main character.

Jeremy dragged himself up from the table. "I might ring Sam," he said tentatively. "We could get on with the digging."

I found the number for him and helped him dial. "Don't be too long," I said.

I went into the bedroom to get dressed.

All morning Richard bobbed around in my mind. I carried him carefully, like a valuable package. I saw his quick pointed face, turning toward me on the seat. There was the neatness of his hairline against the pale forehead, as if someone had painted it on. The mystery of the shadows under his eyes. The nape of his neck. I dusted the bookshelves in my room. I picked up pairs of dirty underpants and twice-worn T-shirts and threw them in the washing machine. I vacuumed under my bed. Everything I did had a bounce to it, a breathy hum, as if each action were a star note in a new song.

I ran the duster over Ganesha. He gleamed and grinned at me. Maybe *he* had brought me Richard. Or maybe the planets had all lined up in the right order. Or maybe Mum threw salt in the direction of love last night. I don't know. But certainly the thought of Richard was enough to dull the other thoughts. The nasty ones.

The thought of Richard brought the world back into focus. It's as if it had been waiting outside all this time, leaning on the door, and now it was tumbling in, with all its colors and smells and textures.

I looked at the row of perfumes on my dressing table. Dad often brought back a duty-free bottle from his flights. Mum gave me hers. The bottles were coated with dust. I picked up Donna and dabbed it under my ears. I closed my eyes. I smelled expensive women with pearly teeth and plunging necklines. Sleeping Beauty would smell like that when the prince bent to kiss her.

191

You can't help thinking about fairy tales or gods or magic when you've been kissed like that. Even if you want to be scientific like Grandma and explain it with pheromones or the mating instincts of baboons or something, nothing accounts for the bolt of electricity in your belly and the branch of lightning that shoots up your veins. You suddenly know what you're *for*. And the lightning only happens with *that* person, doesn't it, in that time and place. (I knew that forever after, amen, observatories around the world would make me pant.) Imagine if I'd never gone to that place, if it had rained that night or Jeremy had lost interest or there'd been an earthquake. I never would have met him. It is luck, isn't it? Think of all the words there are for the miracle of that meeting—*destiny, fate, magic, enchantment.* It has the timing of fairy tales. The inexplicable feelings that change endings and cancel out evil.

I only wished I could have moved the whole thing backward or forward. I wished I had met Richard months ago, or months in the future. Not smack bang in the middle of the greatest disaster of my life.

When the phone rang, I was on the toilet. Can you believe it? Jeremy answered it, and I heard him say, "*I'm* not doing anything today. I don't know about Cally. No, she can't come to the phone—"

"Jeremy!"

"What?"

"Tell him I'll be there in a minute."

"Okay. Richard? Cally said she'll be there in a minute. She must only be doing wee. What are *you* doing today?"

When I got to the phone I snatched the receiver and gave Jeremy a good pinch on the arm.

"Oww!" he yelled. "Oww oww, Cally pinched me! That hurts, you scumbuggit. I'll get you for this, you stink-butt wee-head! I hate you!"

He was wailing and shouting so loudly that I couldn't hear anything, even though the receiver was pressed tightly to my ear. The noise must have woken Mum, because she came rushing out into the kitchen in her chilly nightie. She was still removing slices of cucumber from her lids. Cucumber is good for cleansing tired skin. You put it on just before bed.

"I'm going to pick up the phone in my room, Mum— will you put this one down?"

She nodded over Jeremy's head. He pressed his nose into her tummy, flinging his arms around her bottom like a drowning man. He was such a drama queen. He had cucumber in his hair.

I dashed out of the kitchen.

*H*ope is bubbly and oxygenated and energizing. It's like carbonated water in sunshine. It sparkles in a glass on a table that overlooks a valley of blue water, dotted with boats. You can hear the masts tinkling together in the wind.

That's where I wanted to go on Sunday.

But harborside cafés are expensive. Neither of us had much money. And anyway, I only wanted the sparkling water as a backdrop for our celebration.

"Why don't we go to the beach?" Richard's voice on the phone was a little deeper. "It's a beautiful day."

Collapsed bikini tops loomed. I feel so much more comfortable with my clothes on——I wish I didn't, but there it is. There's a lot to be said for preserving illusions.

"It might be a bit cold to swim now," I said cautiously.

"Yes, you might be right. But we can go for a walk round the rocks, and up onto the cliff."

We arranged to meet at eleven.

I had a shower and worried about what to wear. In my room I decided on jeans and a nice silky blue shirt I'd had for years. I'd put my suit and towel in my bag and hope I wouldn't need them.

Mum and Jeremy were still in the kitchen. Mum was making coffee and Jeremy was doing something with his magnet set on the floor.

"Where are you going?" He scowled, seeing my bag.

"To the beach, with Richard."

"Oh, can I come?"

"Who's Richard?"

"He's a boy I met at the observatory. It's all right, Mum, he's not a bank robber or anything, I know his father. He's a teacher at my school. Mr. West."

"What happened to Tim? I thought you were still seeing him."

"Why can't I come? I met him, too! I promised on the phone that I'd come."

"Tim's gone on holiday. We, well, we don't have all that much in common, really."

"That's a shame. He seemed very polite. Well, which beach are you going to? Take something warm, because I don't like the look of those clouds."

"I could take my spade. I could dig holes and tunnels in the sand. We could make castles. Will I get my Speedos? I'll only be a second!"

"No, Jeremy, I'm sorry. I'm just going by myself. It's a grown-up sort of thing. Hey, what about Sam? Isn't he coming over?"

Jeremy shook his head. His shoulders sagged. "Sam's *busy*. He's going to lunch at his auntie's. They're going to have chocolate cake, because it's his mother's birthday."

Mum raised her eyebrows at me. I knew that look. "Couldn't he come? He won't be in the way. He'd have such a nice time in the fresh sea air." I looked away.

"No one ever invites me anywhere," said Jeremy.

Mum's eyebrows practically shot up into her hairline.

I went to the door. I didn't look at either of them. "See you later, then. Have a good day!"

I could hear Jeremy start to cry as I reached the gate.

*T*he only known portrait of Caroline Herschel as a young woman is a silhouette. It was painted before she left Hanover to join her brother William in England, in 1772. She's in profile. We see only one side of her, in matte black. There is no light or shade.

The man in front of me in the bus to Manly had a portable radio. He was jerking his neck back and forth in time to the music, like a chicken pecking in a yard. He turned up the volume. I could hear the words now—it was an old song, "When a Man Loves a Woman." It made my blood pound. I thought of Richard's mouth. I wondered if Caroline Herschel had ever felt like this. Perhaps when she discovered her first comet. But did she have this dissolving, runny kind of excitement, as if her bones were made of whipped cream? We'll never know. History gives us only one side of her, a black silhouette.

I sang the words of the song under my breath. I looked out the window. Beyond the rooftops and trees a slice of sea lay like icing on a cake. I wanted to remember this bus ride—the song, the anticipation like an infinitesimal pause between notes, the sugar-frosted horizon.

We passed the deli where Mum bought her caramelized tomatoes. Sometimes she throws caution to the wind and buys two hundred grams. I saw Carlo, the deli man, arranging buckets of flowers outside the shop.

The bus driver whistled "When a Man Loves a Woman" at the red light. He stared at a girl in a short skirt crossing the road. I wondered if we only ever see one side of people—even people we love. How did Mum see Grandma, for instance? In the mold of Caroline Herschel? When Mum was little, she only saw Grandma's profile, proffered to the sky. She must have seen Ruth from the back, her shoulders hunched at the table as she studied her maps. That night when I was twelve, Mum said, "Your grandma always looked at the sky more than she did at me."

When you take a photograph with the sunlight behind the subject, the person becomes a silhouette. It's hard to get them in the right position, with a balance of light and shade. Part of the moon is usually in shadow. Sometimes it's almost invisible.

Richard has shadows under his eyes. The color of his eyes is grape green—the seedless kind you can get in summer, fresh, tight with juicy flesh. But it's darker underneath his lashes, more like evening.

If you're a sneak like me and you read people's diaries, you get a glimpse of the other side. The part turned away from the light. You can see details shining through, islands of truth you never would have imagined. But around them float areas of exaggerated shadow.

As the bus turned the corner, past the aquarium, I smelled salt water. A rush of feelings crowded into my throat. I saw Jeremy's face in the kitchen, his lips saying "please." I imagined him in his red Speedos, filling his blue bucket with sand. He kneeled at the edge of the waves, shrieking as the sea gushed into his tunnels. I saw Tim racing up the beach after a surf, flinging himself down on his Mambo towel. Droplets of water scattered on his skin like dropped pearls.

Salt rises up from the sea, dissolving into the air in clouds of sea fog. I breathed in salt and the slur of waves on sand, and I thought, *This could be something new.* I didn't want to feel guilty. I knew how to do that. Mournful, like bells tolling in an empty churchyard. The imminence of Richard was igniting me. I could tell sleeping cells, strands of thought waking up. I could tell them to Richard. We would discover things together as we talked. He would listen. He would look at me and say wonderingly, "I'd never really thought of it like that. You animate things, Cally, you bring them to life."

Did Grandma, did Mum, did old Caroline Herschel ever

ride like this, toward heaven? Did they struggle like me? Caroline Herschel's top lip was full and round, generous. It sat like a promise above its companion. Her chin was a small circle, like a child's. You can see the straight line of her nose and rise of her throat in the silhouette. Perhaps she was very beautiful. She was William's assistant for half a century. In the early days of his career, she even put food into his mouth, when he was busy grinding a mirror and dared not take his hands from it, allowing it to cool. On nights when he was sweeping for "nebulae" Caroline sat at a table near the telescope, recording descriptions as her brother shouted them out.

She became a skilled comet hunter. She was rewarded for her work. But what I wanted to know was, did she ever feel her bones turning to whipped cream? Did she ever want to live in her own house, have her own children, be a blazing star herself? Perhaps she wouldn't have found the comets if she'd done that. It's not fair, is it, that you have to parcel out your passion, as if you were slicing pastry into an even number. Something gets lost in the slicing, I bet. Caroline Herschel's top lip was so articulate. It was poised, ready, as if saying "*p*."

As soon as I stepped off the bus, I saw Richard. He had his back to me. He was leaning against the stone wall, gazing out at the harbor. There was the dark hair, curling like the tail of a *g* down his neck. Beneath the curl was a small round vertebra. When I'd put my arms around his neck, that little bone had felt like a pebble under my thumb. I'd rippled it back and forth under its veil of skin, the way you roll a river stone in your palm.

A green-and-gold ferry glided into the bay, like a plump bird landing on a pond. I hurried toward Richard, willing him not to turn around. All the way in the bus, past the bank and the bread shop and the deli that sells caramelized tomatoes, I'd been hoping that he wouldn't be there first. Have you ever seen those old movies where lovers run through high grass to meet each other? It was a very sixties thing. My mother reruns those scenes on video. She loves them. My father reads the newspaper. Anyway, the lovers run with open arms, long hair flying, eyes locked, galloping like young horses across the fields. This kind of scene always made me nervous because the poor things had such a distance to cover, and it would be so easy to trip. Imagine if you fell flat on your face at your lover's feet.

I didn't want Richard to see me run. I'm no athlete. I wanted to surprise him. I wanted to be perfect.

The 163 bus stops near the tobacconist and the milk bar at the wharf. People were streaming out of the ferry toward me. They jostled past with flinty elbows and fluorescent shorts. Hats and baseball caps bobbed together in an undulating rainbow. I wove through the crowd, grateful for the camouflage, dissolving like an oil smudge under a brush of bright color.

I felt like a spy as I hurried along. Eyes on the ground, looking for cover. I put on my dark glasses. But, like James Bond, I longed for adventure and dangerous revelations.

The curl at the base of Richard's neck grew closer. I could see it over a man's yellow Hawaiian shirt. I felt tired suddenly at the thought of disguise. I imagined charging into the spotlight of Richard's gaze. I'd throw off my sunglasses and hold out my arms. A spurt of bile came into my throat. It tasted like green ginger wine. I rubbed my lips together. There was an acidy chemical taste. I'd spent ten dollars on this black lipstick, you'd think they'd at least have given it a nice flavor. It cost so much to be cool. You had to look practically dead. Maybe Richard wouldn't like black lipstick.

"Hi, handsome," I said coolly, tapping Richard on the shoulder. He jumped like a startled rabbit.

"Hello!" he practically squeaked.

I grinned. The line of his back had looked so relaxed, but maybe backs are unreliable. "Sorry I gave you a fright. I didn't mean to."

"That's all right," said Richard, and grinned back. "I was far away." He pointed out to the harbor. "This is a dreamy place."

We laughed. Maybe he had gone over our every word on the bench, too. Was it possible? Was there life on Jupiter?

We decided to walk down the Corso, toward the beach. The smell of hamburgers and frying fish made my stomach turn. I thought of that night at the Cross, the fast-food outlets and the gritty mixture in my teeth.

"Do you want to get a hamburger?" Richard said. "I'm hungry already."

"I brought sandwiches," I said quickly. There had been only avocado and sprouts in the fridge, but that was better than standing outside fish shops that made my stomach heave. "I've got enough for both of us."

As we wandered down the Cross, I felt the sun sprawl

over my shoulders. It was warm and mesmerizing. But it made me worry. It was almost bikini weather.

We came to the end of the food shops and bargain boutiques and there was the long blue streak of beach. We found a table and bench on the concrete stretch overlooking the water and sat down. I brought out the packet of sandwiches and gave Richard the one with extra sprouts. (I hoped he didn't mind herbivore food.)

"Ah, good, avocado," said Richard. "My favorite!"

I nodded, my mouth full.

We talked in little bursts, in between bites of sandwich and picking sprouts out of our teeth. We looked at the ocean. Far out, beyond the ruffle of waves, heads bobbed about like small black watermelon seeds.

Richard asked me about school, my family. I tried to talk normally, but it was hard when there was such a sense of danger. Or was it excitement? Everything was too bright. The sun was dazzling, glancing off Richard's shirt in waves of light; the sea was sapphire; the sand glinted. I felt as if I were in a war and I'd be blown up any minute. Maybe I would say the wrong thing and set off a land mine.

"What do you think you'll do when you finish school?" Richard asked.

"You mean what am I going to be when I grow up?"

"Something like that."

"I don't know." I suddenly felt exhausted. I wished I didn't care so much. "At the moment I just want to get through the week."

Richard looked at me. The gold flecks in his green eyes

were like flashes of sun. I shivered; it was as if he had X-ray vision.

I wished we had met after eight, under the cover of evening.

"What are you sitting on?" Richard said suddenly.

"A wooden bench, same thing you're sitting on."

"Ha ha. No, I mean, what is it you're not telling me? You look all worn out and weary with something, and I have no idea what it is."

I knew I should have worn my other lipstick. "This is just my usual look," I said. I started to babble. "It's called cool—you train your face to look immobile in the face of catastrophe and you appear years older than you are. With this black lipstick, you can achieve the vampire effect with accelerated decay. At least that's what my father says."

"Can you reverse the look when you're thirty?"

"Ah, that's the question. Will we all still be alive at thirty, chatting on benches in clean air, eating food that won't give us salmonella?"

There was silence for a while, and it wasn't comfortable. It was what you might call pregnant.

"Anyway," I blurted out into the gap, "what about you? What do you need to be forgiven for? You know, you said that thing at the observatory last night, something about the water and the quiet there, that it was forgiving."

"Oh, that was just something to say."

"Oh."

Silence. I watched the watermelon seeds bobbing.

Romance is so much more satisfactory in your head. People say the right thing at the right time when your eyes are closed. Why is real life such an anxious sort of anticlimax?

"Well, that's not really true," Richard said, lurching into the quiet. "It was a good place to come that time."

"What time?"

"Oh, years ago. The observatory was like a sanctuary then, a place of prayer."

"You mean like a monastery?"

Richard smiled. "Not quite. I wasn't training to be a priest or anything, but I guess I did need to confess my sins." He took a deep breath. "Okay, if I show you mine, will you show me yours?"

"Maybe. I can't commit myself. I'm sure my sins are a million times worse than yours."

"Well, I'll risk it."

"That's what stars do." I nodded at him. "See, I had you pegged from the start. You can't expect an old moon like me to take nuclear risks. It's just not in our nature."

"God, you're a smartass," said Richard. "Well, when I was sixteen, I had a really shitty year. It's like everything suddenly went speeding downhill."

"Me too!"

"Yeah?"

"Yeah."

He waited, but that was all. He looked down at a crust of avocado sandwich. "I spent most of that year crying," he said.

"Really?" I don't know if I was more surprised at his honesty or his tears. "You mean at school and everything? That must have been a social nightmare for you. I mean, boys don't, do they?" God, that sounded lame.

"I had some sort of breakdown, I suppose. In the beginning people just kept telling me not to be so heavy. 'Lighten up, Richo!' they'd say—you know, I was filled with this dread about the world ending, and I'd tell people about global warming and tidal waves, or the new breed of killer mosquito. I used to search for news items that would contribute to end-of-the-world evidence. I remember Kerry O'Brien on the *Seven-thirty Report* saying after an item on lead poisoning, 'Well, there's another thing to worry about.' I had such a rush of fellow feeling. I wanted to ring him up at the ABC and commiserate. As far as I could see, every day was another nail in the earth's coffin. And nobody else understood. Only Kerry and I. The world just kept denying all the evidence and saying, 'Lighten up, Richo!'"

"That must have been awful. I wish I'd known you then."

"You did meet me." Richard gave a lopsided smile. "Once I came with Dad to your school. I remember because you were so pretty and I was such a mess. You took one glance and turned back to Dad. You never looked at me again. In that moment I could see those little wires in your brain making the decision. 'Nerd,' they said. 'Absolute dork.'"

"I didn't!" But even as I protested the blush crept over my cheeks. There was a faint image crystallizing of a tall dark-haired boy all twisty with shyness. "You never said!"

"Well, whatever. Mum kept telling me that I wasn't so bad-looking, any girl would be pleased to go out with me. I had all this potential under my skin, et cetera, et cetera. I told her the only thing I had under my skin was pimple pus. She said never mind, girls have always worried far more about the way they look than boys—that's what feminists are fighting, the tyranny of this perfect female body image. Blah, blah. It's hard to believe all that when girls like you swan around, flicking back your shiny hair and showing your long legs. You look like a wet dream. You'll never know how scary you lot are."

"Boys still rate girls one to ten for looks," I put in, "as if that's the only thing that's important."

"I don't. Anyway, this is from my point of view, right, so do you want to hear it or not? Girls the same age won't look at you if there's someone there who's been through the pimple phase and come out the other side—with their provisional license plates and the family car. You feel like a nothing compared with them, just a damp spot on a sunny day. Especially if you have this crying thing."

"But why were you crying?"

"Well." Richard's face was working. "Well. I suppose it was some sort of reaction."

"To what?"

Richard sighed. "I stole some money at school. Quite a lot of money."

"Oh." I couldn't imagine it. Richard, with that assured voice and searching eyes. He was looking down at the table. There was a big white splotch of seagull poo near his elbow. I wondered if I should tell him about the poo. I decided not to. There'd obviously been enough shit happening to him already.

"See, there were some soccer guys who were looking for team members. I'd been practicing like crazy. I would have done anything to be friends with them. Nauseating, isn't it?" Richard glanced up at me. His eyes were a green flash. "They were older, you see. One of them had a motorbike. They went out drinking at night. They said I couldn't go round with them unless I had money to buy beer. They knew my dad was a teacher, and that was really uncool. Christ, they were like pirates, Cally—they got girls, they had tattoos, they didn't give a shit. I stole the money from the canteen. One of them, Wacko, was with me. He ran, but I got caught. I didn't even have a chance to buy one beer.

"When they caught me, I blurted about Wacko. I couldn't help it—I was petrified. The soccer gang never forgot it. I got suspended from school. Mum and Dad were so miserable, it was like someone just died. After two weeks I was allowed back in, but it was even worse than at home. At school, everyone knew. Not just that I was a thief, but I was a coward. I had no friends. Before I'd been an invisible pimply nerd with no friends. Now I stuck out like dogs' balls. Everyone knew who I was, and what I was. It's terrible to lose your anonymity like that. There's nowhere to hide. No way out."

"You must have been so lonely." I didn't know what to say.

"I remember when the crying thing started. I was going for a walk, just a week after it happened. I'd been suspended, and I had all this time at home. My parents were both working, and in the living room there was a big clock. It ticked so loudly, beating out the minutes, like some sort of sentence in purgatory. The curtains were always pulled shut because we had leather sofas given to us by Granddad. Sunlight is bad for leather. It was so gloomy. There was a lone shaft of light that came in around ten. It was like God's voice or something. It made a diamond on the carpet. Everything else outside it was dead. I used to think that if I dared step inside it, I'd be forgiven. I went for a walk in the bush, but the track seemed to go branching on forever. This panic overtook me and I began to run. But the more I ran, the longer the track grew. Everything looked unfamiliar. It was like some horror cartoon, a surrealist painting. I expected to see watches melting over tree trunks. I could never get to the end."

Richard was gazing out at the sea, but I knew he wasn't seeing the waves or the girls in bikinis, or the kids digging moats. He was blind inside his own head. I touched his arm.

"The panic never really went away—not for months. I took some tablets, I can't remember what they were, and they muffled the fear a bit, so that it was more like a sound far away. You know the whirr of a lawn mower in the next street? There was just this terrible sadness, as if I'd lost something I could never get back. I couldn't name it, so I couldn't get it back.

"I had no control over my face. No control over the crying. It was terrible. The headmaster came into our class one day and told everyone that I was having a bad time and to be kind to me. It was so humiliating, and they still said, 'Don't be heavy, Richo.' I remember having these obsessive thoughts about water. I kept trying to calculate how much water I was shedding. I was so heavy and so weak—just like H_2O. There was nothing solid."

I nodded. "You know those rollers they use to flatten new roads? Their wheels are filled with water because that's the heaviest thing there is. Amazing, isn't it, that something so transparent can be so heavy."

"Yeah, amazing."

"The wheels press down on the tarred surface until it is smooth and flat. Did you know that a roller filled with water weighs fourteen tons? That's as heavy as five thousand watermelons."

"The wheels are called drums."

"I know that. So anyway, how did you get over it? Did you just dry up one day, like the Dead Sea?"

Richard's gaze flew back to the table and me. He focused again and gave a half smile. "No, there were no sudden miracles—I just had to get through the week." His eyes narrowed and I looked away. My heart started to thump. When he finished his story, he'd expect me to tell mine. I was dying to, and dying not to.

Richard rubbed his hand over his face. "There were small things. Dad stopped being angry and started to listen. I told him about the water and the sadness. He sent me to a counselor and she suggested I go to another school. Life gradually improved. But I still don't know if it was *all* because of the money thing. That kind of sadness hardly ever has just one cause, do you think? I mean, we're not all identical little robots wired up the same way, getting sad or happy if you press button B."

"Or a bunch of chemicals fulfilling our end of an equation. $E=mc^2$."

"That's right. I mean, another kid might just have said, 'Hey, sorry,' and got on with his life. He might even have used that kind of notoriety to become a hero—you know, a wicked guy with a past."

"A pirate."

"A blackguard with a heart of gold."

"A free radical!"

"He could have gone on, deeper and deeper into a life of crime. Just think, he could have blown up school garbage bins, snatched little kids' lunches—"

"That's hardly heroic."

"No."

I threw a crust onto the ground for the seagulls. "It's all in the way you see things, isn't it? Some people act tough like that to be cool—you know, defiant. I remember Jeremy asked me once, 'Do you see out of your eyes like I see out of mine?'"

"Good question. I often wondered that as a kid. I wondered if my father saw the same shade of red that I did. I had a thing about red. I wanted him to love it as much as I did. Fire engines and sunsets and red T-shirts and Jonathan apples. I suppose no one sees anything exactly the same."

"No, it's a scary thought. You sort of want to be like other people, don't you? You don't want to be an island, floating out there on your own."

"Mmm."

We watched a seagull pecking at a crust, its black eyes darting nervously.

Richard laughed suddenly. "I remember I spent the whole of Year Five trying to talk with an Irish accent."

"Why?"

"Well, there was this new boy, Liam, who'd come from Ireland, and he picked me to be his friend. He sort of claimed me, like a brother. It was exciting to have such an exotic best friend, and I didn't want to disappoint him for a minute. We'd sit together at lunch, and Liam used to eat really quickly, so I did, too. I had constant stomachaches. I was always hungry, but I didn't want him to find any other friends while I finished my sandwich. He was often homesick, and he used to talk about his friends back home. He'd do their voices, and in this game we had—throwing spitballs at an enemy gang—he wanted me to be Patrick, his friend in Dublin. I had to yell out Irish curses as we threw them. Patrick was very fiery, Liam said. I used to practice the accent every night in front of the mirror, and soon I had it just right. I talked like that at breakfast, and at the shops, and when people asked me my name, I said, 'Patrick.' People in the street used to think Liam and I were brothers fresh off the boat from Ireland."

"You wanted to be just like him."

"Yeah. I would have shaved my head, too, if he had."

"What happened to him?"

"Oh, he went back to Dublin."

"That must have been terrible."

"Yes, it was. My father threatened to send me after him. But in a strange way, I felt more relaxed after he'd gone. I actually slept better. I wasn't up for hours learning Irish poems. It really had been such a strain trying to be someone else."

Richard leaned against me. His mouth was only an inch away from my hair. "What I didn't know was, you don't have to be the same as someone else to be close."

"There's your gap thing again. Reaching out across the abyss!"

"It's *your* gap thing, Ms. May. I'm only picking up your theme. Why do you hold yourself so far away?"

His eyes were darker at this angle, forest green. I noticed for the first time that they turned up at the corners, foxlike. Perhaps he would pounce. He looked ferocious, fervent. There was this sort of hum between us, like a live telegraph line. The anticipation was delicious, excruciating. I couldn't stand it. I sort of groaned and he pulled my head toward him and our lips crushed together. He opened my mouth and his warm breath spilled into me and I could taste him on my tongue. I wanted to open further, I wanted to slide open like a cave in a rock, a mossy, moist cave filled with him.

"Stop chasing that poor seagull and come *here*!" A woman's voice behind us made us spring apart. She was calling to a small boy, who came and sat on the opposite side of our bench. He stared at us while his mother lumped a mountain of parcels onto the table.

Richard and I held hands. I kept my head nestled in his neck. It didn't feel dangerous anymore. When our skin was touching I felt safe and damp, like a newborn animal. I wanted him to lick me all over, the way a mother does her cub.

The boy ran his toy car over the table. "Vroom, vroom," he went as it crashed into his mother's elbows.

"Sit still, will you?" she snapped in an end-of-her-tether voice. There were red marks on her arms where the bag straps had been. I smiled at the boy and did a cross-eyed maniac face. He giggled. A Jeremy pang shot through me. I shoved the thought away.

Sitting close on that bench, I smelled the sun in Richard's shirt. There were so many little shadows and valleys in his neck and shoulders, places where you could nestle. I wondered what it would be like to travel over his chest into the hollows of his armpits. It would be dark and hidden in there, silky with hair. I could breathe in his private smell. We grinned at each other. I wanted to tell him more. I ached to tell him how brave he was, the way he'd talked of his shame so openly. Imagine what Miranda Blair would do with information like that. I wanted to tell him how it made me feel—so connected, switched on—and I wished I could give his past back to him, all shiny and transformed with my words. I wished I could make a present of myself, the way he had.

But I wasn't used to people showing me their dark side. I didn't know the right words to use in reply. "I'm really glad you told me" sounded so superficial, like "Great, thanks for telling me, now I'm warned and I'll look out for my handbag." I didn't want to say the wrong thing. It seemed so fragile, this offering of his, and in my clumsy hands it could break. My mother always got a clouded look when we talked about anything emotional. I could tell that she thought what I said was callow, not worthy of the great sea of sorrow that she lived in. I wished I had practiced this, the way Richard had practiced being Patrick.

"Do you want to go for a walk?" I said.

As we got up our thighs brushed together. I glanced at Richard. I wondered if he knew how much I wanted him to touch me. I felt a tide of gratitude wash over me—one day I'd tell him about this, how he made storms break in my skin. He took my hand and we fitted together, fingers laced. I was brimming with light and suddenly, just for a moment, it spread into my veins and through my heart and over my belly. It was like finding the switch in a dark room. It was my light, they were my feelings, and I could have flown all the way over that stone path with the ocean lapping on the left and Richard on the right and the curve of Shelley Beach at the end like a glittering prize.

Richard was pointing to a ship on the horizon. It was so far away it looked as if it were stuck onto the sky with glue.

"It really is a beautiful day, isn't it?" said Richard, stopping on the path.

"It's luscious," I agreed.

"*You're* luscious," said Richard. He ran a finger down my arm.

I laughed with delight. I couldn't help it. It came out as a snort. "I feel luscious—like a juicy fat fruit!"

I began to run, I didn't know what else to do with all this light and energy, I thought I'd leap off the face of the earth. Richard chased after. "Come here," he cried, "I want to bite you!" A man walking his dog stared at us. I let Richard catch me.

"You don't look tired anymore," he said.

"No. Maybe I could be the first woman to run at the speed of light." I grinned at him. But he looked serious, like when we'd first sat down at the bench.

I started to walk again. He was silent next to me. He didn't look out at the ocean. I knew he was waiting. It was my turn.

Oh, bugger it—why couldn't we just enjoy this moment? Why did we have to go ferreting in the dark when there was this big bowl of blue sky around us? I felt trapped, resentful. I didn't want to talk about that. I didn't feel like it. I wanted to go on being a ripe pear in that bowl. You show me yours, I'll show you mine. What was that line about "fearful symmetry"? *Telling* isn't symmetrical. You can't get even. It was all very well for him; his sins were over, in the past. He's confessed and had absolution. Mine were still evolving.

I felt the blanket come down on me. It was like turning off the sun.

I stopped. "I feel a bit sick," I said weakly.

"Let's sit here for a while, then," said Richard, settling himself on the low stone wall.

We sat and watched the boats. We didn't say much. A chill breeze began to blow off the ocean. I put on my sweater and folded my arms to keep the warmth in. We were separate islands on a stretch of stone. I made bits of conversation, feeding morsels into the silence. I hated myself. It was just like it had always been. I wasn't brave enough. I wasn't enough for him. Disappointment flapped between us like a wet cloth.

I glanced at his profile—the unswerving line of his nose, the chin thrust out. He looked at things straight on; he kept

214

his chin up. Richard's brand of bravery was so powerful, I thought, he could probably demolish Miranda like a licorice allsort. She'd be left without a word. And he'd just drive away, the drums of his roller sloshing.

As the sun slid down behind the cliff, we began to walk back. The streetlights were coming on. Pine trees frayed against the rosy sky. Richard's favorite color. He put his arm around me and my shoulder fitted neatly under his arm. I wished I could go home with him like that his favorite teddy bear. I remembered that old Elvis Presley song, "I want to be bop bop bop your teddy bear." Dad used to sing that to me when I was little. He wasn't half bad at the hip swivel then. He wouldn't be caught dead doing it now. Mum would roll her eyes at him and point at his paunch.

As we walked up the Corso toward the wharf, I noticed the pools of light on the concrete. I remembered how the light had filled me up, back there on the stone path. Maybe there'd be another chance. Maybe you can't say everything, not all at once.

We kissed goodbye at the bus stop. There was an oval of warmth where our lips met. But when his mouth left mine I felt flat, like mineral water when all the bubbles have left the glass.

That night, outside my window, there was a crescent moon. The hook of light hung in the mulberry tree. At two

215

in the morning it had risen clear of the tree, over the rooftop. I could just see the dark part of the moon faintly, like the flesh of a ghostly orange.

I stayed there at the window for a while. I looked at that dark circle of moon. It was the shape of possibility, of something barely there. As the moon moved on in its orbit and the earth revolved, the dark part would slowly creep toward the light. And everything would be revealed.

PART
3

They're all dirty scumbuggits, Cally and Mum and Grandma, they're full of poo and nasty bits of wall scraping. They're blobs of mucus and toenail muck. I hate them all. I could step on them with giant boots. No one ever does what I want. They don't think about me. No one cares.

Today is Wednesday. Sam Underwood was coming over. For the first time. We were going to have chocolate cake and get a move on with my bunker. I found another shovel. I had it all planned—we were going to dig together, we might have dug down so far, we could have reached the center of the earth. It's really hot down there, but I had the hose ready. Near the center of the earth we might have found bits of really old meteorite, like the one that fell sixty-five million years ago. It ended everything for the dinosaurs. Cally's the biggest scumbuggit of all. She promised the cake, it was her idea. Why do people make promises and then forget?

It's not fair.

When I got home on Wednesday, I said, "So where's the cake, Cally?" She clapped her hand over her mouth like she was going to be sick. "Oh, Jeremy," she said, "I forgot. We have to go over to Grandma's today. We can make another time with Sam, I promise. You'd better ring him now, before he leaves."

I kicked her in the leg. Then I rang Sam. He was just leaving to come over. He had to go and tell his mum to put the car back in the garage. I heard her say, "Oh, shit." He said *I* was a scumbuggit. He said I must really live in a tent then, or an old shed maybe.

"I'm not your friend anymore," he said. He said that before he said goodbye.

Maybe I'll never see Sam Underwear again. I mean, I guess I'll see him, but it won't be the same. He'll look different. He won't be my partner anymore when we line up. He'll tell everyone that I live in a shed. He'll tell them I smell.

When we went over to Grandma's, no one enjoyed it. I couldn't see the point of it. Mum didn't even come. Grandma went on and on about black holes or something. But she kept yawning. Grandma said that everyone at the conference was excited because a black hole has been discovered in our very own galaxy. I wasn't excited, I was scared. What I wanted to know was, are any of those scientists tracking the meteorites? Can they see any coming near Earth? Could a meteorite get swallowed into a black hole? Grandma said she didn't have any new information on meteorites, except she'd heard that a group of people were looking for a crater in the Amazon jungle. How far away is the Amazon jungle?

Cally said I had to visit Grandma because she had a present for me. It was just a silly old shirt. It had a picture of a crocodile in the corner. Grandma also gave me some money, but you can't even use it here. So what's the point? It's called lira—it sounds like a silly girl's name. Grandma gave Cally a present, too. When Cally said thank you she gave this stupid smile—all her gums showed, it was a pretending-to-be-happy smile when you don't mean it.

I don't care, anyway. I don't like people. I'd rather be a dog. Batman's dog. Tomorrow I'm going to get a move on with my bunker. I don't need any help. I'm not going to let anyone in with me. No one deserves it. When the meteorite crashes, I'll be the only one saved. But when I come out, there'll be no one to play with. So what's the point?

I asked Cally after dinner if she'd heard about the crater in the Amazon. She said yes, that some Brazilian scientists thought a large meteorite fell there in 1930. She said not to worry because most meteorites are turned to gas and dust before they hit the earth. But what about the other ones?

Tomorrow I'm going to get on with my bunker, just in case. There's nothing else to do, anyway.

*T*wo more days.

I can get through Thursday if I have something to look

forward to afterward. I've learnt that from Jeremy. He elaborately selects and designs his rewards, staggering them through the day like the little sugar boosters needed by diabetics. For instance, Jeremy always eats his favorite thing last. Like if we were having lamb cutlets and mashed potato, he'd eat the mash first. Jeremy loves sucking on the bones. Mum looks the other way when he does that. But I think it's a good sign. If Jeremy trusted nothing, he'd go for the bones first, his favorite thing. He must still have some hope, even if it is only that his lamb cutlets will remain on the plate and not be vaporized by falling debris before he can suck them.

It's strange how often in books they don't dwell on the happy bits. Maybe writers think no one wants to read about people having a good time, especially if their own life is a compost heap. Or maybe happiness is harder to write. Even if there is a happy ending in a book, it's often just one line. That's never enough for me. In fairy tales, it's "And they lived happily ever after." But I always wanted to know—*how* did they live? Was she an early riser? Did he bring her coffee in bed? Who did the vacuuming? Did they have lots of children? They never give you any details of the "happily ever after." They never tell you the recipe.

It's a shame, because we all need this information, don't we?

The good bits in my life so far seem to last about as long as a lit candle. Those little breathy mouths of flame are so easily swamped. Winds of misfortune howl all around. At least, that's how it seems to me. But maybe that's just the Line Up Here, Disasters Only Now section in my memory box. Do you find the painful bits go on a lot longer than happy ones? Pain is full of grim detail, of hours and minutes and splinters in the vital organs. You can hold them there in your lap, all those separate pieces, and no matter how many times you turn them over, they won't fit together. But a happy moment—well, it's just one whoosh of feeling, isn't it?—comes whole, like a primary color or the takeoff of a bird into the sky.

That's how I felt with Richard. For a couple of candle lengths, or maybe even more. I felt different after that weekend. I had something to look forward to.

Our art teacher, Mr. Hanrahan, is fond of candlelight. He's always going on about the source of light in a painting. He likes the huge shadows that candlelight makes—it adds drama, he says. Whenever we begin a painting of our own, he makes us put down our pencils and notice where the light is coming from. "A painting without light is flat, dead, formless!" he cries. He raises his arms on the last syllable and even on winter days we can see round circles of sweat in his armpits. He is very passionate and he makes me feel protective. I want to tell him to keep his arms down so everyone isn't knowing how he's feeling all the time. He doesn't understand anything about "cool." Miranda and her gang laugh at him. I don't think he cares.

Anyway, I was sitting there in art on Tuesday and old Hanrahan was raving on about the light. Before starting a painting, he was saying, an artist decides on the light he's going to use—moonlight, sunlight—and where it's coming from. Perhaps it falls on a face in profile, sharpens a chin, discovers the fine bones in a hand. The moon picks out details from the dark. It makes one thing more important than another.

And suddenly I knew what he meant. Richard was like that for me. I was holding him up like a light source—he was my kero lamp in the night, my star in all that dark matter roiling round the universe. I remembered how he'd put his arm around me on Sunday, and I'd fitted under his shoulder. The thought of Richard made my heart leap, and the bleakness lifted. There was something else after Thursday.

I tried to draw his face. There was the chin thrust out, the green eyes and the shadows under them. I rubbed it out. It's funny how the more you try to remember, the more blurred it becomes. His image in my mind was growing shimmery and faint. I tried to hear the tone of his voice, the smile in it. He hadn't rung me since Sunday. I could get only Elvis and the teddy bear song.

Maybe Richard was more of an idea than a real person. Maybe I was making him up.

I took a new sheet of paper. I was starting to sweat. I tried to loosen up, doing quick sketches with charcoal. Maybe I'd just selected Richard arbitrarily—sunlight or candlelight?—because he was there. He was handsome and clever, he didn't bully kids or pull wings off flies. He was a good choice, wasn't he, for a girl to pin her hopes on?

It was just that I couldn't keep his outline straight in my mind.

I tried to see his face when he told me about the stealing, but I could only remember my surprise, and how eager I'd been to see him as brave. Just for a moment I glimpsed rounded shoulders and a shrinking back. His chin looked weak. I shivered. It's hard to tell what's real when you're gazing into the glare of your chosen light source. It's blinding, and you get spots in front of your eyes.

I decided to do something else. I painted a white bird in a blue sky. I'd call it "Hope." It wouldn't be realistic (I can't draw birds); it would be more of an impression, really. As I splashed a little gray into the feathers, I thought about hope and anticipation, and how often they were much better than the real event. But at least they carried you to it. Hope was a kind of transport, I decided. When you do it at school—you know, air, sea and road transport—you should also do hope. Because when it disappears, you don't go anywhere. You just lie on your bed and pick lint out of your pockets.

*B*efore Thursday there were art, English and math. There were avocado sandwiches and history assignments and a salad with pine nuts. Mr. Corrigan, the gym teacher, fell over and broke his ankle. Miranda Blair was first on the scene and she was supposed to go and ring the ambulance. She didn't, you know. She went down to the toilet block for a smoke. Then she went to hang out at the mall.

On Wednesday Mum changed the fridge decoration. She put up a newspaper clipping about the stolen children, with a photo of an old Aboriginal man hugging a toddler. It was his grandson. They'd only just met. "Read that article, Cally. It'll give you goose pimples." I was rushing out the door. The last thing I needed was goose pimples. But Mum's face made me stop.

In the afternoon there was Grandma Ruth. I'd forgotten about Sam Underwood, damn it. I felt dreadful. I could hardly hear what Grandma was saying, I was so miserable with guilt. Jeremy just sat there like a lump of petrified wood. Hope had the shape of something flat under his shoe. Poor old Jem.

Tim rang that night. I sat there twisting the phone cord and Jeremy didn't even bother to nag. He just glanced at me and his expression didn't change, as if he were looking at an empty chair. Tim said that he and the guys were going to stay up at Byron Bay for the rest of the week. They'd cook up some excuse for school. "The surf at Wattigo is unreal," he enthused. "It's too good to miss." Did I mind?

On Wednesday I saw Mr. West coming out of the science block. He waved at me and grinned. I waved back. I hesitated for a second and nearly fell over my shoelace. I'd have liked to talk to him, but I didn't know what to say. I wanted to show him my bird picture. Mr. Hanrahan had exclaimed all over it—he'd waved his arms about and sweated profusely. He even pinned it up on the art room wall. It was the first time he'd put anything of mine up there. When Miranda saw it, she sniggered. She said it looked like seagull shit.

When I woke up on Thursday, it was raining. The curtains were pulled and it was still dark, but I could hear the drops falling like bullets on the awning outside. Jeremy had left one of his tin trucks out on the porch and the water was running down the drain pipe straight into the dumper with a loud *ping! ping! ping!*

I pulled the pillow over my head. I didn't want to wake up.

I lay there for a while, my heart pounding. I can never wake up gently—I'm just suddenly there or I'm not. It makes the nausea worse, all this suddenness. As soon as I was awake, even under the pillow, I started picturing the afternoon, the rain and the traffic, whether I'd get there late, what the doctors would be like, and whether it would hurt. You know the kind of thing.

All day, through lunch and math and history, I kept wishing you could fast-forward life, like you do with a video. The nasty bits could be like ads, just events you have to get through, but quickly. The day dragged interminably. I don't remember much of it. The world inside was louder than anything else.

At three-thirty I flung out the gate and raced home. It was still raining. My hair was sopping by the time I reached our house. I could lick the drops as they ran off my nose. Jeremy was sitting out on the porch. "What are you doing out here?" I asked.

"Watching the stupid rain," he said.

His schoolbag leant against his leg. He hadn't even been inside. I took his hand and a centipede wriggled out. His sweater was quite damp. I could see little beads of rain on the gray wool. He smelled of wet dog. "You're all wet, Jem. Come in and change." Honestly, who was the mother in this family? If it weren't for me, Jeremy would sit out here all night, catching bugs and pneumonia. "Where's Mum?"

Jeremy shrugged. He watched the centipede crawl onto the grass.

I looked at my watch. I had ten minutes to change and catch the bus into the city. There was the run up to the bus stop in the rain. A tide of anxiety began to rise in my chest. It made my voice sharp. "Come on, then. I said, let's get changed."

Jeremy shook his head. He didn't look at me.

I pushed past him and went inside. I couldn't worry about him now. I threw off my uniform and pulled on jeans. I hunted for a raincoat and found it bunched up with my shoes. It hadn't been worn for years. Didn't matter, I wasn't going there to impress anyone, was I? An umbrella would have been better, but there were never any in the house, because everyone except Dad always lost them. There were May umbrellas all over the place, in cinemas, libraries, cafés, supermarkets. Dad kept his elegant black one with men playing golf along the rim in his cupboard. There was penalty of eternal disapproval if you borrowed it. No one ever did.

Quickly I tried my raincoat on. It had three long tears down the front. The sleeves came almost up to my elbows. I crept into Dad's room and looked in his cupboard. The umbrella was standing upright next to his shoe rack like a sentinel. I grabbed it.

I was ready. Seven minutes to go. I went into the kitchen to find Mum. She'd be there buttering pancakes. Or in the living room arranging cushions.

The kitchen was empty. Not even a whiff of melting butter. In the living room, Jeremy's toys were still strewn all over the carpet. I stared at his Lego men with a terrible sinking of the heart.

"Mum!" I called.

The answer drifted back. "What?"

I found her in her bedroom. She was darting around, searching out shoes and a skirt and putting on her lipstick. She picked up her bag and checked her wallet.

"What are you doing?"

She swung around. "Oh, Cally, thank heavens you're home. I've got to go out." She looked at her watch. "God, they'll have started already."

"What?" I could hardly speak. "Aren't you having the meditation here?"

Mum frowned. "No, Cally. Beth rang to say she's really not up to going out, but she can have the meditation at her place. It does her a lot of good. It's all arranged with the others. Now, I've got to rush."

"But Mum, I told you already that I have to go out this afternoon. I'll be out till late. You can't go, you just can't. Christ, don't you remember anything? Who's going to look after your son? You know, the boy called Jeremy out there?"

"Don't speak to me like that, Callisto!"

There was a loud sniff and we both swung round. In the door of the hallway stood Jeremy. "Where are you going, Cally?" he said. "Why can't I come? Why doesn't anyone ever want me to come?"

"Of course Cally wants you to come, darling."

"He *can't* come with me. Children aren't allowed."

"You shut me out, man, you treat me like a kid!"

"Oh, shut up, Robin!"

"Don't speak like that to your brother. What is this place where children aren't allowed?"

227

"Oh, it's just a place. It's, ah, it's a film we have to see for school. It's rated M. He'd never get in."

"Well, that's a shame, blossom, but I didn't realize you had something on—did you tell me? Anyway, you know Thursdays are meditation. I can't cancel on all those poor women. They depend on me." She picked up her handbag and keys. "For afternoon tea you can give Jeremy those pancakes from last week. They're in the fridge. Now don't fight. Bye now."

I stared at her, streaking out the door. "What about Dad? When's the plane due in?"

"Not till seven tonight, darling," she called over her shoulder. She pinched Jeremy's cheek. "Be good!"

We both gazed at the flash of cream skirt that was Mum, disappearing out the door. I looked at my watch. Three minutes to go.

"Right. Go into your room and take off your sweater. Get a dry one, find your raincoat and let's go."

"Can I wear my Batman outfit? Or should I wear the Robin one? Only I don't like the green mask. Why didn't they make a black one, like the one Robin wears on TV?"

"I don't bloody well care what the fuck you wear. Just get it on now, because I'm leaving!"

Jeremy vanished. I banged the wall with rage. I wanted to go on banging, beating my fist against the wall till it fell down. The stupid uncaring bloody bitch.

Jeremy crept out. He looked strangely bulky. I saw bits of black Batman sleeve poking out from under the Robin outfit. The cloak was rucked up underneath. He looked like a superhero who'd had too many desserts.

"You said the *f* word," he whispered. He had tears in his eyes.

"Let's go," I muttered.

I ran fast as lightning up the road. Jeremy hung on to my hand and I hauled him up the hill like a dead body.

"I'm too sad to run," he said.

"Fucking *move*!" I shouted at him.

The bus was there at the top of the hill. There were two people still climbing on. "Wait!" I yelled. We panted along the path, hurtling past a woman with shopping. Something fell out of her bag as Jeremy brushed past. I didn't look back. The doors of the bus were closing.

I shoved my shoe between the doors. Through the crack I saw the bus driver making up his mind. He was looking at my shoe as if it were a squashed cockroach. "Please," I said.

We sat down near the back. I didn't want to be near enough to catch the eye of the driver in the rearview mirror. *What a desperado*, he was probably thinking. *And her lumpy little brother, the superhero.*

I stared out the window. Rain spattered the glass like a million spitballs. When I could breathe deeply again, I began thinking what to do with Jeremy. It was true that children weren't allowed into abortion clinics. Well, it's understandable, isn't it? Who wants to look at some happy kid running around in the waiting room when you're not going to have yours? What the hell was I going to do with him?

The lady on the phone had told me about the children

thing. "Bring someone with you if you can," she'd said kindly. (She'd meant somebody who'd had their peripheral vision for at least ten years, of course.)

I glanced at Jeremy. He did look bigger with two outfits on, that was for sure. And his vocabulary was larger than that of some adults I knew. He certainly wasn't happy, either. Would a depressed lumpy superhero with a spectacular vocabulary look better in the waiting room? But he was sniffing again. Now he was picking his nose. I sighed. No one over twelve does that in public.

"Where's your hankie?"

He shrugged. "Where are we going, anyway?"

"Oh, you'll see. Just somewhere," I said vaguely.

"Don't shut me out, Batman, don't treat me like a kid!"

"Robin, this mission is far too dangerous for you. It's just something I have to do alone."

We played the game and it passed the time while the bus sat in traffic and the rain caused havoc. There's nothing I can do about it, I told myself. Now *I* felt too sad to run. I felt too sad to do anything. Robin let me hold his hand from Cremorne to North Sydney. His hand was very warm and a bit moist, due to all the layers he had on. The windows in the bus were shut on account of the rain. I tried to open ours just a crack but the woman behind me made a *tsk*ing noise, so I left it. There was a strong smell of salami.

At four-twenty-five we drew into the city. My appointment was for four-thirty. We'd cross King George, turn left into St. Paul's and right into Burke. If we caught the lights, I'd be on time.

The bus stopped just around the corner from the clinic.

We actually went past it—number 63, a big cream building—but you're never allowed to get off before the stop, are you? From the window I saw a lot of people standing on the steps of the building. *Jesus,* I thought, *I hope I don't have to wait for hours. Thursdays must be popular.*

The bus driver shook his head at us as we clambered off. "Batman out," said Jeremy.

The street we turned into was lined with plane trees. Jeremy roared in and out of them as if he were a car in one of those driver-training courses. He didn't notice the people on the steps until we were right there.

I grabbed Jeremy's hand and pulled him back. The people turned to look at us. One of them whispered something to her neighbor. Those people weren't waiting to have an operation. Some of them were men. They were holding up big signs and placards on wooden poles. There were pictures of dead babies. One poster said, Don't Kill Your Baby. It was written in red paint, and next to it was the face of a dead child.

Jeremy was staring at the pictures. "Are these people from South Africa?" he asked. "Do we have to help them?"

A woman was coming down the steps toward us. I couldn't see her face. She held the big square sign in front of her. A hand grasped my arm. "Don't kill your baby, girlie," the woman said. "You'll burn in hell."

She was panting hard. The sign must have been heavy.

I wrenched myself away. My knees were shaking so much, I could hardly stand up. Jeremy was staring in bewilderment. A man in a gray sweater shook his finger at me. "It's wicked. You're a murderer if you go in there."

Suddenly the man gave a yelp of pain. I looked down and saw that Jeremy had whacked him in the shins with Dad's umbrella.

"Ya dirty scumbuggits!" he yelled. "I don't care what country you're from, you can't speak to my sister like that!" He tugged at my hand. He was looking wildly around, searching for an escape. The people had all descended, surrounding us. "Come on, Batman, follow me," he whispered. "You need protection, and protection is my racket."

We raced up the steps, pushing past placards and clutching hands. Jeremy held the umbrella out in front of him like a sword. He flashed it from side to side, jabbing it in the air if someone got too close. We stumbled into the doorway, onto calm cream carpet.

We stood there like refugees. I couldn't stop trembling.

"What do we do now, Batman?" whispered Jeremy. I could feel his legs collapsing against mine.

"*H*ang on a sec, Robin," I managed. I saw that the hallway opened out on the right into a waiting room. I took a couple of steps and peeped in. The room was filled with women siting on chairs and couches. There was a table piled with magazines, and an urn and coffee cups in the corner. Some of the women looked fairly old, around thirty or forty; others looked quite young. One girl stared back at me. She was skinny as a pencil—she'd have been in Year 8. She gave a crooked grin. I smiled back. The muscles in my back began to unclench. There was a boy sitting next to her. He was handing her a cup of tea. The people in this room looked so normal, flicking through the pages of magazines, sipping coffee. They looked like the women who shopped at the supermarket, or caught the bus to work in the morning.

"It's okay, Robin," I said. "Let's go and sit down."

Just then, on the left, I saw the receptionist's desk. A young woman came toward us. "Hi," she said with a friendly smile, "I'm Lily. Can I help you?"

Jeremy stepped forward. "I hope so," he said confidingly, "because some people out there have just been very rude to my sister. She can't help it if she doesn't have any money to give them and all their children are sick. It's not her fault."

Lily looked quite unfazed. She nodded sympathetically. "We have a lot of trouble with those people. I wish they'd do something else with their afternoons." She looked at me. "Do you have an appointment? Would you like to see a counselor?"

I told her I did have an appointment and we talked for a bit. She took us over to the desk and I filled out a form and a health checklist.

"Are we at the doctor's?" said Jeremy, his brow clearing.

"Yes, that's it," I said.

Jeremy's brows knitted again. He clutched my hand. "You're not dying, are you? You're not old enough yet. Is it those teenage blues?"

Lily looked up and giggled. "You know, children shouldn't really be here. We just don't have the space. Is someone coming to pick him up?"

I shook my head. I tried to explain about family arrangements getting mixed up and my mother having a case of terminal unreliability. I babbled on and on (I was nervous) until finally Lily held up her hand.

"Well," she said, tapping her chin with a ballpoint pen, "let's deal with you first." She looked down at my form. "I see that you elected to have an IV sedation when you made the appointment."

I nodded.

"Okay. We like to keep you here for a couple of hours after that. You may be a bit sleepy and disoriented. And someone needs to go home with you. Do you have anyone coming? An adult, I mean?"

Oh, shit, I'd forgotten that. *No,* I could say, *I have no one in the world.* After all, it was the truth. I felt like Oliver Twist. *Can I have some more relatives, please?* But it would never work. I hated to lie to Lily, I really did, but there was nothing else I could do.

"My boyfriend's coming," I said quickly. "He knocks off work at six. He'll come straight over after that. He's a car mechanic—boy, you should see him fix a fan belt, he's a real whiz with an engine, everyone at work says he'll be setting up his own shop in no time. He goes to tech at night, it's really tiring after a long day's work, but he's so revved up, he doesn't notice." Jeremy was staring at me openmouthed. I could tell he was about to interrupt, but I was ready with more. I'd flow all over him, like an active volcano, and he wouldn't be able to get a word out. I was really warming to the subject, about how Tim wanted to see me all the time, and the difficulties of juggling an intense relationship with schoolwork, when Lily held up her hand again.

"That's great, Callisto," she said, smiling. She turned to

Jeremy, who had found another ballpoint and was drawing bats caught in a meteor swarm. "Now, Robin, what are we going to do with you?"

I snorted.

Lily looked puzzled. "I thought I heard you call him that?"

Jeremy dug me in the thigh with the umbrella.

What the heck, I thought.

"Okay, Robin—you can put the umbrella down now—would you like to sit with me behind this desk? Your sister will have to see the doctor. It will all take a rather long time."

"Like how long?"

"Well, let's see." She looked at her watch. "Callisto, you'll see a counselor now, okay? And then, if you go in for your operation, you probably won't be out of here until about seven-thirty, eight o'clock."

"That's the nighttime!" cried Jeremy, shocked. "*The Simpsons* are on then! It'll be dark. What about my dinner?"

"Can your boyfriend take Robin home when he arrives? He'll be here soon after six, won't he? Then he can come back for you."

"Who?" asked Jeremy.

"I'll tell you later, Jer—er, Robin. Just let the grown-ups work it out now, okay?"

Jeremy's shoulders slumped. He went back to drawing bats. I noticed a couple of them had succumbed to gravity. They didn't survive the swarm.

I told Lily that yes, my boyfriend could look after Robin. She said, "Oh, good" because she had to leave around six.

My hands were sweating. I couldn't think straight. It was all becoming too complicated. I felt like a beetle in a spiderweb. Jeremy would just have to wait. It wouldn't kill him. I'd make some excuse about Tim later. If I had to leave now and make another appointment, I might as well hurl myself under a bus. I couldn't do this twice.

Jeremy waved reluctantly at me as I went into the waiting room. I saw Lily hand him a stash of fresh paper, and she'd found some colored markers. He was giving her a watery smile. She saw me looking, and mouthed, "He's okay, don't worry." I could have hugged her.

She wouldn't have wanted to hug me. Not if she knew me. I told lies the size of Mount Etna. That's 3,274 meters high. It's the highest active volcano in Europe, in case you're interested. I tried to think about Mount Etna instead of Jeremy as I sat down in the waiting room.

It wasn't long before a small, tidy-looking woman came in and called out my name. "Hello," she said, "my name is Rosa." We shook hands. Hers was firm and dry. "I am your counselor for today. Would you like to come with me?"

She showed me into a square room with white walls. Two leather chairs sat around a coffee table. I hovered above them. There was just us.

Rosa took some papers from a desk and gestured for me to sit down. It was very quiet in there. You couldn't hear the "South Africans" outside. Perhaps the signs had got too heavy and they'd gone home. I couldn't get over how neat Rosa looked. She was a woman in miniature, doll-like, with shiny blond hair that fell to her shoulders in one swoop, like a single brushstroke. The red dollops of her earrings matched her suit. She reminded me of those sleepers in overnight trains—everything was in its right compartment, all folded up tight, with no room to spare. She probably carried a spare pair of tights in her handbag.

How could I tell her about me? I was a bunch of unraveled knitting at her feet.

Rosa asked some general questions and informed me about the procedure. Her voice was light but warm. I could tell she was trying to be cheerful. I thought of Richard, and everyone saying, "Lighten up, Richo, why don't you?" Such a pang shot through me at the thought of him that I winced.

"Is it hard for you to be here today?" asked Rosa.

She was looking straight at me, and there was a crease of concern between her brows. She leant forward, and I felt that the thing she most wanted to hear in the world was my voice. Even if Nazi storm troopers barged in, she'd tell them to wait. She wouldn't take her eyes off me for a second.

No one had ever looked at me like that. Well, only if they'd wanted sex or astronomical information.

It was amazing what that simple question did to me.

I tried to say yes, but I gulped instead. Tears were welling up in my throat and spilling out and I kept trying to say that one word but I was gagged with all this salty H_2O. I don't know where it came from. Rosa just kept nodding. She didn't tell me to stop, or to cheer up, or that it was all right. She handed me tissues and waited.

I wanted to ask her, *Will you keep your eyes like that, all wide and kind and uncritical, while I tell you?* In between all the nose blowing I muttered some things about Tim and the newspaper and the weather. I don't know what she made of it. I desperately wanted her to like me. She was so calm and neat in her red suit, her legs crossed at the ankles in sheer stockings with no ladders or bits of lint trailing off them.

"I understand," she said. "And how did you come to make this decision? Did you talk it over with anyone?"

There was a thick silence. It was grainy, like quicksand. My head was clogged with it.

"Do your parents know about this, Callisto?"

I shook my head. I didn't look at her. I couldn't lie to Rosa. I just couldn't.

"It's okay. I just think it might be good to talk about your feelings. How do you think your father would react to your having a termination?"

I gave a wild laugh. It came roaring out, like something savage in the jungle. Tarzan, maybe, before he met any other humans.

"Well, what about your mother?"

"Mum would just go into a total spin." I thought of her lying in the dark with her mantra, wading into the soothing waters of her meditation. She spent her whole life trying to inoculate herself against pain. *Cally's better off without me,* she'd written in her diary. How could she help? "Mum couldn't cope," I said.

"Okay, so, what about the most important person—you. How do you feel about it? Tell me a little, if you can, about how you came to make the decision."

She was looking at me, waiting patiently, although I knew she must have ten other women out there lining up.

didn't know what to say. How can you describe the undertow? There are no words; it's just a swift current of dread and urgency. It pushes you along, a nameless thing, and it doesn't let you get organized. It doesn't let you think.

I sank into it. I didn't fight it. I spoke to her from the undertow. I could hear my voice sounding harsher, pebblier with the current. Shit, I was like that girl in *The Exorcist*, except I was inhabited by the undertow instead of the Devil. That movie had given me nightmares. Maybe my head would turn around on my neck seven times like hers.

"Take your time," said Rosa calmly. "Take a deep breath."

"It's this feeling of dread," I mumbled. "I don't know, that I'd be trapped, trapped forever to stay the way I am. I couldn't do it, I don't know how to look after myself, let alone a baby."

The woman nodded. I started to cry again. She said nothing, just looked at me as if her heart would break, and gave me tissues.

"Have you considered alternatives, like adoption?"

"Yes. No. I don't want to do that."

There was a girl at school, Cara, who'd had her baby adopted. Her parents made her go away to a place in the country, a home for pregnant girls. She came back to school eventually. She used to wear the baby's name tag around her wrist like a bracelet. On his birthday she would cry all day at school. I saw her once recently. She said she still wanders around, looking for him in prams, at the supermarket. She looks like my mother. She has a secret sorrow.

In that white room, with Rosa's calm ankles and the comfortable chairs, I felt myself floating away. It was such a relief. For just a moment, I became gossamer thin, like a worn piece of sheet, and I drifted above everything. I was wafting toward Jupiter, a breath away from Galileo.

I looked down and saw the girl that was me on the chair. You can see things much more clearly from a distance. She sat at attention, her knees together, trying. She'd try anything to be liked. She'd follow people around who set her hair on fire, she'd lie down on newspaper and apologize, she'd swallow plants like a herbivore. She'd swallow anything, that one. She could never say no. She said, "Yes, please."

It was shameful. Someone down there ought to kick her. Wipe the smile off her face. Imagine Mr. and Mrs. May seeing that girl. Mr.'s eyes would roll in disgust. He'd see her get up from the newspaper, glimpse the dirty black smudges on her thighs where the ink had smeared. He'd see her lying on the grass on her back, bitten by insects. Her undies would show. He'd see her gritting her teeth. Smiling.

I didn't want to go back in there. It was dangerous. It was better to be a ghost.

But there must have been a time, I thought, when I said no. You heard mothers talking about the "terrible twos," when toddlers stamp their feet and say no all day long. Did I do that?

Cally's better off without me, Mum wrote.

Well, I wasn't, I wasn't. How did I know what to do? And now look where I was. The lady on the phone had said, "Don't come to the clinic in your school uniform, dear, change first." She'd said that because no school would want a girl who got herself into this mess. They'd pretend they didn't know you. It was as bad as being a bank robber and getting caught. When they're arrested, robbers always put their coats over their heads as the police lead them away. The lady on the phone should tell women to bring their coats as well as their Medicare cards.

"Do you need some more time to think about this?" Rosa asked softly.

Her voice pushed me back down there, into the white room. "What?" I said. "I mean, I beg your pardon?"

She repeated the question. Our eyes met. As I looked at her, I wasn't thinking of what she was saying, or this particular afternoon. I was thinking of the enormity of living life like this. I saw the way I grabbed on to people like life rafts, barely checking if they were afloat. It was only luck that I hadn't drowned by now.

"Look, I really do want to go ahead with this," I said. I blew my nose. I tried to make my voice firm. "It's just, you know, the sadness. I feel like I'm throwing away a little bit of me. Of what might have been. You know, a possibility. I've never been any good at making decisions."

Rosa waited.

I twisted in my chair. "The thing is, well, do you think I'm doing the right thing? I mean, it won't change my mind or anything, but it would just be good to know, you know?"

Rosa smiled at me. "You are the only one who can make this decision. I think you are extremely brave. And I know you will do the best you can."

I shuddered. Who'd leave all this up to me? But then I felt a wave of certainty. As Rosa said, there really was no one else.

I stood up. Rosa did too, and I took her hand. I felt quite tall. I towered over her, in fact. "I want to have the operation," I told her. "I want a second chance, I really do."

For once, I was trying to do the best thing I could for myself. When I knew how to do that—after about ten years of practice, maybe—I'd be able to do the best thing I could for my child.

Dr. Kavan pointed to a crisp white folding bed and asked me to lie down. He turned back to his desk. He was finding instruments, or putting on gloves, or something. I was wondering—should I take my jeans off now, or wait for him to tell me? There should be a guide for young girls: *What to Do at the Doctor's Without Making a Fool of Yourself*. He was still over there, with his back turned, fiddling on the desk. I didn't like to be bold and strip off before he told me to. I couldn't sit on that clean sheet with my bottom all bare. He'd think I was a slutty girl, always dying to get my pants off. I mean, here I was, in this situation. I left them on.

"Well, now, we'll need those jeans off," he said briskly as he turned around.

It's probably one of the most embarrassing things there is, being examined in the private area by a stranger of the opposite sex. I lay there sweating, my heart pumping away. This was the flight-or-fight reaction, common in stressed animals. You know, a perceived dangerous situation floods your body with adrenaline to help you survive. Embarrassment can practically kill you.

The doctor was nice. When he put his gloved fingers inside me, he didn't wrinkle his nose or shake his head or call me a naughty girl. He just poked about with an expression of detached curiosity. I felt like a quite ordinary flower being inspected by a kindly botanist.

"Good, good," he said. "You're not very far along."

I felt bold enough to ask how far.

"I'd say just a few weeks. The sac is only as big as your little fingernail."

I thought of those pictures held up outside. There weren't any fingernails among them. Someone ought to tell those people. Their signs could be a lot smaller, and they wouldn't have to strain all their arm muscles carrying them around.

He patted me on the shoulder and said we'd be ready to go ahead soon.

Back in the waiting room I found a vacant chair. I put my bag down and went to get myself a magazine. A woman at the urn was dunking a tea bag in a steaming cup. She looked up and gave me a friendly grimace. I grimaced back. For the next half hour, while I had my blood pressure and weight checked and talked to the nurse, I must have exchanged about a hundred of those smiles. And each time I felt a little warmer, a bit more connected. Bank robbers never smiled like that.

Jeremy was still drawing bats at Lily's desk. He came out to show me, although he shouldn't have. He showed me the King Bat, who had black wings shaped like Dad's umbrella. He'd even drawn little green men playing golf along the scalloped edges.

.

"How much longer will you be?" he asked, looking at me mournfully. If he'd been Batman's dog, he couldn't have looked more pathetic. His ears practically drooped. His shoulders slumped. I spied the biscuit tin near the urn. He took a handful and trudged back to Lily, leaving a little trail of shortbread crumbs after him. He looked like Hansel lost in the forest.

Soon it would all be over. I wished I could give Jeremy some of my confidence. I felt quite energetic sitting there, sort of springy, as if anyone could hurl lightning bolts at me and I'd just catch them in my teeth. Maybe it was just the fact that I hadn't eaten anything since breakfast—you weren't allowed to if you were having IV sedation. Not having lunch makes you stay alert. Still, I'd made a decision—all on my own. I wasn't doing this to please anyone else. It was just something I had to do. And I was doing the best I could.

You might think it's pathetic, a girl sitting there in that clinic, congratulating herself in a situation like that. But I'm telling the truth, once you make a decision, you feel better. You really do. And that's the way it was.

*T*he IV sedation method was definitely the best choice. You mightn't agree. Everyone is different. But it worked for me. They attach a little cannula to your vein and drip the stuff through. It makes you sleepy and the world crumples softly all around you. The softness is like a downy pillow, and you want to sink into it, pressing your head down further and further into the feathers, and there's only ever deeper layers of softness.

Sometimes I wish you could have a permanent cannula attached to your brain. But I suppose your conversations would suffer. You'd only talk mush, like a paddock after too much rain.

As the doctor and nurses worked, I floated away again. I thought I saw Richard. I smiled at him. It seemed stupid now, not telling him. The world was infinitely understanding. I couldn't wait to see him again. I'd tell him everything, and he'd say I was the one who was brave.

I think Rosa was there for most of the operation. She pressed my hand and murmured things to me, but I can't remember what she said. For a minute, when her back was turned, I thought she was my mother. My mother with her hair brushed.

Afterward they wheeled me into the recovery room. Other women were lying on stretchers, too. We all had our sheets up to our chins. We were too tired to smile. We were like those white pools of light dropped by streetlights. We lay silent and pale, enclosed in our own circles of thought.

I was quite content to lie there forever. Time passed softly. The doctor came round to see how we were. I had an ache in my belly. It was a dragging feeling, like when you have a period. He said I was doing well.

I began to notice things. There was a print on the wall. It was a Van Gogh, I think, the one with the butter-yellow sunflowers in a vase. I propped myself up on my elbows. I looked at my watch. It was six-thirty.

God, Jeremy. Lily would be gone by now. Jeremy would still be sitting at her desk. I hoped he had plenty of paper. Would anyone have noticed him there? Surely Lily would have given him a drink. I wondered how much longer I'd have to stay here.

When a nurse came in, I asked if she could find Jeremy. "Tell him I won't be much longer, will you?" He must have been starving. He'd usually have had dinner by now and be choosing a toy to take into his bath. It would be dark outside.

It seemed ages before she came back. As soon as she walked in, I could tell something was wrong. You could see it in her face.

"There's no one by the name of Jeremy in the clinic," she said.

My heart clamped in my chest. Then I breathed again. "Oh, sorry, I forgot." I laughed with relief. "His stage name is Robin—you know, as in Batman?"

But her face wasn't changing.

"I'm sorry, but there are no children out there in the waiting room."

"Did you look at the reception desk? Maybe he's hiding under it, or in the toilet? Sometimes he plays games like that."

The nurse bit her lip. "I'll just go and have another look. Don't worry, just try to relax." She helped me lie down. "We'll find him."

I twisted the sheet in my fingers. I was completely awake now. I looked at each of the sixteen Van Gogh sunflowers.

She was coming back already. I could hear her feet on the polished floors. *Tip-tap, tip-tap.* It was a cheerful trot. It didn't sound rushed, like an emergency.

She was smiling. "It's okay," she said. "I spoke to Jenny."

"Who's Jenny?"

"The receptionist who comes on after Lily. She said Lily left her a note——Lily had to leave at six and in the note she said that your boyfriend was picking Robin up. If he was late—Tim, isn't it?—Jenny was to look after him until he arrived. But obviously he turned up on time."

"You didn't find Jeremy?"

"No." The nurse looked at me. She had one of those round open faces. The kind that doesn't tell lies. "Tim must have come for him, you see," she said slowly. She patted my hand. "Are you still feeling foggy? Don't worry, your brother's probably at home by now, wolfing down his dinner."

*T*hey said I had to lie there for another half an hour. Time wasn't soft anymore. It was filled with microseconds. It was amazing how many disasters you could imagine in a microsecond. For instance: One of the "South Africans" hit Jeremy with a sign and kidnapped him. Or Jeremy hit one of the "South Africans" and they took him to jail. Or a meteorite dropped out of the sky and Jeremy fell into the crater.

It was better during those thirty minutes to think about meteorites, things with an absurd statistical probability, than anything else.

I wondered if it was still raining. Jeremy didn't know this part of the city at all. Was he sitting outside on the steps? Why would he do that when it was raining and cold? I remembered him on the porch when I came home that afternoon. Sitting there in the wet and cold.

Oh, please, God, let him be there on the steps. I'll give anything. Make him wet and cold if you have to. It's all my fault. All my fault with this stupid sex business and shouting the f word at him, and him being too sad to run and me making him wait on a vinyl chair in a room full of sad ladies for three hours.

My legs were twitching. I couldn't lie there anymore. Gingerly I sat up. I found my jeans folded neatly on a chair. I pulled them on. My stomach ached. Blood oozed. There was a thick bulky pad between my legs. I bent down to put on my shoes. A line of cramp started under my belly button. It dragged down all the way to where the hair started. But my head was clear. It was so clear it hurt. It was like those windy cloudless days when your skin chafes and your hair goes flat. All the clutter disappears when panic blows through you. It blows everything else away.

D<small>r.</small> Kavan didn't want me to leave. "Are you sure your friend won't be coming?" he asked. "He may have struck a lot of traffic. You know, with the rain, and peak hour. I'd like you to wait a little longer. . . ." He trailed off. "How do you feel?"

"Fine," I said. "Look, I'll get a cab." I opened my bag and checked in my wallet. "See, I have enough money. I was going to use it to buy a book on contraception but—"

The doctor smiled.

We argued for a little while longer. It was hard to be stubborn with someone like Dr. Kavan. He'd been so kind and gentle and he'd seen all my private parts. But compared to Jeremy, everything else was fading in significance.

Dr. Kavan waited with me until the cab arrived. "The clinic will ring you tomorrow, to see how you are," he called after me.

"No, I'll ring you," I called back.

Outside, the steps were empty. Ten horizontal slabs of concrete. No little boy.

I zigzagged along the length of each step. Just in case. Maybe he was hiding. Maybe he'd shrunk like Mrs. Pepperpot and fallen into a crack in the concrete. Jeremy could vanish like that. But he always got the giggles.

The street was empty, too. The protesters had gone home. A fine curtain of rain blew across my face. It made puddles in the gutters. Jeremy loved to jump in puddles. I always yelled at him about that, because the water would go through his boots into his socks and he'd get cold. Then he'd get earache and have to suffer the onion treatment. I'd tell him all this and he'd stop. He always listened to me.

"Wait for me," I'd said. So where was he, for God's sake? It was so dark—there was no moon, no pinprick of stars in that blanket of cloud. The main streets were lit, but the alleyways and lanes would be thick with shadow. Jeremy was afraid of the dark, like me. Why hadn't he waited like I'd said?

The taxi driver hooted. He was idling at the bottom of the steps.

I climbed in the front. I didn't feel very well. "Could you drive slowly along this street and around the block?" I asked him. "I'm looking for someone."

"It'll cost you extra," the man said. He was picking his teeth with the wrong end of a match.

"That's okay," I said.

We cruised along like hit men in the Mafia. I peered out through the window. The glass was foggy, so I wound the window down. Drizzle sprayed into my face. Cars tooted behind us. Headlights swam down the smooth black streets.

Nothing. The only person I saw was an old tramp rifling through a garbage bin.

"Listen," said the taxi driver, "someone's going to run into the back of us soon. You can't drive like this in the city in peak hour. Let's go, okay?"

I nodded. I gave him my address.

Jeremy knew his address. He knew his phone number and his birthday and the velocity of winds on Jupiter. Surely he could figure out how to get a taxi home. Maybe that was what he'd done. Maybe he'd thought it'd be an adventure, like Robin chasing Tony Zucco through the city streets. He probably told the taxi driver to "step on it" and "follow that car."

I couldn't wait to get home now. My heart was pounding. My legs wanted to be running, racing through red traffic lights, making cars screech to a halt.

I'll make a deal with you, I thought as I stared out the window. *If you let Jeremy be all right, I'll never ask for another thing. Nothing else matters, anyway. Jeremy is everything. He's big as Mount Etna. Every other disaster is a pindrop, a silly whisper, the movement of a curtain in an empty room. Jeremy is only five. He hasn't lived any life yet. He hasn't even had a candlelength of happiness. I've had two. Take me first.*

I didn't know who I was talking to—God? Ganesha? Fate? Who *should* you talk to in these situations?

I just wanted to talk to Jeremy. We were on the bridge now. In lane three. My stomach hurt. It was a dull ache, like a rope pulling. My throat ached, too. My hands felt so empty. I remembered holding Jeremy's hand. I'd dragged him up the street. "Fucking *move*!" I'd shouted. "I'm too sad to run," he'd said. His fingers had soft little pouches of flesh under each knuckle. My hands tingled where Jeremy had held them. Even when people lose a limb, they say they still get twinges in that absent place.

One of the windscreen wipers was stuck. The cab driver fiddled with it and swore. The wiper lay there paralyzed across the glass, like something too frightened to move. Rivers of light flowed ahead, green running into red.

We were off the bridge. An ambulance screamed behind us. The driver swore again and moved to the left. This is why no one dwells on the happy bits, I thought. They call it "blind happiness," "blind love." Because when you're happy, you're not looking. But you need to keep your eyes open all the time, or you'll lose something. It's like Dad said: You've got to be prepared. Think of all those stars burning brilliantly out there, so proud of their light, and all the while they're quietly dying.

When we turned into my street, I had my wallet out, ready. The porch light was on.

I fumbled in my bag for the keys. The mulberry leaves dripped onto my hair. I hesitated for a second at the door. I didn't think I could bear it. Maybe I could just stay this way, hovering, like oil floating on water. There was the chair he'd sat in this afternoon. You could still see the shape of his bottom in the saggy cushion.

I opened the door. Through the hallway I saw the light on in the living room. I heard voices.

Two bulging suitcases leant against the bookshelf. Mum was sitting on the sofa. She was saying something to Dad, who was turning the pages of today's paper. He still had his tie on. They both looked up when I came in.

"Callisto, where have you been?" said Dad.

"Where's Jeremy?" cried Mum. She leapt up.

I felt everything stop in my body. "He isn't here?"

"No," said Mum. "He was with you, wasn't he?"

"Yes," I said numbly.

"Well?"

"I've lost him."

Mum grabbed on to Dad's arm. "What do you mean? You can't just lose him—like, I don't know, a handbag, or an umbrella! Where have you been?"

My stomach twisted. A clump of blood squelched out onto my pad.

"To an abortion clinic. I've had an abortion."

"What?"

I looked at my parents. Their mouths hung open. They didn't move. They could have been figures in a still life of mine. *A Picture of Horror,* by Callisto May.

"You took Jeremy to an abortion clinic?" My father's voice was quiet. Too quiet. My mother closed her eyes.

They said nothing. They didn't know what to say. They'd never known what to say to me, either of them.

Mum groaned. She made a little movement toward me. She had tears in her eyes. I'd seen that expression before. She wore it with the sad ladies. I didn't want her using it on me.

"What else could I do?" I burst out. "If Mum had been doing her job and looking after her son, we wouldn't be standing here right now!"

"Go to your room, you nasty little baggage! I don't want to see your face."

"David! That's not the way to handle it!"

"Well?" He turned on her. "Where were you? At one of your absurd little meetings?"

Mum said nothing. Her head hung down on her chest.

"Well?" Dad took a step toward her. His voice was louder now.

She flung up her chin. "Where were *you*? When are you ever around to help?"

Dad gave a harsh laugh. "I was coming home—by taxi—because my wife didn't have time to pick me up. She was too busy lying in the dark calling up the spirit world."

"And who else is there to hear me? You decided a long time ago to practically live in another country and leave your family to fend for themselves."

I couldn't stand listening to them anymore. "What are we going to do about *Jeremy*?" I shouted, and ran into my room. I slammed the door and locked it. Dad came thundering down the hall. He banged on the door. He kicked it. His foot must have hurt, because he only had his thin airline slippers on. I heard him blaring through the keyhole— "Where's this clinic? Is it in the phone book? How long has Jeremy been gone?" On and on.

My heart was booming away. Maybe he'd kick the door down. Mum joined him outside. Their voices seeped through the wood. I heard her bleating about getting the car, going to look.

"Look where?" sneered Dad. "You wouldn't know where to start. You go on and on about other people's kids, you're like some broken record, a bloody great bleeding heart—"

"Well, you don't even see what's going on in the world. You're cut off from people. You're like some sort of robot. You're useless. What about that other country you live in? Well? You say nothing about what goes on there—"

"What?"

If Jeremy did get a taxi, why didn't he come home? Maybe somebody gave him a lift. *Oh, God, please, no.* I've told him about that. A policeman even came to the kindergarten to talk about it—"stranger danger," he called it.

Jeremy didn't have any money. Perhaps he went to Grandma's. She could have paid the taxi. Maybe he was there now, wolfing down her spaghetti. I picked up the phone.

"You didn't even read about the Truth and Reconciliation Commission."

"What?"

"In your beloved South Africa. You acted like you didn't know—you're like those people who say after a war, 'Oh, I didn't know that human beings were being buried in shallow graves. I thought they'd all emigrated to Bali.' Or 'I didn't know what that funny smell in the air was. I thought it was fried chicken.'"

"You're crazy, Caroline. You ought to be locked up. I'm very sorry for you."

"Sorry—that's a joke. Robots like you can never say sorry. All around the world *real* people are waking up—the Germans can say sorry, the Rwandans can say sorry—"

"Poor Caroline, she's finally flown off with the fairies."

"No, you're the crazy one—you can't feel anymore. You're barely human. Look at you, in your neat little airline socks. You're like some Ken doll you can dress and undress. You come equipped with your own set of clothes. You never get a hair out of place."

Dad kicked the door again. "Callisto, if you don't come out of there on the count of three, I'll—"

"What, David? What will you do?"

Grandma's phone rang and rang. I was about to put it down when she answered. "Hello," she said, out of breath. "Callisto? I was just putting the garbage out. How are you, darling?"

Her voice sounded so normal, I couldn't believe it. It was like coming out of a horror movie and breathing in calm, fresh air. I wanted to turn the world back four hours. I could curl up on her lounge and she could tell me about the new black hole in our galaxy or anything else in the universe.

"Is Jeremy there with you?"

"No, Cally. Is your mother home?"

I felt like putting the phone down. Jeremy was out there in the dark, in the rain. He was lost. He didn't even have a coat. He just had two layers of nylon. Superhero nylon. I hoped it would protect him.

Nothing else seemed able to.

"I'm coming over," said Grandma.

"Okay."

Grandma. I suddenly felt lighter, like a weight lifter who gives up his dumbbells to the next man.

When I heard her knock, I unlocked my bedroom door. Voices drifted down the hallway. Up and down the scale they went, dueling scores riding over each other.

"Don't be so pathetic, David. It's no use trying to hide it." It was Mum. Her voice was so shrill. "This is my mother you're talking to, not some client you're trying to impress."

I winced. Mum was going to tell her. About me. It was coming any minute. I hid behind the door. Their voices were low now, rumbling, like something boiling in a pot. I could feel the tension building up. Waiting was like holding your breath underwater. When I was little and we played hide-and-seek, I always ran out too soon. I found waiting unbearable—I'd do anything to avoid that moment of discovery, so loud in the mothball dark of the wardrobe.

"Grandma!" I called.

"Callisto!"

She was hurrying down the hall, her gray hair frizzing around her like a springy cloud. I swung the open door. She stopped short suddenly. "You should be in bed. Do you have much pain? What have you taken for it?"

I would have preferred a hug. Maybe she didn't want to touch me now. I was all ready to put my head on her chest. She was so sturdy, my grandma, she was like a fig tree with her solid trunk and ample arms. But she kept them folded. "Grandma doesn't do hugs," Jeremy said once, "she does instructions." Why are people so much better when you make them up?

"Something with codeine phosphate would be best. I'll see if Caroline has any in the bathroom. Now, tell me the name and address of the clinic, and then pop into your pajamas. We're going to take care of things here."

I sat down on the bed. My head felt blurry.

I heard her charging off into the living room. The voices started again. My stomach ached. I lay down for a moment. But I thought I heard Jeremy crying in the dark.

I crept down the hallway.

Grandma was picking up the phone in the kitchen.

"What are you doing?" Mum said sharply.

"I'm calling the police," Grandma replied. "I gather no one has done that yet?"

"Oh, that's right—call in the experts," Mum hissed. "They'll know exactly where he is. As if they haven't got a list a mile long of missing persons. We'll waste half the night giving information and they'll say, 'Thank you very much' and go off duty. Why don't we just get in the car and go ourselves?"

There was silence for a moment and then Grandma said, "I don't think you are in a fit state to drive, Caroline."

"I agree," put in Dad.

"Now, dear, what was Jeremy wearing this afternoon? Did he have his yellow raincoat on? We'll have to explain all this to the police."

"She doesn't know, because she wasn't there." Dad gave a jeering sort of snort. Grandma was hunting for a pen. She found one of Jeremy's Batman ballpoints. Dad was whispering something to Mum. I leant closer to hear. I saw him gently take her chin in his hand. He was looking into her eyes. "I blame you," he said softly. "I blame you for Jeremy."

Mum sank down onto the kitchen stool. She put her head on her knees, as if she wanted to fold herself up until she disappeared.

"Come on, dear, now is the time to be strong," Grandma said. "Was he wearing his school uniform?" She had her pen poised.

"You don't know what it's like to lose a child," whispered Mum.

"Oh, Caroline, we don't know that he's lost," said Grandma. "He might be sitting at a police station eating ice cream. But that's why we've got to ring them. Now let's get organized."

Mum's face was twitching. It looked so naked, with all that weather passing across it. I almost couldn't watch. "You never *said,* you never acknowledged it," Mum went on. "You never said, 'This is the worst thing to happen in a person's life.' All you people walking around, pretending it didn't happen. You talked about other things, like mowing the lawn or the shoe sale at David Jones. It was like not burying him. You just told me to be strong."

"What?" cried Dad. "You're living in the past. Don't put your mother through this again, Caroline. We're dealing with Jeremy now. Pull yourself together, for his sake!"

Mum leapt up. "You," she spat, "when have you ever been

here for anybody's sake? Gany died, your wife lost six kilos in a week and you got on a plane and flew away. Well, I blame you, David May. I blame *you*."

"Gany?"

They all turned around as I came into the kitchen. "Who was Gany?"

"He was your brother. He died when he was three months old. He was my first child."

"Caroline—shut up!"

"Why did he die?"

"No one knows. The so-called experts couldn't make a diagnosis. 'It happens sometimes,' they said. 'We're sorry for your loss.' But I always knew he wasn't happy. He didn't ever really bloom—"

"Oh, nonsense, Caroline," said Dad. "He was a perfectly normal baby. There was nothing anyone could do. Callisto, go back to your room now, please. Now!"

"You said I shouldn't tell the children. You said they'd grow up with a handicap if I did. But how could I forget? How could *I* forget?"

Mum looked so small on the kitchen stool. All the parts of her body were touching each other. Her face was in her hands, her elbows digging into her knees. She looked shrunken. Sorrow like that would make anyone shrink.

It'd make you want to die. *Take me,* Mum must have said, *take me first*. But they didn't.

I took a step toward her. *Look at her poor broken face.*

"Callisto!" said Dad. "Go back to your room now!"

Grandma came over and took my hand. "The Panadol is in the bathroom. Let's get a capsule on the way."

259

Look at her tears dripping through her fingers. I didn't know what to do. How would I know what to do?

I shook off Grandma's hand. "I'll get it myself."

*F*rom my room I heard Grandma talking on the phone to the police. "Dark brown eyes, dark hair, he was wearing a Batman outfit."

"No, that was underneath," I called out. "He had Robin on top. Robin's red."

"And he had a little wart on his thumb," she added. I heard her voice break. I didn't know she'd seen that. Jeremy said Poison Ivy had kissed him there.

Grandma was silent for ages. I bet they asked her to hold on. They probably put that Muzak stuff on for her to listen to. There's nothing more irrelevant in life than Muzak, is there? It's just a waste of sound waves. Especially in a crisis.

I thought of the stolen-children clipping Mum had put up on the fridge. I'd read it, but it hadn't touched me. I hadn't let it. "Most parents know what it's like to lose a child for five minutes—last seen at the school gate," the journalist had written. "Where is she? they ask themselves. Who has her? What is he doing to her? . . . Imagine that feeling protracted—over a week, then a year, then a decade."

I got up and went into Jeremy's room. I prowled around. I picked through his toy crate. Old Jem, he was such a hoarder. There were his old rattles and chewing ring. Where could he have gone? I punched his teddy in the arm. ▶

wished teddies could speak. This one must know all Jeremy's secrets. He told it everything. As I walked out I picked up an old gym shoe lying in the doorway. The black paint had flaked off everywhere and made a little pile of dark crusts on the carpet, like the remains of something burnt. Jeremy had wanted black shoes, to be like Sam Underwood.

I leant against the wall for a moment. Sam Underwear. I closed my eyes. I hadn't bought the cake as I'd promised. I hadn't bought juice. Sam hadn't come to admire Jeremy's bunker.

I threw down the shoe. Little bits of black paint flew off. And dirt.

It was the dirt that gave me the idea. My head practically lit up, like those characters in comic books with lightbulbs in their brains. I found Jeremy's Playskool torch and ran through the hallway, toward the front door. No one saw me. They were huddled down there in the living room like enemies at a conference.

The lawn was slushy with rain. I crouched down as I passed the living room windows. Mum was sitting by herself on the couch. I ran along the side of the house. The cold seeped into my socks. When I got to the steps leading down to the back, I slowed down. The steps had always been cracked and broken, and I'd slipped more than once. But when I shone the torch I saw the old stones had been replaced with bricks. The first step was perfect. The others needed finishing. I smiled. Someone must have been working on it.

Scattered around the brick pylons under the house were

old cardboard boxes and pipes and scores of sweet wrappers. The wrappers glowed brightly likes jewels in the dirt. So much dirt. Loose earth was sprayed all around, covering the carpet of leaves. I spotted a small mountain of mud further up—directly under the kitchen.

I crawled along on my knees. In the torchlight, near the pile of mud, there was a shovel. It was near an old door lying flat in the dirt. I recognized the door—it was the one from my room. The only thing Dad had changed when we'd moved into the house. The wood was all splintered. It was a flimsy thing. I remembered, because Dad had to go away a few days after that and he'd left me with no door. I couldn't play my radio loud or read in torchlight or anything without someone coming to yell at me.

I threw the shovel away near some boxes. Then I tried to lift the door. It slid a few inches across the dirt. My stomach clenched. In the gap, I saw the ground slope away sharply. I dragged at the door and it came away from the hole.

In the circle of torchlight, curled up in his bunker, lay Jeremy. It was Jeremy, my Jeremy. His cheeks were smudged with dirt. Spidery tracks of tears made webs in the black. He was shivering as he slept. He looked like one of Mum's pictures on the fridge. He sucked the thumb that Poison Ivy had kissed.

I lay on the ground next to him. I put my head into his tummy. He slept on. I tried to cry softly. I wanted to laugh, too, and celebrate and do a sailor's hornpipe, but only the tears would come. I smelled the wet fishy smell of his nylon. My forehead moved in and out with his breath. I could feel blood leaking out onto my pajama leg. It made a rust stain on Jeremy's knee. I breathed through my mouth into Jeremy's stomach, sucking in tears. Words and pictures and thoughts and dreams, everything swam into everything else as I cried for my little fish and the fish I once was. I cried for my dead baby brother, who was called Gany, and I cried for Jeremy, who had been digging his own grave.

Dad carried Jeremy inside. All the way, as he stumbled over the half-finished steps, swearing at the stones, he prodded Jeremy for details. Jeremy was hardly awake. How did he pay for a taxi and why did he stay outside worrying us all to death and if no one was home why didn't he go to a neighbor's?

I told Dad that he should have fixed those steps years ago and then he wouldn't be stubbing his toe on them in those silly airline slippers. He told me to shut up and that I sounded just like my mother. "And anyway, you should be in your room."

"You've been telling me that since I was three," I mumbled. "Why don't you try something else?" But he wasn't listening.

"Jeremy!" cried Mum as we came into the house. She pulled at his shoulders. She grabbed him under the arms. Dad didn't want to let him go. They carried him together over to the sofa. He lay with his head on Mum's lap, his feet on Dad's knees.

"I gave Grandma's lira to the taxi man," Jeremy murmured into Mum's skirt. "He seemed pleased."

Grandma choked. "I bet he was. He could have made fifty trips with that money." But her eyes were sparkling with tears. She bent over him, stroking his forehead. I was looking at everyone in amazement. I had never seen so much feeling in this house. It was like high tide sloshing against the walls. Everyone looked different.

Mum wiped the dirt off Jeremy's cheeks.

"I'm cold," said Jeremy. "It was so dark."

Mum wrapped the TV rug around him. She held his head close to her chest. He snuggled in, put his thumb in his mouth and went back to sleep.

Grandma came over to me and put her hand on my shoulder. "Shouldn't you be sitting down?"

Mum looked up at me then. "I don't know how you could do a thing like that, Cally," she said.

"What?"

"I just don't know how you could do it."

My legs began to tremble. I felt my head go light with rage. It was as light as a cloud, it was going to float off my shoulders.

"There are a lot of things you don't know about me, Mum."

I was staring at her as if I could kill her.

She held out her hand. "No, I mean, why didn't you tell me? Let me help you? How could you do this thing all alone?"

"Why didn't you ever tell me about *you*?"

Dad got up, sliding Jeremy's feet onto the sofa. "Callisto, you should be in bed. I'll talk to you tomorrow. I'm only going to say now that I am very disappointed in you. More than words can say." He sounded like he was delivering a sentence.

I felt the tears starting again. He looked away from me as if I were something disgusting that would contaminate him. I wished I had a coat to put over my head.

He turned to Mum. "I'm just going to change out of these wet clothes."

"Oh, no, you're not," said Mum. "Don't you go sneaking out now like you always do."

"I can't talk to you when you're in this state."

"No, you might have an emotion, it's a frightening thought. You always go and make tea in the love scenes on TV, don't you?"

Grandma stood up. "Caroline, you're tired. Overwrought. It might be best to talk about all this in the morning."

"Or maybe never at all. Let's shove it under the carpet, shall we, like we do everything else."

I stood up. Dad glanced at me and his eyes quickly moved away. "Your pajamas are filthy, Callisto," he said. "*You* at least had better go and change."

There was an awful silence while everyone turned to stare at me. I saw their eyes travel down my pajamas, to where the blood was spreading into a map of Europe. I wished I could fall into one of Jeremy's craters. I wished a meteor would fall on us right now in this living room and no one would ever say another word.

But I couldn't bear the silence.

"I'm disgusting, aren't I?" I burst out. "Well, don't look at me, then. Pretend you only have a son. Pretend I never existed. I wish I bloody didn't. I wish all my blood would leak away until I was dead!"

Dad said nothing. His left eye was twitching.

"Oh, Cally," said Mum. She held out her hands to me. She had that look—the deep frown, the head to one side, the lips slightly parted. I didn't trust her.

"You're looking at me like I'm a sad lady," I said. I was crying again. I didn't know anymore when the tears stopped or started. My head was like a tap with a faulty washer. The tears kept leaking out from some ocean inside.

"You are a sad lady tonight," said Mum softly.

"What, now you're going to let me join your club? Why do I have to be sad for you to look at me? I don't want to be like you!"

Mum shook her head. "I don't know. Just give me a hug. Please!"

"You haven't looked at me for years."

"Come here."

I saw the softness in her face, the shine of her hair, Jeremy's head pressed against the pillow of her breast. She was my mother. I didn't know her. I hadn't known the first thing about her.

"Why didn't you help me?" I felt like slapping those open hands. I wanted to rake my fingernails down those smooth arms. I wanted to be enfolded in them too, like a hand in a glove. My head was floating again. "You didn't look after me. Rosa said, 'Why isn't your mother here to help?' I had

266

to make excuses, I had to freak out about Jeremy, there was no one to look after Jeremy, I had no one to sit with me, to take me home, to tell me it was going to be all right. I don't know why you *had* children!"

"Callisto!"

I swung round to Dad. He was holding his eye to stop it twitching. I was so light with anger I felt like a hot-air balloon. I could have floated around the room, torching them all. "All you can say is my name. What else do you know about me? Nothing! What do you know about Jeremy? Did you know he was building a bunker? Digging his own *grave*? What a happy little nuclear family!"

I stood on tiptoes, ready to run. I expected Dad to hit me. And I wasn't going to change my pajamas, either. I was going to bleed all over the carpet if I had to, let all my disgusting blood drown that house and its sorrows.

"Come here," Mum said again.

"No, you'll get dirt all over you."

"I don't care."

Dad just sat and held his eye.

"Why didn't you tell Jeremy and me about our brother? Why did you make it a guilty secret?"

Mum sighed. "David said it would hurt you."

"That's right, blame me," Dad blurted. "You were the one who was going mad with it all. You wouldn't sleep, you wouldn't eat, you kept seeing him, hearing him, it was all you would talk about."

"I needed to."

"You needed to forget, that's what. You had to go on and live your life. I had to get on with mine. You didn't look at me anymore. You didn't care how *I* was, what I was doing. That time I got mugged in Johannesburg and had stitches in my head, you barely asked me about it. You said, 'Is that all?' It was as if I was just some irrelevant noise in your life—"

Like Muzak, I thought. I had never heard my father put so many words together at the same time. Words about feelings, that is. He could talk on about picture frames and gold leaf and gallery prices for hours. But this was like some sort of magic spell. I didn't want to break it.

Dad was frowning, looking down at his fingers splayed on his knees. I could see red creeping up his neck. It was amazing. I couldn't stop looking at his neck. I even felt sorry for it.

"I just wanted you to be in there with me," Mum said. "That was all. I needed someone to listen—to acknowledge the pain. That's all anybody needs. Isn't it, Cally?"

I didn't answer. I was wondering—if I put a hand on Dad's neck, would it be hot? He looked hot. Hot and angry and confused and lonely. I thought of that little Aboriginal girl looking over the fence. I pictured Dad packing his bags while Mum cried on the bed. I remembered looking down at myself in Rosa's room, alone on the chair. I felt all dissolved inside, liquid with sorrow for me and all the world. For a moment I was small again, under Richard's big human tent, where no one is separate from anyone else, and everyone's pain is the same.

Jeremy took a big breath in his sleep. He half sat up, and Dad reached over, pulling him onto his lap. "He'll be getting a bit heavy for you," he muttered to Mum. I saw him put his nose into Jeremy's hair and breathe him in.

Grandma stirred in the armchair. She put her arms into her coat sleeves. "Caroline, I . . . well . . ." She struggled with her sleeve. "Look, dear, not everyone can say how they feel. Sometimes we don't even know. Your father was the one in our family who could use words. But me, well, I'm just not . . . Well, I was frightened for you, like David. We thought it was for the best. Maybe it wasn't, maybe it was the worst thing. I don't know . . ." Grandma's voice trailed off. She adjusted her coat collar.

"You're not leaving?" cried Mum.

"Well," murmured Grandma. She suddenly looked so much older, standing there. I'd never heard her not finish a sentence. The buttons on her coat were done up wrongly. "I don't know that I can help."

"Christ," I said, "not you too. What is this, some jinx gene handed down through generations? Are we all going to throw up our hands and say, 'Oh, it's too hard,' and my children will learn it and their children will, on and on, amen? Even if things aren't said, you feel them anyway." I turned to Mum. "You mightn't have told us about Gany"—I tried to say the name softly, respectfully—"but somehow we always knew, Jeremy and I. We lived with your past, Mum, we lived with it every day. It just didn't have a name. It drowned us, it was like, I don't know, old swamp water, it took the freshness out of everything. We only just kept our heads above water, Jeremy and I. And now, tonight, it felt like we'd gone under. You know, outside that clinic? I just wanted to find Jeremy's hand to hold. I couldn't find it under all that water."

Mum drew me onto her lap. I started to struggle, there

was all that crusted red and dirt from Jeremy's bunker and her skirt was cream, but for once her arms were strong and she wouldn't let me pull away. I sank into her and I wasn't too heavy or dirty. She just let me cry there. She stroked my back.

"You know," said Mum after a while, "when you were born, I was so happy. I clung on to your fingers and I remember thinking, *I'm going to do it right this time*. I held you in my arms and I was holding my future. But your little face made me think of the past."

I looked down at Jeremy. His eyeballs were moving under his lids. He was dreaming. We never had a chance, he and I.

"The first loss is like a black hole, Cally," Mum said quietly. "As the years go on it sucks all other losses, bigger and smaller, into it. It colors them and flavors them. It robs them of their own separate identities until they are just feeding the black hole itself. It's like—oh, Cally, it's like this great empty yawn of grief." She took my hand. "This is your first loss."

I snatched my hand away. "This is nothing *like* yours. Don't make me into you. It's as if you only see me when you think I'm like you."

Mum's eyes receded. She put her hands back in her lap.

"And don't go away like that just because I don't agree with you. I'm just saying that your loss was worse, it was much—"

Mum nodded. "I know, Cally. There is nothing worse than losing a baby. A baby that you've fed and changed and laughed with and loved. I'm glad you didn't go through that. I hope you never do."

"I'm sorry, I didn't mean—"

"It's just that I want you to realize that you've had a loss, too." She closed her eyes for a moment. "Only don't hold on to it, Cally. Sometimes, when you can't have the thing you lost, you hold on to the sorrow. It's the only thing you have. I couldn't see past the sorrow. All this time, all this wasted time. I'm sorry, love. I really am."

It's funny, you hear "I'm sorry" twenty times a day—in the supermarket when someone bashes into your cart, at the shop when the grocer is out of cornflakes. But when you hear it from your mother, that's something else. You'll always remember that.

A planet represents a balance between the gravitational force that seeks to collapse it and the electromagnetic force that props up its molecules. It sounds like an awfully delicate balance. A struggle that makes you shiver. If you added just a little more gravity, a planet could light up and become a star. A slightly different amount and it would collapse.

After that night, in the following weeks, our family was a bit like that. There was this tentative seesaw of goodwill, as fragile as anything. Tempers would flare and someone would rush in and placate. We were all so careful with each other. We were like crystal figurines on a shelf. Dad kept asking me if I wanted a cup of tea. Each time he had to check if I took sugar. He couldn't remember if it was one lump or two. He still had trouble listening to people. But he was trying. You could tell.

It was weird, and sort of nice. He didn't even mention the umbrella. But if you really want to know, it was also rather tiring. It was as if we'd stepped onto a new planet, where there were new rules. And every minute we were learning them. Sometimes there wasn't enough air to go around.

Mum didn't stop talking. It was as if she'd suddenly been released from a wicked spell and was making up for lost time. I discovered all sorts of things about her. Like how she'd always thought I was the grown-up in the family. That I could handle anything. That I was a better mother for Jeremy than her.

"That's such a cop-out," I told her. "You just wanted free baby-sitting." Before, I might have been flattered. It would have appealed to the borrower in me. You know, anything for approval. But I knew what she meant, really. I only had to think of her sitting there on that stool. No one should have had to go through that alone. No one.

Still, I told her, she had gone ahead and had two more children—she must have thought she could manage.

"I know, but I couldn't get on top of things, and you seemed better at mothering than me," she'd say humbly. God, she was exasperating. But at least she was there.

Jeremy loved it. He loved all the words bouncing off the ceiling, he went to sleep with language buzzing in his ear. There were so many words about, he didn't have to gaze intently at people when they talked. He could relax. Words weren't the private, rare little jewels that they'd been before.

And one day he might even take his helmet off when he goes to bed.

Grandma told him he could bring Sam around to her place and she'd show him the medal she'd got for discovering all those galaxies. Jeremy did a cartwheel. She said she'd give them both chocolate cake, too. But only if Jeremy filled in the bunker. It gave her the creeps.

That night, Thursday the fifteenth, I reckon we had our own Truth and Reconciliation Commission. Right there in the living room. It's true what they say about microcosms and macrocosms. You can see the universe in a single cell. That Thursday night there was the hub of international conflict right in our own small nuclear family.

The only thing that annoys Jeremy about it all is that he slept right through it. He can't believe Dad went outside to get him in the rain with only his airline slippers on. He would have loved to see that. But I told him not to worry, because I'm writing it all down, and when he's old enough, he can read it himself.

Jeremy likes to have the last word. It's on account of having that oversupply of fuel in his brain. He says that he's already written his version. It's all there in his head. And when I'm having the teenage blues again and lying quietly on my bed, he'll tell me about it. The way he sees it.

EPILOGUE

*D*on't worry, I'm not going to give you the recipe for life or anything. I don't know if any of us has turned out all right yet. We'll have to wait a few more decades for that. But I do want you to know about Richard.

Of course, I told him everything about the night of Thursday the fifteenth. I suppose you knew I would. He's the kind of person you can tell those things to. He's such a good listener. After that night, I felt I'd never be scared of anything ever again. (Well, almost.)

Richard has his own place now. It's a one-bedroom flat in the city. I stay there most weekends, and we go to the movies or cook dinner together. At first, on Saturday nights, when I was rushing off to Richard's, Dad would say, "Have you *got everything?*" in this really significant tone. Sometimes I'd make him sweat and pretend I didn't know what he meant. He'd clear his throat loudly and get really busy with his mail or something. He won't say it, looking me in the eye. I can't, either. I guess it must still be really hard for Dad. For both of us.

But he shouldn't worry. Not about that, anyway. If I get pregnant again, it will be because I really want to.

As if I could forget.

Richard is working extra nights at the observatory, but he's always pretty poor. When he asked me to help him decorate the flat, I brought a whole stack of *New Scientist* magazines over, and I framed my painting called *Hope*. He put it smack bang in the middle of his bedroom wall.

I've decided he isn't an arbitrary light source. We actually have a lot in common. Science, naturally, but also, we see the world in a similar way. Sometimes I feel that if we were artists, we could draw the pictures inside each other's heads.

He says my thoughts are too weird to illustrate.

He says that, but he finishes my sentences. I finish his. Who knows, one day we might become great inventors together. Or we might just sit at home drinking tea and talking all night. I don't care.

When we climb into bed, there's the weather. Sometimes, when we're lying naked together, a stillness comes, like the eye of a hurricane, and in there we whisper to each other in our language.

*W*hen I go back home alone, I take those times with me. I look in the mirror of the May bathroom and remember his eyes smiling at me. I'm trying, I really am. But often, just out of the corner of my eye, I glimpse something. It's the dark coming down. It comes with an ache, a dragging menstrual pull.

On the news last night I saw all these people protesting outside an abortion clinic. They were holding placards and signs. I kept looking for that man with the gray hair, but he wasn't there. There's a debate going on in Parliament about abortion. All the people debating are men. A senator said that lots of women have their abortions in spring because they don't want to look fat in their bikinis!

You can tell that he has never been pregnant.

People like him make it all so much harder. I mean, when they're waving placards and spitting at you, you can't admit a moment of weakness. You can't tell about the feeling afterward, the sadness. You just say you're fine. And you spit back, if you've got the gumption.

But I think Mum was right. You have to tell the sadness, otherwise it grows in you, like the shadow of the child you didn't have.

Every time I watch a movie on TV and the baby dies or is hurt, the tears come. They just spurt out, as if something struck an underground spring. Maybe it will always be this way. But even so, knowing that, I don't think I would have done anything different.

I wanted my second chance. I needed it like oxygen. I wanted to grow up first. Richard and I might have children one day. I'd like to. I think Richard would be a fantastic dad. And I'll make sure our babies don't have to borrow their light. I'll give it to them gladly. I'll be as tall as a skyscraper, as strong as a horse. I'll give my babies endless helpings of love, just as a mother should. And when they're old enough, they'll have all the fuel they need to make their own. Little rockets of energy they'll be. They'll have pockets of happiness inside them, like microchips of joy. Well, I'm going to try.

Writing things down makes you feel good. Telling someone is even better.

That's the closest thing to a recipe you'll get from me. I can only tell you what happened the year I was sixteen. And that's the way it was, the whole naked truth of it, if you really want to know.

ABOUT THE AUTHOR

ANNA FIENBERG is the author of many well-loved and award-winning children's books in her native Australia. *Borrowed Light* is her first young adult novel. Anna Fienberg lives in Sydney.